ADVANCE PRAISE FOR
The History of Great Things

"Elizabeth Crane has written a novel that is both unprecedented and fantastic (a word I mean in every sense). Without question, the unconventional narrative is compelling in a can't-stop-reading kind of way. But there's more to this book than a keen story cleverly told. Her every page thrums with wisdom, buzzes with truth. What did I learn after reading *The History of Great Things*? I learned that love survives death. And that no one ever really goes away, even if they have. And that all sides have many stories. And that we make our own happiness. This is unlike any novel I've ever encountered and it's absolutely wonderful."

—Jill Alexander Essbaum, author of *Hausfrau*

"I cannot remember the last time I simultaneously cried and laughed as hard as I did while reading Elizabeth Crane's glorious, tender knockout of a novel, *The History of Great Things*. Wait, yes, I can. It was the last time I spoke to my mom about life."

—Amber Tamblyn, author of *Dark Sparkler*

"Like everything Elizabeth Crane writes, *The History of Great Things* is wonderful fun to read—smart, insightful, and witty—but it will break your heart too. It stares down the poignant question so many daughters want to ask: 'How well did my mother really know me?'"

—Pamela Erens, author of *Eleven Hours* and *The Virgins*

"In her signature prose style, full of verve and wit, Elizabeth Crane unpacks the problematic relationship between mother and daughter that will resonate with anyone. By telling each other's stories, the mother and daughter in *The History of Great Things* reinvent each other, their relationship, and the possibility of empathy. You will cry, weep, and be glad you went along for this very particular beautiful and heartbreaking ride."

—Emily Rapp Black, author of *The Still Point of the Turning World*

"I've long been an admirer of Elizabeth Crane's absolutely unique voice—no one else working in contemporary American letters sounds quite like her. This is an important work, fearless in both structure and vision, with Crane's razor-edge fusion of intelligence, humor, and emotion informing every chapter. Get ready, world: this one's going to be huge."

—Jamie Quatro, author of *I Want to Show You More*

The History of Great Things

ALSO BY ELIZABETH CRANE

When the Messenger Is Hot

We Only Know So Much

You Must Be This Happy to Enter

All This Heavenly Glory

The History of Great Things

A NOVEL

Elizabeth Crane

HARPER PERENNIAL

NEW YORK • LONDON • TORONTO • SYDNEY • NEW DELHI • AUCKLAND

HARPER PERENNIAL

P.S.™ is a trademark of HarperCollins Publishers.

FIRST EDITION

Designed by Meghan Healey

Library of Congress Cataloging-in-Publication Data has been applied for.

ISBN 978-0-06-241267-6

16 17 18 19 20 OV/RRD 10 9 8 7 6 5 4 3 2 1

for Susan, my sister

and for Alice, champion, who always says *keep going*

Binghamton, 1961

You're late. Two weeks, forty-one hours late, nine pounds, ten ounces. That's a lot. That's like a bowling ball coming out of me.

—I've heard this part before, Mom.
—Just let me have my say and then you can have yours.
—Fine.

So you're a giant bowling ball coming out of me. If bowling balls were square. It hurts like a bitch. Honestly. No one mentioned this detail to me in advance. I may as well be pushing out a full-grown adult. Wearing a tweed pantsuit. Think about that. That's what they should tell kids in sex ed. Not that sex ed exists now, because it doesn't. Sex exists. Not ed.

It's 1961. Your father is in the waiting room, of course, because that's the way it is at this time. No dads, no home video, no breathing techniques. All fine by me, though I wouldn't hate for someone to mention to me that Pampers exist now. Your father is escorted in as soon as they've cleaned you up (god forbid the father should have to see that?) and handed you over to me all wrapped in a pink striped bunting, and when Fred comes over it's very dear, actually. He peeks down into the bunting, and I see a pleased look on his face that's different from any I've seen him have before. He's not usually terribly expressive, as you know. But I can see how he feels about you already. I hand you over and realize he's never held a baby before, that maybe we should have practiced with your cousin or something, because you're a little unsteady passing between us, but once he's got you he's got you.

The next day, we take you home. You're a good baby, thank god. Sleep through the night, don't fuss too much, drink formula like a champ—nursing is not considered "modern," even by doctors (by most, it's considered icky), and I am perfectly happy to accept this wisdom. And you are exceptionally beautiful. A thicket of dark curls on your day of birth that soon soften to a light brown, dark eyes that soon turn blue—I still don't know where those came from, since Fred and I both have green eyes, but it's fine, because your blue eyes are huge and you're nicely plump, with deliciously squishy baby legs even though my insides and my crotch still feel like the baby Godzilla just left my uterus. Grandmother Crane sends a beautiful layette from Marshall Field's: a delicate linen dress, a hand-crocheted cardigan, with matching bonnet and booties, though the whole set gets ruined pretty quickly, not very practical for a baby. I told her I'd just as well have stuff from Penney's, but of course that wasn't good enough. By the time you're old enough to walk, between Mother and me, you have an almost exclusively handmade wardrobe. She knits some absolutely darling little sweaters, and I make dresses, some of them smocked; sometimes I make matching dresses for us, and for your doll Bibsy if I have some selvage left over. In any case, you're a very well dressed, absolutely beautiful little girl, everyone remarks on this, and I am very proud.

Until the tantrums start, around the typical age, two and a half or so. I won't be around for some of these, but one time there's a particularly huge fuss about cleaning up your kitchen set. *Time to clean up! But why? Because it's suppertime. Well is it suppertime or cleanup time? First it's cleanup time, then it's suppertime. But why? I'm not finished! Because it is, Betsy. But I'm not finished! Yes, you are for now. No! No! I'm not! I'm not finished! I will never be finished!* I had read in Dr. Spock that you're supposed to throw your child in a bathtub of cold water during a tantrum, but on this occasion there's no time for that, and now that it's happening I can't imagine how there'd ever be time for that, you'd basically have to have a bathtub full of cold water ready to go, though with the increasing frequency of your fits it might be worth it. So I run to the kitchen and grab a glass of water and throw it on you, and sure enough, you do stop yelling for a brief moment, no doubt because you're completely stunned. *I'm going to tell my daddy on you!* you say, and I have to leave the room, otherwise I will laugh.

—I'm thinking you have an unfair advantage, at least when it comes to my first eighteen years, because you were there.

—Not always.

—Good point.

Muscatine, 1936

Okay. Muscatine, Iowa. June of 1936.

You're born in Muscatine. Edna, your mother, has been a homemaker since your older sister, Marjorie, was born a couple years earlier. Before that she worked at the Heinz factory for a while. Walter, your father, is the editor of the *Muscatine Journal*. Member of the lodge.

—*Which lodge?*

—*I don't know, some lodge. A lodge is a lodge.*

—*Don't tell him that.*

—*Mom, Grandpa's long gone.*

—*Well, so am I, Betsy, but you're talking to me.*

—*Okay, whatever! Let's say it's a Moose lodge.*

—*Let's say? You don't think we should try to be accurate?*

—*Well, it's not a memoir. It's just a story.*

—*But it's a true story.*

—*It's* not *a true story, though. That's not what we're doing. Do you think you know my story?*

—*Yes. I don't know. Maybe. More than you think.*

—*Lemme just keep going.*

You're kind of a sickly baby. You have the croup a lot and your father is always at work or at the lodge, doing lodge things, making secret lodge greetings with the other men in their fezzes, smoking cigars and telling bawdy jokes. Your mother's tired all the time though she never complains about it one bit. Marjorie isn't any much easier than you, she hasn't had the croup, but she's a handful. Won't go down for a nap, not ever. Always loud and asking annoying questions nonstop and by the time you're born she's already got an opinion about everything.

—I dunno about the croup, but so far the rest of that is pretty believable.
—Shhh!

But you're a good kid. You and Marjorie share a double bed until she goes to college, and you fight a lot (or, all the time). You think Marjorie is a pill and Marjorie thinks you're a pill and you're both right, but it's a different era, and you're well-behaved kids, nobody rats their hair or makes out with boys, none of that. Well, Marjorie comes home and kicks you out of the bedroom one night for a sleepover with a girlfriend (you are part miffed to be kicked out, part happy to get to sleep downstairs in the den by yourself), and when you go back upstairs to brush your teeth you hear her giggling and giggling with her friend Effie and you hear some boys' names you haven't heard before, Roger and Ted, and Effie asking Marjorie to tell her everything, *everything!* about what it was like, and you don't know what *it* is, you're maybe eleven at this time, but you know it's something you will never, ever do. You just know.

When you're fifteen, your first boyfriend takes you to sophomore prom for your third date. *Told you*, you say to Marjorie, sticking your tongue out at her. *Be careful or I'll cut that off, sassy-pants.* You ask her, *How come you're not going to the senior prom, Marjorie?* knowing full well that she didn't get asked because her boyfriend just dumped her for the most popular girl in school. *Prom's stupid*, Marjorie says. *Only prisses go.* The boyfriend is cute enough, a bit of a dullard, on the debating team, *Bo-ring*, picks you up in his dad's Buick, you're wearing a pale lavender tulle dress you and Mother made together, absolutely dreamy, and having a boyfriend is definitely better than not having a boyfriend, your sister was right about that. The girls who don't have boyfriends are either ugly or are tramps who'll go with whoever. You want to get a pin. Sooner or later all these boys want hanky-panky, though, so each year you solve this problem by simply trading in last year's guy for a new one; in succession these boys are heartbroken—this is the heartbreak of three boys' lives, though you'll never know it. You join the school chorus, switching after years of humdrum clarinet, something you're enthusiastic about, maybe for the first time.

Your father doesn't know that Effie's great-grandmother was colored (Effie herself doesn't know this yet), because if he did, she would for sure not be sleeping in a room with you and your sister, would not be over at the house at all. You know this because of that time you invited your friend Ginny over to play dolls and didn't think to mention the color of her skin. In retrospect, you should have thought to mention it, since Daddy had more than a time or twenty or thirty made his views on the subject clear. You've heard him come home from work grumbling about how *ever since that pinko Truman's been in office the world's gone to heck in a handbasket. Robinson in the majors, and now they're voting in the House? Malarkey.* It'll be years before you add any of this up, you don't know who Robinson is or whose house he's talking about, you just know to steer clear when he gets on a tear like that. Still, when Ginny comes over and your father comes home from work and you ask if Ginny can stay for dinner all he says is *No*, but you haven't ever seen him look like that before, like there isn't a more horrible thing in the world to him than Ginny being there for even another minute, and you're fairly sure Ginny knows that too, even though her being a little girl is maybe the only reason he doesn't say anything more before he goes and gets your mother. Grandma quietly (though visibly ashamed—she's a good Christian woman who isn't in the habit of sending people away, colored or not) helps Ginny gather her things to go home.

After, Ginny and you are forbidden even to speak at school, so you ask questions: *Why not? Why not? What did she do?* (You almost ask *How will you know if Ginny and I speak at school,* but that's likely to result in a swat on the bottom, plus you're sure he *will* somehow know if you and Ginny speak at school, you never forgot him telling you that newspapermen have *eyes and ears everywhere.*) Your father tells you he's disappointed that you don't already know, which is disappointing to you. *Those people should stay with their own, Lois,* he says, which is a punch to your little gut, *Those people*—what this means about what Ginny did wrong, and what you did wrong by bringing her over—and you make a plan in your mind to be friends with Ginny when you grow up.

—Okay, you're pretty good at this.

—Thanks, Mom.

—I mean, that might be made up, but it could have happened. Maybe it did happen.

—Well, but it's important that everyone understands this isn't what actually happened, only what could *have happened.*

—That's what I said, Betsy. It could have happened. I said "could." In this case, it's fairly close to what actually did happen.

—Yes, but that's not what I want. I want it to be only things that could have happened but didn't. I want the characters and their relationships to be real, but not the exact circumstances. Only similar, believable circumstances.

—But wait, why does it matter what the reader thinks about it?

—Because it's the whole premise of the story. We're sitting here having this conversation because there was so much about the other's private lives that neither of us really knew. You know what I mean: I wasn't alive when you were a girl. I might know a story or two you told me about your childhood, but a lot of times it was just like, "Daddy wouldn't let me have my black friends over." So this way I can make *that a more fully realized story, filling in details I couldn't have known. We can even make up whole scenes based on nothing more than scraps of information. I know where you were married. You know where I went to college.*

—Sure, I get that. I'm just saying it could *be true. I still don't see why it matters how people read it.*

—I don't know, Mom. Because it just does.

—That sounds like a Lois answer.

—I am your kid. I'm never unclear about that.

Marjorie Did It

The Christmas when you're seven, after much discussion, your mother and father decide it's time to bring home a puppy, a West Highland white terrier. This is, without a doubt, the greatest thing that has ever happened in the history of great things. Marjorie is less sure, because when Daddy brings him out, he hands you the puppy first, so in this moment Marjorie has never been more sure that you are the favorite, whether or not that's true. The puppy is supremely cute, a wiggly little sausage of white fuzz—but this moment is altogether different for Marjorie from the one you're having. You're slow to pick up on anything beyond the puppy licking your face, in spite of the fact that Marjorie is whining that she wants her turn, and Mother quickly takes the puppy from you to hand it to Marjorie, who gives you the raspberry. *Let's name him Whitey!* you say, your father says *That sounds like a good one.* Marjorie rolls her eyes. *Yeah, that took a lot of brainpower, how ever did you come up with that?* she says, to which you say, *Because he's white!* as though that isn't the very reason for Marjorie's little barb, which has gone right over your head. *Tell them the rules, Mother,* your father says, sitting back down in his chair. He lights a cigarette and rubs the eczema from his arms, an unconscious habit that your mother cannot break him of and which has left a fine white dust that no amount of daily vacuuming can fully remove from the deep recesses of the chair. You will later say you felt you knew that dust better than you ever knew him. *I swear,* Mother says, *one day this chair will be made entirely of your father,* an image you can't quite make sense of. He's got one of those nubby beanbag ashtrays that sits on the arm of the chair (which beanbag has its own weather system of dust), and a pocket on the side for his *Reader's Digest*s, his primary occupation when he's not at work or the lodge. Mother explains all the work that goes into having a dog: feeding, walks, grooming; she will supervise, but this is to be your responsibility. *And if you don't keep it up, sayonara, Whitey!* your father says. Neither of you kids has ever heard the word "sayonara" before, but you get the gist. And because you are good kids, you both care for the puppy well, walking and feeding him on schedule, though ultimately you and the puppy become so inseparable that Marjorie gives up trying and you happily take on her Whitey chores just so you can say he's *your* dog. At one point you make the case for letting him sleep in your bed, to which Daddy laughs in your face. *Lois already hogs the bed as it is!* Marjorie says. *Do not! Do so! We'll both stay on my side, I promise! No dogs in the bed,* Daddy says. *That's that. I win,* Marjorie says. You give her a big wet raspberry close to her face, she gives you a shove. *Daddy! Marjorie shoved me!*

Now you're eight, Marjorie's eleven. Whitey is overall a great dog but has gotten into the habit of barking incessantly when no one is home and then again for another hour or two after you get home from school. The neighbors all around have complained and you have tried various things with no success: alarm clocks, stuffed toys, putting him in a crate in the basement; all seem only to make him bark more.

One afternoon you come home from school and there is no barking and there is no Whitey greeting you at the door. *Whitey! Here, Whitey!* Nothing. *Marjorie, where's Whitey?* you call upstairs. *How should I know? He's your dog*, she yells down. Mother emerges from her sewing room to tell you not to worry, she put Whitey out in the yard to chase a squirrel. *Phew!* you say and head for the back door. *Whitey!* you call, but he doesn't come running, and you don't hear him and you don't see him and you're not worried yet because he has a long staked chain for when he's outside and sometimes he sleeps in a cubbyhole under the back porch, which is exactly where you find him, but which is weird, because he usually wakes up when he hears you call him. *Hey, Whitey*, you say, and something moves in your stomach you've never felt before, it isn't nausea, it isn't butterflies, it's a new and terrible moving, and you bend down and reach out to Whitey and he is as still as the ground beneath him, and you start to shake, and you say, *Whitey*, even though you already know, you've never seen anything more dead than a smushed spider before but you know Whitey's gone, and you burst into tears, calling *Mommy! Whitey! Mommy! Mommy!* Though you always call your father Daddy, you almost never call your mother Mommy. She comes running outside, sees you crying, *Whitey!* you say again, she looks under the porch at Whitey and back at you, takes you into her chest, you're heaving now, *Shh, child, it must have been Whitey's time to go to heaven*. Marjorie comes outside and asks what the crybaby's crying about this time, sees Whitey under the porch, goes a bit white; Marjorie's tougher than you but it's still a lot for a kid to take, her cute dog dead under the porch. Marjorie says nothing, just sits down. You look at Marjorie with suspicion. She's not upset. You've read a half-dozen Nancy Drew books. The quiet ones are always the suspects.

Your father digs a grave for Whitey in the back, puts him in a cardboard box. The only thing worse than seeing Whitey in that box is seeing your father close the box. He puts the box into the hole in the ground, shovels the dirt back onto it. The four of you are standing around the grave, staring at the hole in the ground. *Can I go inside now?* Marjorie asks. *Shush*, Mother says. You've never been to any kind of a funeral before. Your mother asks if you'd like to say a few words. *To Whitey?* you ask. *Can he still hear me? In a way, yes*, she says. *You know how the lord watches us, and we say prayers to him, even though we can't see him?* You do know, though you have never understood this; the concept is frightening, that entities are watching you that can't be seen: newspapermen, the lord. *Good-bye, Whitey.* You have no words. Your frown is like a caricature of a frown, chin out, lower lip forward and trembling. It's the worst kind of sadness you've known, but you can think of nothing else to say. You stand there silent, Marjorie sighs and huffs loudly, waiting for the go-ahead to leave. You remember something from *Brenda Starr.*

I will avenge your death!

That night, you position yourself at the very edge of the bed, as far away from your dog-murdering sister as you possibly can; a centimeter closer and you'd be in real peril. *I know what you did*, you whisper to Marjorie, facing away. *What?* Marjorie asks. She hasn't heard you. *I know. I know.*

Good Luck

It's 1942. You're six, Marjorie's nine. You and Marjorie are getting dressed for church. Marjorie laughs hysterically upon noticing that your blouse is inside out. *No it is not! Look at the seams, dum-dum, that goes on the inside, not the outside. Shut up!* You're *a dum-dum! Hey, I don't care if you want to embarrass yourself.* Mother hears the scuffle and comes in, screwing on one of her real pearl earrings. *Girls! What's this fuss about? Marjorie called me a dum-dum! Lois said "shut up"! Girls. That's enough. Lois, sweetie, let me help you fix your blouse.* She takes your blouse off and turns it inside out, helps you button it up. *Told you*, Marjorie says. You stick your tongue out at her. *Enough, girls. Goodness, you're on your way to church, this is no way to behave. Why do we have to go anyway, Mother? Lois, we've talked about this many times*, she says, helping you on with your sweater. *Because that's where the lord is*, Marjorie says with no affect, not helping to convince you. You have heard that the lord is other places too, specifically wherever you are. You have talked about this many times, or perhaps more correctly you have been *talked to* about this many times, but you are coming into an age when new information sometimes causes confusion, where there are gaps between answers and questions, when you could ask about ten different questions in response to *That's where the lord is*, though this will come to no good. There's usually a one-question-per-kid allotment about such matters before you are shushed and given the customary *That's just the way it is*, or *The lord works in mysterious ways*, which is creepy and unsettling, because that could mean anything; if the lord works in such mysterious ways, couldn't he just creep right into your room at night and spy on you and take your things and who knows what else? But you keep it to yourself, store up your questions. *Go downstairs and get your coats on, girls*, Mother says, *I just have to remind your father when to take the pie out of the oven before we go. How come Daddy doesn't ever have to come to church?* you ask before you can remember to be quiet. Remembering to be quiet has proven to be a challenge. *Because he's the man, Lois.* You have by now gathered a certain amount of information about what the man does versus what the woman does. The man, as you add it up, does whatever he feels like or doesn't, and the woman does everything else. The why of it, you have no idea.

I want to be a man when I grow up, you tell Marjorie. Marjorie laughs, says *Good luck*. You have no idea what's so funny.

At nine or ten, during science class, you mix some chemicals together that burn your eyes, and after this you have to wear glasses. Mother wears glasses, so you don't mind—you like being like your mother—but Marjorie calls you "four-eyes" and so you try not to wear them any more than you have to. Marjorie says *Ha-ha, good luck getting a boyfriend, four-eyes*, and nine- or ten-year-old you begins to fear you'll never have a boyfriend; even though you have previously not been so sure you wanted one, you want one now because Marjorie thinks you won't ever have one, and that is enough to make it a priority in the near future, when people start having boyfriends, which is thankfully a few grades away yet. You have no idea how beautiful you are. When you've asked *Am I beautiful?* the answer more than once has come back *Charm is deceitful and beauty is vain*, but the meaning of this phrase is never explained to your satisfaction. You are told further that *the lord shall cut off all flattering lips and the tongue that speaketh proud things*, triggering a series of nightmares in which your face ceases to exist from the nose down. Nor are you clear on the difference between metaphorical and literal, and by the time you learn about this in English a couple of years later it will be far too late. You will be told how gorgeous you are, often, in that already-too-far-away future, long past the time when it might have settled in your mind as true. Marjorie has always known, but she's always been jealous, so she won't be the one to point it out.

Hurricane Betsy

Your father gets offered a teaching job in Baton Rouge, nine hundred miles south, and takes it.

Hurricane Betsy arrives when you're about four. The worst hurricane in forty years, say the news reports. Fred and I find this real funny, since it hits us in Louisiana not long after your lengthy tantrum period has finally come to an end. We lose power for several days, a couple of small trees, but we're lucky overall. You imagine, based on your knowledge of *The Wizard of Oz*, that your house could up and fly away with you in it and land somewhere else, that this might be exciting, like, what if it landed in New York City, where Mommy keeps going? You don't have any clear picture of New York at this point, though I've sent you a copy of *Eloise*, so you more or less imagine your house blowing onto the top of the Plaza Hotel, and you and Mommy and Daddy together again, everything pink and stripey and happy and to-gethery. Your father explains to you the difference between a hurricane and a tornado, what the winds and rains are capable of doing. A flat, wet house does not sound so great.

I'm going back and forth between there and New York often during this time, but your dad takes good care of you while I'm away. When you're not at school, he's on the floor of your bedroom pretending to be the mommy in the kitchen with no complaint, and knowing him, no concern at all about the irony of that; he's at the edge of your bed reading you books, there are never enough books, he reads you the same books over and over, *The Bad Child's Book of Beasts*, *Hop on Pop*, gets you new books from the library every week. You ask for one more book every night and he reads one more and you ask for one more again and he reads one more again and if you wake up from a bad dream, which happens often, because sometimes he lets you watch *The Man from U.N.C.L.E.* (just because the sounds of Napoleon Solo and Illya Kuryakin's names please you), even though you don't understand most of what the show is about and the overall tension level makes you dream that you're being chased through your kindergarten by Soviet spies, he comes and sits with you in the dark and tells you that all Soviet kindergarten spies have been apprehended by Solo and Kuryakin, not to worry. He takes you to the zoo, he brushes your hair, he makes sure you brush your teeth; he's not so good at doling out punishment, but generally you don't need too much of that. He writes me to say that you're the best, brightest daughter ever, and that you learn to read when you're three, can't get enough of it. You write me letters like this (transcribed by your father, of course):

Dear Mommy,

I can only write the alphabet letters now but I can read! I sound out the words and Daddy is happy. We read all day. I am a big girl now. Daddy says so. Daddy plays kitchen with me and puts my bathing suit on me and turns on the sprinkler outside and I run in it. I hope New York is fine.

Love,

Betsy

That Ain't Right

One afternoon when you're about five, you're next door at your friend Linda's house making a fort out of blankets and sofa cushions that is intended to be a home in which you are the dad. You have volunteered to be the dad, even though Linda says she was going to make you be the dad anyway because *House decides, Betsy.* You start to say why you actually *want* to be the dad; Linda almost asks why any girl would want to be the dad and not the mom, which is obvious to you but not to her, but she stops herself because she doesn't want to risk you changing your mind and then having to explain to you what *House decides* means. Linda is a nice Southern girl, and you are also a Southern girl now, technically, though you were born a Yankee; maybe that's a mixed blessing, but of the two I think it's the better. You make pretend dinner in the kitchen, pretend pork chops and pretend frozen peas from the pretend refrigerator (a scratchy sofa cushion, set on end) while Linda pretend vacuums the floor. *What would you like for dinner, dear?* Linda asks, and you put on a deep voice and say *I'm making pork chops and peas*, and Linda says *What, no, the daddy doesn't make the dinner*, and you say in your own voice *Sure he does*, and Linda is now wondering if you live in Backwards World, says *No, the daddy goes to his work and then when he gets home he sits down at the table and asks where dinner is.* This is the first you've heard of this; there may have been a moment when some version of this happened back in Binghamton, but you have no recollection of it. Your dad teaches music at college, which to you means he does this by some kind of telepathic singing magic, because he is almost always home when you're home. Yes, you do go to kindergarten, so you don't know that he is gone for some of those hours, but he is there to make oatmeal or eggs and toast in the morning, and he is there to take you to school, and he is there to pick you up from school, and he is there to play with you after school, and he is there to make dinner, give you a bath, read you books at bedtime, tuck you in, come back in when you have nightmares, and he's there for more of the same every other day of the week. *What?* You look at Linda like she's crazy. *Nuh-uh*, you say, *Yuh-huh*, she says *Ask anyone*, and you say *I don't have to ask anyone, I know what's true*, and she says *You don't!* and you say *I do too! My daddy makes the dinner!* and Linda says *No he does not*, and you say *He does too!* and Linda asks *Well why doesn't your momma make dinner? That's the right way*, and you tell her your mommy goes away to work, and Linda shakes her head and says *Oooh*, like this is just terrible, says *That ain't right.* You say *Don't say that!* She says *Well it ain't. The momma takes care of the babies and the daddy goes to work.* You say *Shut up!* kicking down the cushion that's holding the whole structure in place. Linda says *Oooh, that's not nice, I'm telling.* You stop yourself from saying she's lucky you didn't kick her. You say *Well,* I'm *telling, too*, even though as soon as you say it you're not quite sure what it is you might be telling.

You run home and enter the house yelling. *Daddy! Daddy! Linda was mean! What? I'm sure she didn't mean to be, come tell me about it. I told her the daddy makes dinner and she said that ain't right. Isn't right,* he says. *Isn't right,* you say; you're prone to picking up poor grammar habits, he's prone to nipping that in the bud. *Well, pumpkin, we are doing it just a little differently than some people do it right now,* he says. *What do you mean? When I was growing up,* he says, *more often than not, mommies stayed home and daddies went to work. That's how my folks did it, although my mother was a schoolteacher briefly before she married my father. Waaaay back before I was born, if women worked, it was usually before they got married, or it was in very specific fields: schoolteachers, nurses, like that. Now things are changing, and some mommies are also going to work. It might seem different to Linda. But that doesn't make it wrong. It's not wrong.* When he says these last two sentences, you're not fully convinced that he's fully convinced. You're a perceptive kid, but you're four, not in any position to challenge him. Fred's changing with the times, semi-reluctantly. He has the sense that when you grow up, you might be able to do whatever you might like to do, and he wants this for you, though he misses me and wishes I didn't have to be away quite so much. *C'mon,* your father says, *let's bake some sugar cookies. I got a couple of new cookie cutters—a horse, a dog, and a house, and I got us some blue sprinkles. Okay!* you say. *Can we get a real horse and a real dog too? Umm, I think you're going to have to make do with baking and eating them for now. Fine.*

—*Did that really happen?*

—*Didn't you just finish saying you specifically wanted things that* didn't *happen?*

—*I did.*

—*So I'm doing it your way.*

—*Well, it seems believable.*

—*What does that mean? You think I can't guess?*

—I think maybe you could guess but you wouldn't want to.

—All right. That's fair enough. It may have been true once, but things are different now, Betsy.

—Huh.

—Look, if I only tell you what I know for sure, your part of the story is going to be very short and possibly not as interesting as mine. You kept a lot of things to yourself, Betsy.

—That's true. You could have kept more things to yourself.

—You'd be surprised.

—Or not.

New York City, 1967

Your father and I sit you down and explain what divorce means, that he and I have grown apart, that we both love you very much but that we are not going to live together anymore, that he has accepted a teaching job in Iowa, and that you will visit him there, but you will come with me to New York City, where there are opportunities for me that don't exist in Iowa. I can see your little brain wheels speeding up, that you are imagining that his work in Iowa is only temporary, just like when I was away working when we lived in Louisiana, but you don't ask any questions, so at first I assume you're fine, that you understand. We tell you to just keep being the brave and strong little girl we know you are, and things will be fine, almost like they always were. Your father helps me pack up our things for the move, though after everything is divided up neither of us seems to have much, and when we get to the apartment it suddenly feels rather big: it's only a two-bedroom, but we don't have much more than a single bed for each bedroom, four Victorian parlor chairs, and a love seat for the living room.

In the weeks after our arrival, from your height of forty-two inches, you begin to store away vast files of information about our new city. It's hard to tell exactly what conclusions you draw, only that your eyes are always wide open, that you're aware of your surroundings and that you have not yet made sense of them for yourself, because I get asked a lot of questions I don't have good answers for. *Where are all the houses? People don't really live in houses here. Why not? Maybe because it's such a small island? It's an island? Where is the beach? There is no beach. I thought islands had a beach. Not this one. Why aren't there more trees? There are more trees in the park. Why is there so much trash in the street? I don't know. What is that man doing with his pants down? I don't know. Don't look at that. Why is that lady's skirt up so high? Because she's trampy. What's trampy? Never mind. Why is everyone a different color here? Because everyone doesn't hate people who are different colors here. What? Never mind. What does* pendejo *mean? I don't know. What does* fuck *mean? Never mind. How could that guy fall asleep in the middle of Broadway? He might not have another place to sleep. Why not? Maybe he doesn't have a job. Why not? He's probably lazy. Why is that lady shouting at nobody? That lady's just crazy. It seems like there are a lot of crazy people here. There are. Why is it so loud in the subway? They're trains—trains are loud. Why is it so loud here, everywhere? Because millions of people live here. Why do those cigarettes smell so bad? All cigarettes smell bad. What's that smell? I don't know. What's* that *smell? I don't know. What's that other smell? I don't know. Why is everything so smelly? Why is there writing on everything? Is it okay to write on things here? I thought it wasn't okay to write on things. What are those people doing? What are* those *people doing?*

Your reserve of questions is endless, and eventually I give up and tell you I don't know everything, which happens on the first day of first grade. On the walk to school, you say *Daddy knows everything, let's ask Daddy*, at which time I say *We'll talk about it after school*, and you look up at your new school, which does not look like your old school, it looks to be covered in a hundred years of filth, dark and dirty and massive, like if you go in you will very obviously not come out, it looks like a big giant haunted house from a scary movie, not like your kindergarten in Louisiana, which was painted white and had a flower garden in front. *Where are the flowers? Well, there might not be flowers at this school. Where is the playground? It's right here, honey,* I say, pointing to some girls doing double dutch. *That's an alley, Mommy, that's not a playground,* but it is a playground, it's clearly connected to the school, and even if it is a crummy one, it's definitely a playground, and you pull on me, trying to go back toward home, away from the doors of the school, you say *I don't want to go to this school,* and I say *You don't get to pick, this is your school, come on, it'll be great, you love school,* and you say *No, I don't, this school looks like jail.* You start crying for your father, *Where's Daddy, where's Daddy, I want Daddy, I want Daddy,* ceaselessly loud, gulping, inconsolable crying for your father. *Daddy lives in Iowa now. What? Whyyyy? Remember, we told you before we came here, Daddy and Mommy don't live together anymore? No you didn't tell me that! Yes, honey, we did, you and I live here now, it's your first day of school! No! I don't remember anything! Sweetheart, you'll make new friends, you'll learn all kinds of new things. No! I don't want new friends! I want Daddy! Come on, remember how much you love school? No! I don't! I only love Daddy! I want to go back! I want Daddy!* I remind you, again, that we explained about where Daddy was, and that you'd see him as soon as he sent us money. *We don't have money? Not enough. Why won't he send it? He says he doesn't have any more to send, but that isn't true, his parents have plenty. Why won't they send it? Because your grandmother isn't a very nice person and she hates me, now come on, honey, let me walk you to your cubby. Noooo!* It's all I can do to get you to take off your jacket and hang it up. *Honey, you have to stop crying. I can't! I will never stop crying!* You cry when the teacher gently takes your hand. *Don't goooo!* It is reported to me later that you have cried all day. We go through this the next day and the next day, until I become sure you'll never stop, and you don't stop until around Thanksgiving, I suspect mostly because you're finally exhausted.

Around this time, a girl in your class named Alex says hi when you get placed in a special group of kids who can already read. Another girl named Liz is also in this group, and the three of you become fast friends, having playdates at each other's houses. We don't do this at our house often. Because why? Because I can't deal with it. That's just the truth. I can handle one friend over at a time, if you play quietly in your room. So you go to the other girl's houses, where you're free to get more rambunctious (though you're not what I'd call rambunctious anyway), where there are siblings, where there are toys and games and snacks other than celery and cream cheese. Alex and Liz are both nice, bright girls, much more outgoing than you, and one day at Alex's house you and Alex and Liz are playing psychologist, which is what Alex's mother does for a living. Alex is usually the psychologist in this game, since she knows the most about it, and Liz volunteers to be the first patient; you're undecided at this point, so at first you just watch and learn. Alex sits in an armchair in the living room and directs Liz to sit on the sofa. *Wait!* Alex says *I forgot something*, reaches for a box of tissues to put in front of Liz. *I don't have a runny nose*, Liz says, a little defensively, and Alex says *It's for if you have to cry*, and Liz says *I don't have to cry*, and Alex says *You might feel like crying soon*, and Liz says *I won't!* although she does feel a tiny bit like crying already just because she doesn't understand what Alex is talking about, and even Alex doesn't exactly understand why there is crying in psychology. Alex herself has briefly been to a child psychologist, when she was four, doesn't remember it so well, only remembers playing with some blocks and puppets. What Alex knows about adult psychology she has learned from her mother's gentle explanation that sometimes people need to talk about their feelings, and also from what she picked up walking past her mother's office door and hearing occasional loud sobs and complaints about husbands and not feeling understood by anyone.

So tell me about your feelings today, Alex says. *My feelings are fine,* Liz says. *No, you can't be fine, it's boring if you're fine,* Alex explains. *Okay, I'm feeling mad!* Liz says. *Great!* Alex says. *What are you feeling mad about?* Liz doesn't know what to say now, because of course she isn't really mad. *Are you mad because your parents are divorced? No. It's okay if you are. My mom says it's normal to be mad or sad about your parents being divorced. Well, I'm not. Are you sad? No! Okay, fine! What are you mad or sad about then? I'm not mad or sad. Have you ever been mad or sad?*

At this point, you think about when you've been mad or sad, and if you've ever been mad or sad because your parents are divorced (you have for sure been sad), and what to call the other feelings you've had that aren't quite mad or sad. Is confused a feeling?

I was sad last week when I stayed over at my dad's and I had to leave to go back to my mom's. Good! Very good! But then I was also sad when I had to leave Mom's to go back to Dad's.

Wait, you get to see them both? you say. *Sure, silly, everyone does,* Liz says. You say *No! I don't!* Liz says *You don't what?* You say *I don't get to see my dad anymore. Not even every other Wednesday? No.* Liz gets to see her dad every other Wednesday? What does Wednesday have to do with it? That doesn't make any sense—

but it still sounds way better than seeing your dad on no day. Alex can tell by your silence and the slight downturn of a frown that something isn't right here. *Oh no*, Alex says, *you better take a turn getting some psychology now. Liz, you get up now and give Betsy that seat.* You and Liz trade places and Alex says *So what are those feelings like, not to see your dad?* Alex has the idea that the word "feel" or "feeling" should be in just about every question she asks. *Bad*, you say. You've only last week stopped having round-the-clock bad feelings about this, and you are not in any hurry to get them back. *Bad, yes, very good*, Alex says. *Why is that good?* you ask, it doesn't seem good at all, bad and good aren't the same, how does she not understand that? Alex doesn't know. *Well, it just is, that's all.*

Your plan for when you get home is to ask me why can't you see Daddy every other Wednesday, but when you get back, I am crying. So you table the question for the time being and bring me a box of tissues and ask me if I want to talk about my feelings.

Funny Little Girl

When I'm not traveling, I take you to as many Broadway musicals as I can scrape together the cash for, which isn't many, so instead I bring home records: *Carousel*, *Oklahoma!*, *Godspell*, *The Sound of Music*, *Mary Poppins*, *My Fair Lady*, *Fiddler on the Roof*. In 1969, in heaviest rotation, by a lot, is *Funny Girl*.

Of course, you listen to these records mostly when I am not home, when no one besides you is home, which, yes, is often. There is usually a stretch of time—say, if I am out for a voice lesson—that is long enough for you to play an album at least twice or to play your favorite songs: "People," "My Man," "Don't Rain on My Parade," "I'm the Greatest Star" ("*I'm the greatest star by far but no one knows it*"). You save your allowance money for a set of fake nails from Woolworth's, finding that a sailor shirt alone won't quite complete the experience. You have seen *A Happening in Central Park* on TV, studied it. You borrow one of my falls, which is not even a little bit close to your own hair color. You spend a good amount of time setting up the fan to blow your dress around dramatically. And by "your dress" I mean one of my dresses, a peach chiffon mini with bell sleeves, chosen because it will blow the best and because it has a bow in the back like Barbra's.

Always, you sing facing into the big mirror over the living room sofa. Before the song begins you hum the overture because you *feel* the overture. There is no fake microphone; you don't need one. You *are* the greatest star by far that no one knows of. It has been raining on your parade for years now. Oh your man, you love him so, he'll never know. You have no man (or boy) right now, there isn't even an object of your affection at the moment, but this resonates no less on that front. You are utterly certain in the deepest part of your eight-year-old soul that he is in the universe somewhere, that you are tragically separated by forces you don't fully understand but are no less real and true: he goes to another school, he lives in another city, he's one of those boys from *Tiger Beat*, he lives in another country, his mother is mean and keeps him locked in his room (and he knows he should be with you too, which makes it all the more tragic). You don't know which, but it's for sure one of these.

The fake nails never stay on, so often in the middle of your Barbra-style gesturing, one or two fall to the floor and you have to stop and stick them back on, move the needle back on the record. Always, you end by falling dramatically backward onto the sofa with wide-open arms, like you've seen in the movies, with a loud and overdramatic sigh, exhausted from all the singing and feeling and singing-feeling.

When you grow up you will for sure be either a Broadway star, or a veterinarian, or a police, or probably all of those things. Until the following year when you read *Harriet the Spy*. Then you will for sure be a writer. Or a spy.

You hear the click of the lock on the door, jump to your feet. You don't know that I've just heard you sing the entirety of "Don't Rain on My Parade" from outside the apartment. *You have a good voice, Betsy. Moooom.* You turn red; a compliment from your mom means a lot to you, especially given your plans for a Broadway career, but you don't dare admit what you were doing, not to me, not to anyone. You don't really dare anything at this point, you only dream. When you grow up, you won't be scared to sing outside of the apartment, you're sure. *I wasn't singing. I didn't say you were. I was playing dress-up. Okay, Betsy, if you say so. Just know that it's not all about talent. If you want to be in the arts, be prepared for a life of disappointment and poverty.*

—Just FYI, Betsy, this is not me acknowledging that I ever said such a thing. Because I didn't.

—Okay.

In the Year 2000

In sixth grade, you and your class collaborate on a play. It is set "in the year 2000" at the opening of the tallest residential building in the world: three hundred stories, with balconies that "see across the country." You play the mayor of New York, presiding over the ribbon cutting; you're wearing a corduroy blazer and one of Victor's new wide ties (which looks even wider on you). In attendance at the ribbon cutting are Shamed Former President Nixon, Not Shamed Former President Shirley Chisolm, Don Corleone, Bobby Fischer, Billie Jean King and Bobby Riggs, Shelley Winters, Burt Reynolds, Secretariat, a veterinarian, and the ghost of Bruce Lee. It is meant to be Pinter meets Pirandello. *We've been reading them in school*, you report, leading us to second-guess our choice of private school after all, but your enthusiasm is nothing if not sincere. The experience of writing this play has been an inspiration, the laughter of your classmates at your contributions has sunk into you on a cellular level; you feel like your true voice is reaching the people! It's all you've ever really wanted, you know this now. Each character has at least one line about what it's like in the year 2000. *Nowadays we have the ability to shrink our animals so we can carry them in our pockets!* the veterinarian says. *Don't even think about it*, Secretariat says. Throughout the play, there are numerous long pauses and a play within the play in which Shelley Winters swims up from the Hudson River (*We can breathe underwater now!*) to moderate a debate between Nixon and Chisolm about whether or not Nixon should be allowed to breathe anywhere (this little political bit, you feel personally, is your strongest contribution), which leads to more long pauses and various characters jumping in and pointing out that most of these people probably aren't still alive in the year 2000, that we're practically near death ourselves at thirty-nine.

After the play, I shake the hand of Nina, the adorable little girl who played the veterinarian. *You were so great!* We follow this immediately with *You were great too, honey!* though as far as you're concerned that's too little too late. (That you become friends with Nina the following year is almost remarkable.)

The three of us take a taxi home. You are silent for the duration. Victor and I chat about work; your brain feels like it could melt from the heat of your anger; you go straight to your room, close the door. *What's with her?* you hear Victor say behind the door. You fling the door open. *This was the most important day of my life!* Victor laughs. *Don't laugh! What are you talking about? It's a school play. You had two lines. I wrote them! I'm going to be a writer when I grow up!* Victor laughs again. *Weren't you going to be a singer last week? A year ago you were going to be an impressionist. I'm going to be a writer. Nobody knows what they want when they're twelve, Betsy. I thought I was going to be Vic Damone when I was twelve.* Victor's laugh, right this moment, is the worst sound of all sounds ever made. They should use Victor's laugh to get people to reveal state secrets, you think. *Shut up! I can be a singer and a writer! I'm going to be a singer and a writer and I'm going to write about* you! Victor doesn't take this as the threat you mean it to be, laughs again. *Stop laughing! Stop always laughing at me! I'm going to be a writer!*

Iowa City, Version One

The final custody agreement is reached, so you will now make two annual trips to Iowa to visit your father, including one month each summer. Iowa is, to you at this time, basically earth's greatest place. You have three new brothers right there to play with, you can ride bikes in the street, and there are always several gallon-size tubs of ice cream in the freezer, chocolate and butterscotch toppings and sprinkles in the cupboard, a running stream of grape Kool-Aid coming out of the dispenser in the refrigerator door. Fred and Jeannie pile you all into a Winnebago for camping trips, take you to your brothers' Little League games, you all go bowling, play pinball, play board games after nightly dinners of pizza and hot dogs; you make Super 8 movies, watch *All in the Family* together, stay up as late as you want. Fred teaches most summers, but still has plenty of free time. One of the things you do together as father and daughter is go to flea markets. He's forever hunting for Jew's harps, old Iowa sheet music, and antique Iowa postcards; you're currently hunting for any memorabilia having to do with Fred Astaire. *Oskaloosa 1929, Betsy! Technically not antique, but a nice clear postmark. That's great, Dad! Can I get this top hat from* Top Hat*? How much is it? Ten thousand dollars. Sure thing!*

—Okay, I see you trying to make a point here, but way to hit it a little hard, Mom. Can we maybe try again, this time with a smidge of realism?

—Fine.

Iowa City, Version Two: Kegger

Summer of 1973. You're twelve years old. You're in Iowa for the month of August with your father as per our custody agreement. Like me, he has remarried: a young widow named Jeannie who has three boys, your age and older. Next time you visit you'll have a new half sister as well. Iowa City is only slightly less exotic to you now than it was a couple of years earlier, when you first visited. But you're just on the other side of the age where drive-ins with the family and lemonade stands and riding bikes around the neighborhood are endlessly entertaining. The topics in rotation on your daily, hour-long phone conversations with Nina are boys, boys, boys, clothes, books, boys, and boys. Your brothers are close to your own age, about twelve, fourteen, and seventeen, something like that. Possible options for Nina someday. You get along well with all the brothers, though the seventeen-year-old is generally not very interested in you or your brothers, given your youth. He's interested in girls and getting stoned and if there's beer he's interested in that too. Tonight, the fourteen-year-old knows where there's beer. Your father and Jeannie are at the Bix Fest in Davenport, back in the morning. The fourteen-year-old wasn't planning to invite the rest of you along, he was just planning to go to a keg party at his bud's house, but failed to make sure the twelve-year-old hung up the other extension of phone before discussing party details with his friend. *Oooh, I'm telling!* the twelve-year-old says; the fourteen-year-old hangs up, says *Shut it*; the seventeen-year-old enters, says *What's happenin', little brothers*; he's probably already stoned. You enter the room mid-discussion. *He's going to a kegger!* the twelve-year-old says. You don't even know what a kegger is, mostly because you mishear this as "kigger," though it's clear that whatever this is, he's not supposed to be going to one. *Righteous*, the seventeen-year-old says. *We'll all go. I'll drive.* The fourteen-year-old says *You guys suck* to his brothers. *Come on, Bets, you too*, the seventeen-year-old says. You don't want to ask what a kigger is for fear of looking like an idiot, so instead you say you were thinking of just watching *Toma. It's summer, Betsy, it's a rerun, come on, this will be way more fun.*

The four of you spill out of the station wagon at the kegger, which right now is six eighth-grade boys and somebody's little sister standing around a small back yard listening to rock music on a transistor radio and passing around a dinky bowl of stale Bugles and a bag of Hy-Vee-brand wavy potato chips. Your brothers all know immediately that this party is pretty beat, though the fourteen-year-old might have had a good time with his buds if you guys weren't there totally ruining that vibe. You, however, feel a little bit like you're in a movie, or at least an after-school special. In New York, you're a good girl; your crowd isn't nerdy, exactly, but you and Nina aren't exactly hitting the discos at this point either, and so this to you seems as exciting as the TV-movie moments before the cops or the parents bust in and ship everyone off to juvie. A boy with shiny blond hair down to his shoulders hands you a Dixie cup with beer and you accept it happily; you haven't tasted alcohol yet, but if this is what everyone is making so much fuss about, you're not sure you've been missing anything. There are bits of wax from the lip of the cup floating in the beer, indicating that this paper cup may have been someone else's first. But you take a hearty sip, try not to make the face that says this is your first time, and it turns out that the sensation that follows is actually A-okay. You're thirsty, so you gulp half the cup down, not realizing how quickly the booze will act on the popcorn and ice cream you had for dinner; the result turns out to be both enjoyable and instructive in the event of future keggers. You thank the blond boy, notice that he's wearing a striped T-shirt and bell bottoms, *very cool*, and that he looks a little bit like that kid from that TV show with the family that you like, that heartthrobby one who's always on the cover of your *Tiger Beat* magazines. *Do you go to Northwest?* blond boy asks. *I don't think I've seen you before. No, I'm from New York. No shit! New York City? Uh-huh. That must be so rad*, he says. *Is this like the most boring thing that's ever happened to you? No, I'm having a good time.* Three waxy cups of beer later, blond boy and you are inside in whoever's family room this is, on the sofa, watching *Toma*, and his hand is on your knee and your knee is on fire. In your mind you go from knee on fire to blond boy writing you love letters for the next four years until you graduate from high school and can move to Iowa, to do this forever as Mr. and Mrs. Blond Boy. His name is either Andy or Randy or Brandon; too late to ask again now. Andy or Randy or Brandon leans in to kiss you and now you're five beers in, which has allowed you to forget that you're about to have your first kiss just six feet away from your three new brothers. You have no idea right now if this is a good kiss or a bad kiss, it's just his lips on your lips, but it's a cute blond boy and he's kissing you and it's the greatest thing that ever happened. For a moment you think of stopping him, just so you can go call Nina long-distance, but that will have to wait until tomorrow.

Unfortunately, tomorrow is maybe not the worst thing that ever happened, but it's not in any way good.

Technically, it's already tomorrow when the four of you arrive back at the house to discover Dad and Jeannie's car in the driveway. *Oh, shit,* the fourteen-year-old brother says. You file into the house to find Jeannie on the phone with someone's mother. She takes a big sigh, folds herself in half in relief. Your father looks vaguely dismayed. He doesn't want to have to tell you that if I got wind of any part of this, I'd hustle him back to court in a second, but he knows it's true. It's plain to see that the four of you have been drinking. *Everyone to the table,* Jeannie says, starts by saying how worried they were, none of you home, how many phone calls they made. *The most important thing is that you're all safe,* Fred says. *But there are consequences,* Jeannie says. The seventeen-year-old is grounded for the rest of the summer; he was in charge, and he should have known better. The fourteen-year-old and the twelve-year-old get no baseball for two weeks; you're grounded for a week, and no TV and no phone privileges until you get home.

Unable to use the phone, you spend the day writing an epic letter to Nina. The previous night's romance is still stirring in your center; this could be part beer-hangover, but you don't recognize it as such, in spite of being grounded. What you mostly feel is deep and true love. You peek into your father's office to ask for an envelope and a stamp. He's smiley as always; last night's events will not be mentioned again until 1996, at which time he will claim he hardly remembers, whether he does or not. Hard to know with Fred, sometimes. Anyway, when you hand him the letter and he sees how thick it is, he says *Oh my, this may need extra postage!* Not unthrilling to your dad—the postage, that this is something he can give you. He reaches into his desk drawer, where he keeps his mail supplies: envelopes, all denominations of stamps, and his little hand scale. He folds the six-page letter in thirds and stuffs it into the envelope, clips on the scale, gives the pointer a second to find rest. *Hmm, looks like it's just on the line here, so we'll definitely need to add four cents. Which ones do you want?* He opens his folder of stamps. You point to the Robert Indiana LOVE stamps. *Nina will like those. She has a poster of that in her room. Excellent choice.* You really want to tell him you're sorry about last night, but you have no idea what to say. So you hug your dad for the stamps like he's just given you a new puppy, and he knows.

The blond boy calls after dinner. Seventeen-year-old brother answers and is about to hand the phone to you, sees the sad look on your face, remembers your punishment, tries to mitigate the situation on your behalf. *Uh, she can't come to the phone right now, can I give her a message? Okay. Okay. Sure thing.* Seventeen-year-old hands you the scrap of paper with a number and says *Randy wants to know if you've seen* American Graffiti. Randy! You knew it. You've seen it and loved loved loved it and would see it again. Your dad hears this, sees your disappointment, and says *You can call back and tell him why you can't go, if you want.* Jeannie looks mildly irritated with Fred for bending the agreement like this, but you're not her kid, so she keeps quiet. You want to call Randy back, but having to tell him you're grounded and can't even talk on the phone is the definitely worst thing ever. Fred's still working on burying the shock that his little girl came home drunk last night, but he doesn't want to cave all the way on your punishment, which wouldn't be fair to the boys.

Randy's not home when you call back; just as well. The sound of his blond voice on the phone would be too much. You leave a message.

The following afternoon, Randy shows up at the door in his best butterfly-collar shirt, holding out a blue Ring Pop, says *I already got you this*, he looks sad, and you're sad too, because this is the next greatest thing that's ever happened: by giving you a ring he is obviously saying that he was indeed hoping to be with you forever. Your father comes to the door to see who it is. *Hi, Dr. Crane, Oh, hi, Randy*, you're stunned that they know each other, turns out Randy is the son of a respected colleague. *I was just going*, Randy says. *Okay, well, it was really, well, you know. Maybe I'll see you next summer.* You nod. Next summer is twenty years from now. You wave apologetically as he leaves. *Well, you know what, you're only here for another week, Betsy. Randy's a nice boy. Maybe we can add on another day of being grounded at the end. I'll talk to Lois.* You love your dad the best.

—*Do you really think that?*

—*I don't know. I've thought it.*

There Are Like No People

You're a sophomore at a nice private high school on the Upper West Side. We've chosen this school because it's safer than the public school in our neighborhood.

—Hey, Mom, can we talk about that?

—What about it?

—Does anything about that strike you as—not quite right?

—What's wrong about it?

—I guess I just wonder if you were worried about my safety more than you were about my education?

—Sure I was.

— . . .

—The neighborhood was still rough then, Betsy. The school you would have gone to had a reputation for being dangerous.

— . . .

—I don't understand what you find so wrong with what I'm saying.

—What about the quality of my education?

—We didn't pick just any school, if that's what you mean. This one didn't require uniforms.

—Okay. Moving on.

Tonight's dinner conversation is not to your liking, even though it's not all that different from any other night's dinner conversation. Mostly business. You see it otherwise.

Can I be excused? you ask.

This is the real world. Get used to it, your stepfather says. *It's not my world*, you say. *Don't be naive, Betsy. Stop always saying that! You think because you have one Jewish friend who isn't greedy that what's true isn't true? Well, who is good, to you, Victor? Seriously, what people are okay? Are we okay? Obviously not all white people are okay, because I know how you feel about Jews and gay people.*

You better shape up, Betsy, he says.

You go to your room and close the door to call your best friend. *They're so prejudiced, Nina. It's awful*, you say. *Oh, Betsy, I'm sure they're not*, she says. *There are like no people they don't talk shit about. I'm sure they don't mean it. Don't be naive, Nina.*

You are decades away from recognizing what you just said as having anything to do with anything.

Later, when I think you may have calmed down, I knock quietly on your door and open it a crack. *It's just me.*

I can see that you're not over it.

Betsy, you know how Victor is. Don't let it get to you, I say. *Why am I supposed to be the one who changes?* you ask. *Because he won't. Well, I won't either. Mom, why don't you ever disagree with him? Considering some of what you've told me about Grandpa I would think you would have something to say. How can you complain about his prejudice when you have your own? That was totally different*, I say. *How was it different? It seems exactly the same. Have I ever said you couldn't be friends with someone because of their race or religion? Because that's what it was like when I was growing up. But what difference does it make if you still think and say awful things about them? We would never say those things to their face. I know! That's my point! Betsy, come on, we have Jewish friends and gay friends, I've sung with people of every color and background. There are always exceptions. Oh my god! Well, there are. So you agree with him. Not on everything, no, of course not. How come when he gets going on me you never say anything? What? You never defend me, ever. It's like, when he goes off on me is like the only time you don't have something to say. Sweetheart. . . . Forget it, Mom. Can I be alone now please?*

Cornices

A junior in high school, you haven't been dating yet because you go to a small school and there aren't a lot of choices. By winter, Nina is on her second or third serious boyfriend already; it is decided that they will fix you up on a blind double date with them and his friend Ed. After some deliberation, you pick out a striped button-down shirt and the gray cashmere V-neck sweater you got on sale in the men's department at Charivari, with a pair of high-waisted jeans and blue Wallabees. *Maybe a nice necklace? I could lend you something. No thanks, Mom. What about a pair of boots instead of those, honey? It's snowy out. Yeah, I can see out the window, Mom.* You look at me like I have no idea what's good. *You could bring a pair of heels. Heels with jeans? Don't act like people don't wear that now. I've seen the pictures of Bianca Jagger. Wait, you know who Bianca Jagger is? Yes, Betsy. So that means you know who Mick Jagger is? He's that hideous-looking rock singer, right?* Do you want to bother picking this apart? The fact that your mother knows who Mick and Bianca Jagger are, or the fact that she finds him hideous? You guess not. *Well, anyway, I'm not going to a disco, I'm going on a date. What's Nina wearing? What difference does it make what Nina's wearing? You just called Nina to find out what she was wearing. Yes, because Nina likes to dress the same as me, Mom. Oh.* This isn't the complete truth, though, because while dressing identically to Nina is unacceptable, neither do you want to wear something radically different. *Okay, what about a scarf? Do you want to borrow a scarf? People don't wear scarves, Mom. I wear scarves. Mom, it's 1977! I know what year it is. Well you don't seem to know how we dress now. What are the boys wearing? How should I know! I heard you ask Nina just now. Don't listen to me in my room! I wasn't trying to listen to you. It's not a big apartment. Well, don't tell me what to wear. I can dress myself. I know that, I'm just thinking you might want him to ask you out again.* You look at me like I've stabbed a basket full of kittens. Way down in you there's one tiny cell of your being that wants to challenge me on this statement, to look into it more deeply, to ask about a dozen questions about the idea behind this statement, but you aren't there yet. It's a cell that isn't a fully realized idea that can be formed into words. *I thought I looked cute in this! Well, you always look cute, you'd look cute in a paper sack, but I wouldn't send you out in that either. Get out of my room! You better watch it, daughter.*

Ed, it turns out, is gaga for you. When he comes to pick you up at our house for your second date, I can tell he has spent hours picking out his clothes because he's wearing a nice pair of pressed slacks, Gucci loafers, a checked button-down shirt, and a crewneck sweater. Ed comes to pick you up and he sits down with us and he's all pink in the face, can't stop smiling, like the girlfriend sweepstakes has come to his door with a bouquet of balloons and you wearing a prom dress, a tiara, and a sash. Ed is richer than Croesus and takes you to Windows on the World on your first official date, and you talk about school, where you might go to college. He's applying to Ivy League schools, but you wouldn't get into any of those, which is fine, you don't care all that much, and he says it's not that important even though he's not so sure that's true; all he cares about for the time being is making you happy. At any given moment he will say or do whatever he thinks might accomplish that goal. You don't look at him much on this date; even though the conversation is good, you aren't very good at eye contact, and also he has to compete with the view. Ed maybe didn't fully think through his choice of restaurant, because you are given to dreaming, but he wouldn't know that, and when you look out those windows, uptown, you may as well be floating right out of them and over the city, looking at water towers and rooftops and cornices; you could do an aerial tour just looking at cornices alone, wonder who made them, what went into cornice-making, was that a job, cornice-maker, when did beautiful cornices go out of fashion, what happened to all the cornice-makers when that happened; or you could take a turn west and tour your life here so far, you could go up and down streets and note the ones you've walked on and the ones you haven't, noting how very many you haven't, wondering how there could be so many people on this small island, just like you did when you were six, whose idea was that, wasn't there ever a time when anyone, planners or whoever, stopped to say *Hey, guys, this island isn't all that big*, had some kind of city-planning meeting, a bunch of round men in old-timey three-piece suits, smoking fat cigars, *We'll just keep going uptown*, they say, a lone skinny man says *It's not infinite*, the round men say, *The sky is!*; you float back out, wonder what happened to the skinny man, fly over to the East Side, swoop down over a Fifth Avenue penthouse, railings and trees wrapped in lights, imagine a future with Ed, your future in general seems so far away, but it's hard to picture yourself in a life this nice, like, there's a nice life for you out there, you're pretty sure, less swanky probably, and you wonder what really is to come, where your place is. You want to ask him if he thinks about those things too, you imagine that rich kids might not really wonder about anything, that they don't have to, that a certain course is already set for them, which may or may not be true; what may be just as true is that, either way, Ed would like to take your hand and join you out there above the city, and talk about other lifetimes when it was the Brooklyn Bridge that towered over everything, or a time when bums on the Bowery still wore suits and ties and hats, or when your entire family together could barely afford your nine-dollar-a-month rent, but there was still something about these times, a certain type of shared experience that you know doesn't exist now. But these don't seem like first-date conversations, which is too bad, because Ed would pretty much spend the rest of his life listening to whatever you had to say; you could be that couple that meets in high school and stays together forever, if you wanted to be; he would always love you like this if you let him, would entertain any romantic notion you put forward, would absolutely take you back to any one of those eras if he could. Instead, you talk about movies you like, and music, and you talk about Nina, and her boyfriend, how they're the perfect couple. (She's wealthy, too, and also boys are paying more attention to her than to you, not because she's more beautiful, yes, she's beautiful, but because she's warmer and more open and friendly than you are. That's just the truth.) About twenty times during dinner he wants to tell you how pretty you are, but he never says it, even once, because he doesn't want to scare you, and also because he figures you hear it all the time. He doesn't know yet that at this point you haven't heard it from anyone besides your mother; this is your first date with anyone, not just him. He takes you home in a taxi and gets out to kiss you good-night on the cheek, and the next day you tell us *It was nice*, but that's all we can get out of you, pretty much all we ever hear about it for the duration, even though you date him for the next few months, though you've known since the aerial tour of the city that there was something else ahead for you, even if you didn't know what just yet. He tries again and again to get you to do anything beyond kissing, but when given the choice between saying you're not ready for more and swatting his hand away, you're willing to swat for the length of time that you're together rather than actually talk about it.

Victor and I find out you've broken up with him around two months after the fact, maybe a month after we first asked why we hadn't seen him lately. You'd mentioned that he was going to Gstaad or someplace with his family, but that was a while ago. Also during this time we never have to pry the phone out of your hands to make a call, or if we do it's because Nina's on the other end. Eventually you tell us that you and Ed broke up months ago, that you don't want to talk about it. *What? Oh no, honey, I'm so sorry*, I say, and you say *I broke up with him, it's fine.* It's not really fine, you liked Ed a lot, and you very much wanted a boyfriend, you just didn't think Ed was the one. Later on, I find out from Nina that Ed was pretty crushed about it; you know how Nina sometimes lets things slip.

—Am I right?

—Well, I'd tell you now, but I don't want to spoil your idea of me.

Like Paris

You first meet Frederick in your freshman year at Iowa, second semester. The University of Iowa, about an hour from Muscatine, seems like Paris to you at this time. You share a dorm room with a gal named Joyce from Cedar Rapids who strikes you as positively cosmopolitan, who has actually been to Paris and is happy to talk about it all the day long. Joyce has a navy gabardine dress with impeccable seaming that she bought in Paris, a dress with *Madame de Something-or-Other* on the giant label on the back of neck, in the most elegant cursive you've ever seen. Your first thought is that you and Mother could sew a dress just like it, but something about that label conjures entire worlds; it's practically the size of a dance card, finely stitched aubergine letters slanted against an ivory background, with the word PARIS in a boldly serifed font below. (You don't know what a serif is yet, but you can tell class when you see it.) You major in music, to some concern of Mother and Daddy, who aren't sure what one does with such a degree (you explain that you can be a music teacher, which is true, but not at all what you have in mind—not that you're altogether sure what you do have in mind just yet, something vaguely—*bigger*), but their real hope is that you'll meet a nice young man to marry and create a family with sometime after graduation. It will not displease them when you meet this goal well before graduation.

The aforementioned nice man is also your music history professor. He's not quite as dreamy as William Holden, but Fred is handsome, with dark hair and twinkly green eyes, and you are no different than about six other girls in that auditorium in that you're absentmindedly doodling hearts on the end pages of your textbook (an antique sheet music design), though yours manifest as musical notes with hearts for noteheads and delicate ribbons in place of the flags. Absolutely nothing untoward will occur during class, will not even occur to him (he has zero idea that even one girl is looking his way), but at the end-of-year department picnic, he will offer to refill your cup of punch, and as he hands it over he becomes aware that you are an adult female and you become aware of his awareness, and no one will think anything of it when he begins to court you; this is the last class you will have need to take with him. He will drive to Muscatine every Saturday for the rest of the summer, meeting your parents (who are elated that you have landed such a worldly, scholarly, handsome man), always in a tie and jacket, even for an ice cream cone and a walk by the river. He hands you a ring on New Year's Eve that year, and two summers later you will be married in Muscatine, in a dress your mother made, five bridesmaids at your side.

There isn't quite enough time to plan the dream wedding—your studies take up all your time, you're preparing to graduate in June and have been giving thought to a graduate degree—and after putting it off as long as possible, you and Mother decide that it will be at the Methodist church up the street where you've reluctantly been going to services since you were born. There was some talk about having it at the Cranes' estate in Mount Pleasant, but that set your two polite mothers into utter disagreement, while you stood by, nearly invisible, in the discussion. This negotiation is almost like a Mafia sit-down, but with polite middle-aged Midwestern mothers. Mrs. Crane opens the dialogue by saying with great pride that she has hosted several weddings on the lawn, that it is an absolutely lovely and scenic place for a wedding, and that for these occasions they have a set of Doric columns they keep in the barn to use for an aisle or an altar. She comes armed with photos of Fred's sister's wedding; it is undeniably picturesque, with the old ivy-covered barn, the rose garden, and the pond in the background. Your mother counters on your behalf that it is your preference to have the ceremony here in Muscatine, at your own church. She added that last part; the church is *her* preference. You'd prefer to have it at the Plaza in New York, with nary a minister in sight, a vision from a picture you saw in *Brides* magazine, a fantasy. But there are only two options on the table, and of these you would definitely prefer Muscatine, mainly because that's where your friends and family are and you want to be sure everyone comes. Mrs. Crane counters that they would *of course* be willing to foot the bill for the entire thing, which gives your mother a moment's pause; as parents of the bride, they will be funding the wedding, that's just the way it's done, though their income has always been modest and your mother knows the Cranes are quite well-to-do. Mrs. Crane picks up on this pause, but your mother cannot have everyone in town knowing that they let someone else pay for their daughter's wedding (even though they have just recovered from Marjorie's wedding, which set them back $675). She thanks Mrs. Crane for her kindness and says *It's settled, Lois really wants to have it here*, and so you will have the ceremony at the church here and the reception in the ballroom at the Hotel Muscatine even if it costs you another pretty penny and that will be that.

You and Mother pick out a Butterick pattern at the fabric store downtown, strapless but with a lace overlay that has cap sleeves, nipped tight at the waist, a full skirt. You both *ooh* and *ah* over some of the fabrics; this might be the most fun part, doing this with your mother, choosing a pure white satin for the bodice and skirt, a gorgeous floral lace for the overlay, with a scalloped edge around the neckline. Even the tulle for the underskirt and veil is dreamy. But when you get home and Marjorie sits you down at the dining room table with a to-do list the length of her arm, you're suddenly not sure you shouldn't have gone to a justice of the peace and called it a day. On Marjorie's list: bridesmaid's dresses (she would prefer mid-calf to the just-below-knee-length pattern you've chosen), gloves, flowers, dinner, music, invitations and RSVPs, favors for the table, place cards, cake. Marjorie is excited but also serious. This is a big job; studying for the music theory final is infinitely more appealing than wedding planning right now (and this class has been a total drudge, confusing from the get-go, where is the theory?), and you say so, and Marjorie asks *What's wrong with you? This is your wedding, the most exciting day of your life*, and this idea fills you with horror, frankly, that you might get only one exciting day, but all you can come up with to say is *Nothing's wrong with me, what's wrong with you?* and Marjorie says *I don't have to help you, you know*, and you say *Then don't*, and Marjorie gets up from the table and you say *No wait, do*, and it's a bummer to have to ask Marjorie for help in this way, especially when she sits back down and says *I thought so*, smiling while you glower. She might as well have a list that says *house, cleaning, cooking, wifely duties, baby, baby, grandbaby, grandbaby, grandbaby, grandbaby, dead, done, the end.*

For the most part, the next few months are a blur of wedding planning. Mother and Marjorie are so excited about it that they hardly notice that you find the planning not nearly as much fun as they do. At the printer's, a discussion of fonts lasts an hour, until you can't tell a roman from an italic, and you've definitely stopped caring. For one entire afternoon, you sit and wrap candies in scraps of tulle tied with a bow and a tag that says *Frederick and Lois Crane, August 12, 1956*—why is his name first, on everything? You address envelopes, you address return envelopes, you lick stamps, you lick envelopes, you come to despise envelopes and whoever invented them. You fold place cards and hand-write the names of the guests, make seating charts until your fingers cramp. *Can't they sit wherever they want? It's buffet anyway. Heavens no, Lois, do you know what will happen if Cousin Carol sits next to Bernie Hofstrad? I guess I don't. Well you don't want to.* You get an A-minus on one of your music theory papers because there was no time to proofread it a second time, and since you can't abide the idea of graduating from college with less than a 4.0 GPA, you beg the professor to give you one more chance to revise. That spring, you finish college in three years—no surprise there. Your parents attend the graduation; they are beyond proud to have two college graduates for daughters; but there's no doubt that everyone's primary focus is the wedding, and there's no real celebration beyond milkshakes at the drugstore counter downtown. Your twentieth birthday, the same weekend as your graduation, is almost forgotten. Mother makes a sheet cake, Daddy gives you a Brownie camera (*For your honeymoon!* he says), and then it's back to wedding planning.

One afternoon, in the midst of all this, you try to steal a catnap; you lock the bedroom door, hoping to clear your head, to remember why you wanted to do this in the first place; it's all moving so swiftly, as though of its own accord. But Mother needs to hem your dress, and Marjorie's knocking on the door in a frenzy, because somehow boutonnieres got overlooked, and *if they don't have any white rosebuds left would you settle for carnations, and did you remember to call the minister, that was your job*, and you yell *Goddammit, Marjorie, just let me rest for five minutes!* and Marjorie says *Ooh, you took the lord's name in vain!* though really she just thinks it's funny, adds *There's no rest for the wicked!* and you yell *You're wicked! You're wicked! Leave me be!* and pull a pillow over your head.

Come the big day, Daddy walks you down the aisle with a big grin, you see Fred at the altar absolutely in love, and you're grateful; he's handsome and he's solid, you're sure he'll take care of everything, of you, that you've made the right choice, that there couldn't be any other choice—even though for a minute, walking toward the altar, you picture yourself taking a detour through the pews and out a side door, jumping into your father's Chrysler for destinations unknown, for that other life that will be exactly right, even if you don't know what that is right now. Des Moines, maybe! You went there once on a chartered bus with your high school chorus to hear the orchestra; it was positively magnificent. What exactly would you do in Des Moines, though? What do people do in big cities? Do people go to the orchestra every night? You try to picture elegant Des Moines cocktail parties on the nineteenth floor of the Equitable Building overlooking the city, clinking crystal stemware and talking about important things and being generally clever and erudite. Are you erudite at all? You think of yourself as clever. But clever enough for Des Moines? For anywhere that isn't Muscatine? You hope, but you don't know. The not knowing is what snaps you back into the aisle headed for the altar, where you promise to love, honor, and obey, and hope the future takes care of itself.

To New Friends

You're at college for all of three weeks before you meet the guy you decide is the one to give it up for. It's the fall of 1979, just pre-AIDS. Or, well, not pre-AIDS, pre–people knowing about AIDS. Christ, I hope you don't have AIDS.

—Mom, I think you would have known if I had AIDS.
—Well, I wouldn't have wanted to.
—I don't think I even know what that means.
—Okay, whatever, you don't have AIDS, it's fine.

The point is, no one is thinking thing one about condoms at this point. Or you're not. Getting pregnant and/or contracting herpes are the worst possible outcomes you personally can imagine, but after four or five spritzers you are not thinking about either of these things, much less a fatal disease that hasn't yet been discovered.

—Spritzers? You think I drank spritzers?
—No?
—Spritzers kind of make me sick just to think about.

—*Okay, Scotch neat.*

— . . .

—*So let me get this right, you're worried about me getting your drink of choice right, but not so much about getting pregnant, herpes, or AIDS.*

— . . .

Once you've had enough tequila shots, you start flirting with Steven, the guy down the hall you've got a crush on. These tequila shots also go a long way toward helping you forget that he's recently been dating one of your roommates, or at least move you in the direction of convincing yourself he's fair game at this point. He's cute, much cuter than the boys back home, longish wavy brown hair, twinkly eyes, like a Jewish Warren Beatty, and he's maybe a little bit funny: he asks you if heaven is missing an angel and you're about to say to him *Seriously?* but then he says *Just wondering, I mean, if an angel goes missing, would anyone even notice?* You giggle, but maybe that's only because you've had the necessary number of additional tequila shots for this to seem like it means something even though it's really just absurd. Either way. Tonight, your dreams of romance are elsewhere. You're going to get this out of the way. You're already too drunk to notice that his jeans are ironed with a crease in the front, because this could otherwise be a problem. (Any time a man's jeans are overthought is justifiable pause for consideration as far as you're concerned, which is the opposite of what makes sense to most people, but you will stand by this in perpetuity.) Time has a way of morphing when you drink, so that your seven-and-a-half-minute conversation (covering the half block from *What's your major* to *Where are you from* to *Do you know so-and-so*) becomes sufficient even though most of these questions lead to conversational dead ends. (*English* to *marketing* nearly puts the kibosh on the whole operation right there. You have no idea what marketing even is.)

You overlook: That everyone you know sees you leaving the bar together. That you can see them whispering to each other. *Not cool.* That you hadn't planned for the steady and rapid loss of your buzz on the six-block walk back. That there's not much more to say on the way back to the dorm than there was after he'd said *marketing.* After a long block of silence, you say *So, marketing, what is that, exactly? I guess the easiest way to say it is that it's about how to sell things. It's not that interesting. So why are you majoring in it? I dunno, what else would I major in? Something that does interest you? I'm not really interested in anything.* This is a sentence you're sure you've never heard before. Where does the conversation go from here? Who isn't interested in something? What could that even mean? What goes on in the head of a person who isn't interested in something? Nothing? You may not know what matters to you, but at least you know what interests you. You can't form a sentence. He senses your confusion, probably because in your inebriated state, your face is a screwed-up caricature of a confused face that you might ordinarily try to conceal. *Okay, well, I'm interested in sports. . . .* Never have you been so relieved to hear someone say that they're interested in sports—the one subject among all existing subjects you might be the least interested in—if only because it relieves you of the surreal analysis going on in your head. *I guess I'm just not interested in anything that you could major in. You could major in journalism and be a sports writer. Uch, I hate writing. I don't even like reading.* And here again the conversation ends.

At no time does it occur to you to back out. Or, it does, it does occur to you to back out, but for some reason that doesn't seem like an option. You already said yes, and you hadn't accounted for variations of mood or circumstance that might lead to a change of plan. So you also overlook that, when you get to his dorm room, he asks his roommate to come back in half an hour. At this point, not having done it yet, you don't know how long to expect—a half hour? three hours?—but you certainly get it now that in a half hour you're out of here, which leaves you with a now fully formed watermelon in your stomach of *maybe this wasn't the best idea.* Fortunately he's got a bottle of rum back in his room, which will help wash that right out. Never mind that rum is fully disgusting. Not the point. He motions to his unmade bed; it's a dorm room, there's a desk chair, but that's it. *Sit, sit,* he says, weirdly casual, like this is an actual home where you're going to pretend for a minute that you're not going to do what you're for sure going to do. He toasts *To new friends*, that's not good, even though you're no more interested in friendship than he is, but whatever, you raise your glass and knock back the rum. He takes off his shirt and pants, even though he hasn't kissed you yet. It's not one of the all-time great seductions. You may not know what to do, but you've seen a movie or two, which honestly you were planning to use as a rough guide, but you can't think of any movies where the guy starts by taking all his clothes right off. Are you supposed to take yours off now? Because that's not going to happen. Your idea of a perfect seduction is Katharine Hepburn in wool trousers with a glass of whiskey in one hand and Spencer Tracy kissing her in front of a fireplace just before he gets up to leave. Steven is now down to just his royal blue bikinis. He got past the dreaded creased jeans somehow, but this has to be a deal-breaker. He doesn't read, but that you can actually put aside; this, however, cannot be unseen. This has got to be a rule, somewhere, that the late-in-the-game revelation of royal blue bikinis is an exit pass.

This can't be how this goes. He hasn't even kissed you yet. You've never done this before, and weren't expecting *From Here to Eternity* or anything, but maybe some small pretense of romance? You really should go. Right? You can do that. Change your mind. People are allowed to change their minds. How far is the rum? The rum is right there on the floor beside the bed with the cap off. How could anyone leave an open bottle on the floor? That is a booze loss waiting to happen. You grab the bottle and take a swig, put it back down, look around for the cap. He looks at you somewhat expectantly. You look at him expectantly back. He reaches over to help you take off your shirt, moves down to undo your belt, leans you back onto the bed, kisses you exactly once before he's got his hand all the way into your pants, pushing them down just far enough so he can stick it in. No mention of birth control of any kind has been made by either of you before he moves his dick in the direction of your pants. At no time do your hands move away from your sides. You wouldn't know where to put them even if you were inclined to put them on some part of him. You have definitely not had enough to drink, but you suspect that if you hadn't had whatever number of drinks you've had, you might be in for a fair amount of physical pain. To be sure, once it's in, it feels like nothing approaching good, though there's little in the way of sensation, leaving time to contemplate the pointlessness of this exercise. Your intention was to "get this over with." Should you call it a success? That's a stretch. Steven makes some unattractive noises before his body goes limp on top of you, rolls himself off. Jesus, why would anyone want to do *this* more than once? You look up to see if you can reach the rum, have to stretch a bit, almost knock it over, take one more swig before getting up to go. *Okay, I'm gonna go.* Better to at least pretend as though he hasn't already set a timer on this. *Okay.*

Outside the room, Steven's roommate and a couple of other guys you recognize are sitting on the floor, laughing. They might be laughing because Steven just got some with you and you're now slinking away, or they might be laughing because someone made some joke about something else entirely, but the effect is the same. You plot ways to avoid running into any of these people ever again, which could be challenging.

When, a few weeks later, your period is three days late, you have cause to consider your options in the event that you might be pregnant. Your period's been late before, but this is the first time there's been any reason to worry about it. But there's no worry really. You are pro-choice. It's a bunch of cells. There is not even one fragment of a thought in your head that this could be the beginning of a baby, or that this is a medical procedure with any risks, however minor. You know about *Roe v. Wade*, although you don't know who was who pro or con, or why, and you honestly don't even care to be grateful for Roe or Wade or whoever it was who is totally doing you a solid right now. All you have to worry about is where to get the money for it. Otherwise, there's no more than a vague *I'll cross that bridge if I ever come to it*, and then your period comes, so the bridge is still at a safe distance. You might have three or four other pregnancy scares in the future, but those bridges aren't even built yet.

Still, you won't do sex again for a while.

Bright Future

The fall after you and Dad get married, he takes a year in Germany as a Fulbright scholar. You are twenty years old and have never traveled out of the country before and you are terribly thrilled. You ship a box of books and sewing supplies ahead of your arrival, as you'll need something to do. Your main objective is to be a perfect wife. You rent a small furnished studio apartment near the university; there's not much to it, but you will do your best on your tiny budget to make it homey: a couple of small plants, a fine linen tablecloth from the flea market for five marks (it has a small coffee stain, but you read Heloise and know just how to get that out with a little baking soda). During the year you will pick up more things along the way: a watercolor from a street artist (*It's so dear, Mother, and just two marks!* you write home), patterned curtains you whip up from some fabric remnants she sends. On weekends you and Fred explore parks, wander through museums, attend concerts at the university, budget down to the penny for a bus tour of Europe. You purchase a harpsichord on layaway, which is beyond over budget, but a piano is out of the question financially (not to mention that you wouldn't be able to ship it home), and you will both make good use of it.

Early on, there's an audition for choristers for an upcoming recital. You ask Fred what he thinks about you auditioning and he says he thinks it's a marvelous idea, so you go in, and though you are not yet trained, they remark that they are stunned that you yourself are not a Fulbright scholar, and they offer you a few solo lines in the recital.

This, of course, is one of those life moments on which an entire future hinges, and you simultaneously know it and don't. It burrows down into you, this recognition, locks in there the way a butterfly screw opens up behind the wall, and you are sure that this is the thing that will truly give you to yourself. You practice for four solid hours a day. You have never been so excited or nervous in your life, not going to college or getting married or even flying on an airplane to Europe. The performance goes well; you get to take a small but special bow, during which five seconds the applause goes down into that place in you that makes you feel absolutely alive; it is one of the greatest things in your history of great things. You are swarmed afterward, and Fred lets you have your moment, but he's beaming almost as though it's his own. You cannot stop smiling, write home a handwritten, five-page, double-sided, exclamation-point-riddled letter about it. *All the faculty thinks I have a bright future as a soloist if I want it!*

Two weeks later you take an overly long afternoon nap. You don't feel ill, but you don't feel well, and you have no name for this odd, uncomfortable unwellness, for a second you think you might be with child, but you have been cautious about that, marking your calendar diligently and counting the days, so that surely can't be it, and it passes, and you are terribly relieved when it does.

—This is quite accurate, so far.

—I do have the letters you sent to Grandma from then.

—Oh! I didn't know that. I'd like to read those. But, wait, I wouldn't have written to Mother about anything like that last thing.

—I know.

Matters

Junior year, one Saturday night in your dorm room at GW, it seems like a good idea to drink a six-pack or two of beer because you have a paper due for rhetoric class, and halfway through the semester you still don't fully understand what the word "rhetoric" means, much less how to write a paper on it. *What* does *"rhetoric" mean?* you ask your roommate. Kimmie is practically a hippie compared to you, wears peasant blouses and patched dungarees, ends a lot of sentences with the word "man." *Is that a rhetorical question?* she asks, laughing a bit more than is warranted, handing over a small ceramic pipe. *No,* you say, *it's not, I don't think I get it. It just basically means persuasion*, she says. You exhale a lungful of smoke, say *Huh. I thought it was more, like, philosophical than that. It could be*, she says, *but in itself it just means how you get your point across.* You've now got a buzz on that prevents a real understanding of what "in itself" means here. *In itself*, you say out loud, and then it starts to ring around in your head, with added visuals, you picture same things in same things, books inside of books, pens inside of pens, pipes inside of pipes inside of pipes, infinite same things in infinite same things. *Whoa*, you say, a minute later or three hours later, one of those; neither of you has even a remotely accurate perception of time right now, and if you can't understand the concept of rhetoric you definitely can't understand the concept of time. *In itself. What does that even mean? Okay, look*, Kimmie says. *What is your topic? Rhetoric. No, your paper topic. What are you going to write about? I don't know! Well what does it say on the syllabus? Syllabus? Yeah, the syllabus, that piece of paper they give you with due dates? I don't know if I still have that. It usually helps to have that. Syllabus. That's a weird word. Syllabus. Sillibus. Sllbs. That's a weird word, right?* In your rhetoric notebook, folded among the notes you took in class that you can't read because of your atrocious handwriting, you discover the document. Kimmie takes it, runs her finger down it to find Monday's due date. *Okay, easy-peasy. You get to pick your own topic. Basically all you have to do is make a statement about something that matters to you, and then argue a case that it's true. Something that matters to me? Yeah, something that matters to you. Uch*, you say out loud. You have no idea what matters to you, especially not after nine beers and three hits off Kimmie's pipe, which you now notice is shaped like a nude man with a tiny bowl acting as his erect penis. *Whoa.*

Kimmie begs you to go out with her after your pre-buzz is fully on, one more hit before she goes, paired with another room-temperature beer that hasn't had time to chill in the mini-fridge. *You're not going to get any work done now*, she says. *It's ten o'clock already*. You say *I have to fry*. Kimmie falls over laughing. *You said you have to fry! No I didn't, I said "try"! Whatever, are you coming, or not? No, I have to figure out what matters to me.*

Your roommate exits laughing; you weren't meaning to be funny. You honestly do not know what matters to you. Being drunk and stoned at the moment doesn't help, but stone-cold sober the question would be no less existential. You climb up to your bed, the top bunk, with your notebook and a pen. You open the notebook to a blank page, write "What Matters to Me" across the top, with a number one below it on the left-hand side of the page. Nothing comes to mind, so you write a two below the one, then a three below that. You could just put the stupid pen down on the paper and scribble, maybe it would come to you that way, but it seems too important to just write any old thing down, "peace on earth" or whatever. Stuff like that matters to everyone, doesn't it? What matters to *you*? Right now you can't even remember what *interests* you. You write down "Matter," next to the first number. Now you're on to something. Next to number two you write "What is matter?" Then you cross that out. "What is <u>the</u> matter?" That's not right either. What the fuck *does* matter to you? You care about things. You want the people in your life to be well and happy. You've always liked writing, but does that *matter*? Could that be a thing that matters? You know that whatever matters to your mom, you don't want to matter to you—heaven forbid. That made sense when you thought it a second ago. Oh yeah, right, because you'd be engaged right now if that were the case; forget that there are no viable candidates just yet, at least you have the good sense to know that if you can't even figure out what matters to you, even the best candidate would end in disaster. Then again, you don't want to do the opposite of what your mom did either, because she always told you she did the opposite of what *her* parents did. If you do the opposite of the opposite, is that the same as doing the same? You could just relax, maybe experiment a little. But that's not really your thing, not the experimenting, definitely not the relaxing. You want a boyfriend; you sometimes think a boyfriend would be not so much what mattered to you most, but the thing that would cease your cosmic loneliness long enough for you to *fig-*

ure out what mattered to you most—because the truth is, boys do take up a lot of space in your head, even if it is usually just one at a time.

Another beer will probably help. You climb down off the bunk; your foot gets stuck between the bars toward the bottom. You fall backward—no big—you get up, grab a beer, but suddenly popping open a beer is physically demanding, your right hand doesn't have the strength to pop the tab and your left hand is made of mush, and the beer drops to the floor and spills all over the shaggy throw rug. You try to pick up the can to salvage some of it, but it falls right out of your mush hand as soon as you lift it, which is a bummer, because when you go to the fridge to get another, you discover that that was the last one, and you don't have it in you to go get money from the bank, which isn't open anyway. You go pee, come back with the crusty rinse cup from the sink, try to push the spilled beer out of the rug into the cup with the side of your hand; this results in nothing more than some slightly wet fuzz on the lip of the cup, and you wonder how one would wring out the rug while it's still on the floor. You put the cup upside down on top of the rug, pinch at the rug fibers with your fingers in the hopes of flipping the cup quickly with the liquid still in it, this method also unsuccessful. Somehow you climb back up to the top bunk (tomorrow you won't remember this part), look at what you wrote, scribble something on it, pass out, wake up with the notebook in front of you, not realizing you'd even passed out, scribble a few more words, pass out again, scribble some more.

You want to matter in the world. It matters to you to matter. Yes. You'll figure out how later, maybe. Sadly, though, in the morning, you won't remember this; just as well since it's not a suitable paper topic anyway.

Climbing down from the bunk the next morning, you find that your left wrist has swollen to the size of your face, and you are certain you can see it throbbing like something's in there trying to get out. At student health they ask a bunch of questions for which you don't have answers. Nothing new. They X-ray your hand; there's a small fracture. For about two seconds you think that this could be a consequence of having been drunk and stoned, before blaming it on getting the short straw on the top bunk.

—That is really interesting, Mom.

—I always thought I could have been a writer.

— . . .

—What?

—That's not exactly what I meant.

—What did you mean, then?

—It's just . . . plausible.

—You should give me more credit.

—You should give me what I already have.

—I don't have any idea what you're talking about.

—Let's just move on.

—You move on.

Entry

You graduate from GW in December, a semester late, because of the drinking and not going to class sometimes. It's almost remarkable that it's only one semester, but you pulled it together when you were on the verge of flunking out—drank only on weekends after that, which helped improve your grades, anyway. Junior year you switched your major from English to broadcasting, when you realized it was the only major that would get you out of school before 1992. Not that you have any big ideas about what to do with this degree. You don't even have any small ones. You might like to be a newscaster, if it didn't require hair spray and a suit. The truth is, all you really want right now is a job where you don't have to wear a suit. I try to tell you that you have to at least have one suit for interviews. *Why should I spend money I don't have on a suit I'm never going to wear? It's an investment. That's not what an investment is, Mom. An investment is when you expect or hope to get more money back than you put in. Don't be smart with me. Everyone needs a suit sometime, Betsy. I don't want to need a suit. I'll take you to Jersey to the outlet malls, my treat. You always want to treat me to things you think I need, never what I really need. You're twenty-two years old. You don't know what you need.*

You move back into your old room at home with us even though this is not ideal for anyone. Our apartment hasn't gotten any bigger in the last four years. After a few weeks you land an entry-level job at CBS News; unfortunately, they put you on the graveyard shift. One night, during your three a.m. lunch break, one of the local weathermen sits down next to you in the commissary, asks if you mind having some company. You tell him you don't mind at all; the weatherman is super cute, even though it's hard to tell with the suit and the combed hair and the moustache, which you are way not into. It's 1984. Didn't people stop having moustaches about five years ago? You're not really up-to-date on weatherman style; maybe this is überhip on the weather scene. The commissary is a bleak landscape at three in the morning. The room has no windows, dropped ceilings, and fluorescent lights; it's like a grade school cafeteria without the noise, which would be a welcome relief from the odd, steamy silence. The only other person here is a janitor eating some pudding on the other side of the room. *Roger McMenamee*, the weatherman says. You say *Hi, Betsy Crane, yeah, you do the weather, right? I do, but at 3:25 a.m. I'm sort of the tree falling in the forest of weathermen.* You smile. *So . . . if you talk about the weather, is that like, work? Exactly. Esoteric subjects are wide open, though. Oh good. I was hoping to talk Derrida tonight.* He laughs and asks what you did to get yourself on the late shift. *I guess I graduated from college with no previous work experience?* He nods. *Oh, that's good. You have a chance of getting out then.* You aren't really sure what he's talking about. *I drank my way onto overnights.* You smile, assume he's joking. You are not yet at the point where you might talk about your own drinking mistakes. Everyone drinks in college. When you do talk about your drinking mistakes, it's with a certain amount of pride. That time you and your friends got lost on the Beltway back to DC after a house party in Arlington and mistook the Peruvian embassy for your dorm is still hilarious to you, even though it was not hilarious at all to the Peruvian diplomats, who nearly had you taken away by the cops. Roger the weatherman has a curious smile on his face as you tell him this story, nods in a way that you can't totally break apart, and you're usually good at reading people. He asks what department you're in; you tell him you're sending facsimiles in the traffic department, ask if he knows what a facsimile is. He laughs, says he knows what the word means. You say *Well, it's like sending a letter over the telephone very slowly.* He thanks you for educating him, you tell him you didn't know until you got there that traffic wasn't traffic, like car traffic; he laughs again, finds you charming. *Would you like to dine together again, perhaps somewhere with fewer mayonnaise-based choices?* You say *Sure, I'd love to.*

Dinner with Roger the weatherman is surprisingly fun. He's funny. You are big into funny. *So did you study . . . weather in college? It's called meteorology,* Roger says. *But no.* He tells you he didn't go to college at all, that he was a comic before he was a weatherman. *No kidding? Actually, all kidding. Okay, I gave you that one. So . . . how did you get into weather then? Believe it or not, I was recruited,* he says. *They found me at a comedy club, where I also happened to be bussing tables, and when they told me what the salary was I told them I had always wanted to be a weatherman. I used to bus tables!* you say. *I knew we were soul mates,* Roger says. He's kidding, but he's flirting-kidding, and it's fun.

The waitress comes to take your drink order. You ask for a vodka and soda. Roger says he'll just have the soda. You try to hide your disappointment that he's making you drink alone, but he gets it. *Trust me, you don't want me to drink. I don't? Well, maybe you do. Are you into drooling and public nudity? Not so much,* you say. *Yeah, not too many women are.* He said "women." Weird. *Also, my employers didn't care for it so much. They gave me a choice between overnights and nothing. So you just quit? Well, the network sent me to rehab last summer, that helped. They sent you to fix up a house?* Roger looks as confused as you do, takes him a beat to realize you don't know what he means by "rehab." *No, rehab, like, a facility, a place people go to dry out. I've been sober for seven months now. Wow,* you say. What do people say to this? "Congratulations"? That seems weird. "Hey, congrats on . . . the most boring existence possible?" Definitely weird. *Huh,* you say. *So, you like,* never *drink? That's what sober means, yeah. Huh.*

You're not quite sure how you and Roger are going to move past this, but he changes the subject and you manage to pace yourself over dinner so you hopefully don't look as buzzed as you are. Roger's not an idiot; he's counted how many you've had—four, to be exact—and yes, you did sit there for a good hour longer than most dinners because it's been so fun, but he definitely knows you're buzzed. He also really likes you. Which tonight means he puts you in a taxi and kisses you on the cheek.

But this job pretty much sucks, because you're trying to sleep during the day when I'm trying to practice. Fortunately for everyone, it lasts only four weeks; a career in news holds zero interest for you, the very word "career" is one you're uncertain about, as it implies commitment and ambition, which you've told me more than once is *not what you're about*, so you sign up to take a bartending class, less to forge a career in bartending than to buy some time in which you hope a brilliant noncommittal career plan will come to mind. When no such thing happens in the next week, you get a bartending job, which lasts roughly the same number of weeks as the CBS job, which is to say not many. This takes you into spring, when you take a job with a children's talent agency. It doesn't pay well, but it holds some small promise for career advancement, and as desk jobs go it's not the most boring ever, and you like your coworkers, and you now have a tiny bit more than zero dollars in your savings account. Thank god, because you can't take living with us much longer and we can't either. *You can't stay here forever. It's unhealthy. What does that mean? It's bad for our health? It's bad for our mental health, yes. Victor lived at home until he moved in with you. No he didn't, he had an apartment. He lived there for a week. Well, it was different. Yeah, it was longer. His parents had a bigger place. With one bathroom. I'm not discussing this any more, Betsy. You have a month. And then what? You'll put my stuff on the street? Don't test me.*

The Brother Plan

The summer after you turn twenty-four, you're unemployed again; Nina suggests you get a job on Fire Island. The idea of a summer at the beach is never a bad one; you spend a lot of weekends out there as it is, why not three months? Nina says that one of the families on her block is looking for a mother's helper. She knows this is something you wanted to do back in high school: you love kids, and working with them in some way has always seemed like a vague career idea that might get you to a less vague career idea. Unfortunately, there's nothing vague about the pay: there is none. Instead, you get to live with a family at a beach and get one day off per week. You give some thought to this, but you still have rent to pay in the city. Specifically to me and your stepfather. You have overstayed your post-college welcome by a year, and have agreed to our "you'll pay us two hundred dollars a month for our troubles or you can go find another place" rental terms, but you're already behind three months, and unlike your father's handouts, your mother's loans always come due. So the plan is modified. Nina convinces her parents to let you stay with them for the summer, so the revised plan is that you'll get a waitressing job. You have experience, but one after another of the more upscale restaurants turns you down (you are not big on putting on so much as a decent blouse and slacks for these interviews, figuring that if they like you they like you), and you turn one offer down when it's suggested that the shorter your skirt, the better the tips. You're finally hired as a server at one of the diveyer bar/restaurants in town, the kind that smells like beach and stale beer and serves burgers to people without shoes. Good enough. You get to tell me you were right: someone has hired you for who you are, in a T-shirt and a ratty jean skirt. Bonus: you can wear that same costume to work, you don't even have to pull your hair into a ponytail, and you get a meal before every shift and a free pitcher of beer after you cash out.

For a few weeks, everything about this is fantastic. That Fire Island has no streets, and no vehicles bigger than a golf cart, makes it ideal, at least to begin with. By day, you lay out at the beach in a slick of baby oil and a string bikini, flirting with the lifeguards; by night you flirt with the bartender and the guy who sits at the door. You and Nina are both single at the same time (or, more accurately, Nina is currently as single as you always are), and she usually meets you in town after you get off work to hang out with friends, find other boys to flirt with, maybe go dancing. You're not saving a ton of your tips, but your back rent slowly gets paid down. You and Nina fantasize about living there year-round, writing novels about your mothers. You both know that the fantasy is very different from the reality: winters on Fire Island are bitterly cold, transportation on and off the island is limited, but the main thing is that very few people live there all year. The plan is to get boyfriends who would also live there with you to offset the need for other human contact. Nina sets this plan into motion as soon as you discuss it—not that it wasn't already in motion, at least to the extent that Nina is rarely without a boyfriend. You set your eyes on a pair of brothers who already live there year-round. You've always liked the younger one, who has curly brown hair and dimples and some amazing dance moves. Really, his amazing dance moves are all that matter, until he asks you to dance one night and tells you you're a good dancer. This fast-tracks him into being a candidate for The One. Nina hasn't come out this night; she's out on a date with the guy who runs the produce market. Back at home you discuss your evenings: her date was a dud (she only went because she doesn't like to hurt people's feelings and couldn't think up an excuse fast enough when he asked); there's only so much to say about cucumbers, as far as Nina is concerned, but no, there are many different varieties, plus *Cucumbers can become all different kinds of pickles*, as Nina learned over the course of her two-hour dinner. You, however, are really digging that cute younger brother. You're both excited about the brother plan, but Nina will have to get to work on the older brother ASAP.

The next day, you're on the lunch shift. Lunches are usually kind of slow and you're always bummed to miss a sunny afternoon at the beach, especially for a crummy haul of tips. Nina's home on the back deck working on her tan and her novel. You're not too concerned about her getting ahead on that part of the plan for now; you're having too much fun. You've got plenty of ideas, you're just storing them up. Right now you're *living life*.

You're pulling your bike up to the Solomons' house and cute younger brother is just leaving. He says *Oh hey! See you in town later?* and you say *Sure!* As plan-making goes, such fuzziness on Fire Island is as good as a formal invitation to dinner. This is promising.

What you don't find out until after he walks away is that cute younger brother has just invited Nina to go all the way over to the Pines for tea dance and dinner. *He's going to pick me up and take me in a water taxi! But Nina, that was* my *brother! I thought you liked the other brother! Nina, we talked about this just last night! Yes, I thought you meant the other brother! I didn't! Well, okay, maybe it won't work out with us. There are like sixteen things wrong with what you just said. What do you mean? I can't explain it to you if you don't already get it. But the other brother is so cute, are you sure you don't want to go out with him instead? Yes, I'm sure! All right, well, I guess I'll cancel then. Nina, it doesn't matter now. He obviously wants to go out with you and not me. Like every other guy who ever sees you ever. Betsy. Well, it's true. It's not true! It's totally true. Ed totally loved you, Betsy. That was almost ten years ago. And it was a fluke. Betsy, listen to what you're saying. No,* you *listen to what you're saying. Have a nice time on your date with your stolen brother. That's not fair. Nothing is, Nina. Welcome to my world.*

At times like these, your best idea, always, is to go back to the city. It's not going to be better there, but leaving where you are is always the very first solution to any problem. Nina convinces you not to go, says she's sorry; she goes on her date, you go to town and get drunk, which is a close second to your preferred solution to any problem. You remember nothing of this night, but when you wake up in the morning your left hand is the size of an oven mitt. There's a dull ache, but your head hurts worse, so at first you hardly notice. At the breakfast table, Nina reports that her date was a dud again, just no chemistry with cute younger brother, really, but he's nice and she thinks you and he really would probably be a much better fit. You've now had about a half ounce of coffee, enough only to look Nina in the face and hope she gets that you have problems with what she's just said. *Come on, Bets, what's the big deal, we've dated the same person before. Remember Paul Pearlman?* You manage a giggle. *It's hard to forget a guy whose signature move is taking you to the pharmacy to buy you a Flower Power sticker and a packet of Sen-Sen. Will we ever figure out what he was thinking? No. But we must never forget,* you say. *Look, it's not Fire Island if you and your best friend haven't had some overlap,* she says. You decide it's not worth arguing, even though you will probably have to cross cute younger brother off your list now. You're reaching for the sugar bowl when Nina notices your hand. *Betsy! What? What happened to your hand?* You look down. *Hm. I dunno. I think I might have fallen off my bike. I'm not really sure. It's fine. It's not fine! It's purple!* She rushes you over to the doctor's cottage; he X-rays it, sees your previous fracture, notices the way you brush that off when he asks about it, says it's just a sprain this time, bandages it up, gives you a half-dozen Darvon for the pain, tells you not to drink and to take off work for a few days. *Hooray!* Nina says. *We can both sit on the deck and write!*

This is what comes of that:

> Once upon a time there was a young woman still living at home whose mom ruined almost everything. So the young woman went to Fire Island to spend the summer with her best friend, but then her best friend stole the guy she was interested in, ruining almost everything else, so she went and got drunk and broke her hand. At this point, everything was fully ruined.
>
> Once upon a time there was a young woman who dreamed of being a writer but somehow it was her mom's fault that she didn't actually do it. So one summer the young woman went to the beach with her best friend to write, but she realized she didn't have anything much to write about besides her mom

ruining her life. The young woman's second-best idea was that great writers drink, that if she took up drinking in earnest, she would soon be struck with brilliant ideas that weren't about her mom. But when this didn't happen, she drank more, because that's what drunks do. They drink more. Nothing any better happened after this, believe me.

Once upon a time there was a brilliant young writer in New York City in the nineteen-eighties who was discovered walking down the street by an important book editor who could totally tell that she was brilliant and a writer just by looking at her. The important book editor told her there was an opening in the literary brat pack and that she'd be perfect for it and that he would explain over a six-martini lunch. *You are expected to behave badly. It sells books, but you'll be rich and famous. Perfect!* said the brilliant young writer. She handed in her manuscript and got a six-figure advance for her first book, and was on the cover of *New York* magazine, which got her another six figures to pose for a liquor ad with a typewriter and shot glass. For a time she went on international book tours, had mad love affairs with everyone else in the brat pack, but then she discovered cocaine, blew all her money up her nose in just a few months, and had to move back home again with her mother. Whose fault this all was, obviously.

You knew before you started that when you try to write about me it always comes off bitter. And you are bitter, but you don't want to come off that way. So you scrap your three paragraphs and work on your tan instead, offer to read Nina's pages while you're doing that.

What sucks harder than the fact that she has pages at all is that her pages are really good. You've always thought Nina was a better writer than you, and now you know for sure. Everything comes easy for Nina. She gets all the cute boys first, she doesn't have to work, and she's just naturally a good writer. *It's good*, you tell her. You fear adding words to this compliment, because more words will likely indicate resentment, whether you mean to or not, will quietly or not-so-quietly attempt to diminish her confidence. So you move straight to self-pity. *I suck*, you tell her. *What? You don't suck! You're a great writer, Betsy! I'm a lazy ass. I can't just sit around and write. I have to earn money. But someday we will earn money doing this! Don't be naive, Nina. What's naive about it? We will! You will, maybe. We both will! You don't know what will happen. I can't sit around writing and calling it work. My mother will ask me where my writing paycheck is and if I tell her it's coming in the future she will laugh in my face. She's a singer! She started somewhere. Yeah, but that's different. How is it different? I dunno, she told me it's different, that's all. Well, it isn't different, Betsy. It's the same.*

By the end of day one, Darvon aside, your skull feels like it's three sizes too big for your head. You're sure one drink later tonight won't hurt a thing. The Darvon are gone anyway.

Brava

You and Dad come back from Germany and move to Binghamton, where he has a teaching job.

—You forgot about Minnesota, Betsy.

—I'm just conflating. Nothing happens in Minnesota that's all that different from what happens in Binghamton.

—That's probably true.

You move into a little Cape Cod, excited to set up your first house. Your budget is still laid out down to the penny, so you sew more curtains, shop sales, make a braided rug out of wool flannel remnants for the living room, take it apart about four times until it lays flat. You fix supper for Fred most every night, broiled, buttered chicken breasts with frozen lima beans, pork chops with frozen green beans, Jell-O or vanilla ice cream for dessert, Mother's three-bean salad in the summer, nothing fancy. Sundays are his turn to cook but he would just as soon have TV dinners, which are fairly newly popular, and which Dad considers to be one of the brilliant innovations of their time, so when his turn comes it's either Salisbury steak with peas, mashed potatoes, and apple pie, or he'll fix up some braunschweiger sandwiches on Hillbilly bread. For a while you're pleased with yourself for being such a good homemaker, write letters to your mother thanking her for all the ways she taught you to save pennies, but once the place is all decorated, you're not altogether sure what to do with your time. You're thought of as a good faculty wife, whatever that might mean, showing up with a smile to cocktail parties in a smart wool sheath, pearls, and circle pin, and you know Dad never so much minded that you wanted a career as much as he just hadn't fully understood what that might mean, and that he hadn't thought about it at all before you got married. You're not even sure how much you did, honestly. You knew you wanted more than what Muscatine had for you; that was about it at the time.

There's a small opera company in Binghamton, and you and Fred have attended a few performances there, though you secretly think most of the singers are positively dreadful, that you would be better than any of them. But you and Fred have been trying to have a baby, and soon after this you get pregnant; you're only twenty-two, and this is what people do, though you have some lingering uncertainties about whether it's what you really want, or at least this soon. Still, when you eventually miscarry, you find yourself unexpectedly sad. You imagine a boy (though you'll never know), standing over his changing table, tickling his tummy, observing the utter perfection of every part of him, his long eyelashes, his chubby fingers, thinking how lucky he is to be a boy. The image vanishes though, and your mind takes you somewhere else: you've failed. This is not something you have much experience with—none, to be precise. You have never known anything but triumph, no matter how small; you got straight As throughout school, you behaved like a proper young lady, always, never once got in trouble, although you haven't forgotten that time you brought your friend Ginny over to play, how even though you weren't punished, you had failed to see that your judgment was utterly wrong. This new but gripping sense of failure settles in as though it had been there the whole time waiting for the best opportunity to come forward, like a creature with a mind, as though you are fully made up of whatever the chemical components of failure might be; you now clearly see where you've been made of failure all this time, that you will simply have to work your absolute hardest against this from here on. Shortly after this, you consider trying again, wonder what it would be like to have a little girl to dress up, to pass down all the things your mother taught you.

Your friend Audrey is about your age, already has two kids, a boy and a girl just over a year apart. Audrey is the perfect mother; she was in nursing school when she got pregnant the first time, decided to finish later. You spend a great deal of time at Audrey's with your friend Inge, observing Audrey's endless patience with her toddlers (she laughs when you tell her this, but it's more or less true, she's a gentle soul); mostly, though, you are making notes in your head, as you are fairly sure that your patience is a finite resource. *Fred is ready*, you tell them, *but I might want to wait a while.* You love having Audrey's baby in your lap, his tiny fingers gripping your thumb, but he is crying soon enough, so you hand him over to Inge, who has no plans for children herself, but who also has a good way with a baby. You fall a bit silent, realizing that if you have a crying baby, your handoff is likely to be at work. In her soft German accent, Inge says *Not efryone has to haf babies, Low-is. Dan and I aren't going to.* You've known this about Inge, but it's an idea in your head that people who don't have babies *can't* have babies, that if you choose not to have babies, there's some extreme reason, like a family history of leprosy or hysteria or who knows what, not that you might simply prefer not to be a parent. At the same time, there's a speck of a thought that this doesn't seem quite right: Who decided this? It seems like something that was decided. Inge is one of the most rational, even-tempered people on the planet, capable of making a decision on the basis of her own research or perhaps even her own instincts about what's right for her, but why doesn't that seem to apply on this issue, or at least not to you? You don't feel like you have a choice. A part of you loves the idea of having a child. Another part feels like having kids will be a terrible, terrible idea.

Soon enough it happens, and when you're about three months pregnant, barely showing, you attend another faculty gathering where the director of the local opera company learns that you're an aspiring singer and invites you to audition for an upcoming oratorio. You haven't been practicing recently, an hour here or there, having gotten caught up in making house and babies, and you tell him so, but he insists that it can be casual. You ask for a couple of weeks, during which you practice "Caro Nome" several hours each day, and when it comes time to audition you wear an A-line maternity dress you made just for the occasion (though you still don't really need maternity clothes yet) from a light gray wool that was on sale (you are especially pleased with the sleeves, which are not always easy to line up right with the armholes, sometimes it's necessary to rip them out several times before you get the seams to match up in a perfect line underneath the arms). The maestro greets you with kisses on both cheeks, even though he's from Albany. When you're done, he jumps to his feet, claps, yells *Brava!*—

laughs with joy—and he is not humoring you because you're Dr. Crane's wife, he's genuinely moved. This is all you. The maestro says he can't wait to introduce you to the world and this is the absolute greatest thing that's ever happened in all your twenty-three years.

Who Has No One

Nina is getting married. You are not at all fond of her fiancé, the two main reasons being that he's not that into getting to know you, and that he takes up most of her available time. Nina hasn't abandoned your plan to be famous authors, marry best friends, live next door to each other, and have kids (who would either be best friends or marry each other); she's just followed through, while you've been held up in a bunch of saloons along the way. She's asked you to be her maid of honor, which as far as you know means walking down the aisle and standing next to her, possibly in a horrible dress. That seems manageable enough, though you're not looking forward to it. It's maybe not so surprising that she's getting married before you; Nina's an always-has-a-boyfriend type and you're a wait-for-some-movie-star. Still, a part of you, a big part, feels like this is something she's doing to you, or at least something that is happening to you with some sort of cosmic intention. Frankly, this seems emblematic of your life in general. Your worldview is perilously close to being fixed on Life Is a Series of Events Specifically Designed to Fuck with Your Head. That's a worldview, right? You're from New York. What else would it be?

—I think this might be true, but I might be conflating your worldview with mine.

—There's some overlap, Mom. Or there is at this time, anyway.

Unfortunately, it's difficult to have this conversation with the person you most want to have it with. It's obviously not reasonable to suggest to Nina that she's doing this to hurt you, getting married, but what you can't quite work out for yourself is how she can't anticipate your needs about the whole thing. It doesn't help right now that Nina's worldview is, in essence, the opposite of yours. She believes deeply in prevailing goodness. So when you propose to her that these events are being designed with nefarious, Betsy-sabotaging purposes, and she asks who it is that might be designing them, your response is a simple one. *God*, you tell her. *I didn't know you believed in god*, she says. *I don't, really*, you say. You both can't help but giggle, but you're going to stick with it. *That makes no sense*, Nina says. *It makes perfect sense! How does that make any sense? I don't know exactly, it's just what I think. Maybe something happened in a past life where I did believe in god, and then something shitty happened and I stopped believing in god, and even though I don't remember any of this now, the god I once believed in is punishing me now.* Nina laughs. *Don't laugh!* You both laugh. *Don't laugh, I'm not kidding! Okay, I believe you, I believe you, but it still doesn't make sense. Don't tell me what makes sense! God isn't about what makes sense, everyone knows that. Betsy, come on. Listen to what you're saying. It's what I think.* It is what you think. It is really what you think, and you're going to stick with it for a while.

At this point, you've been to a whole lot of weddings. You've been to weddings at the Plaza and the Pierre, outdoor weddings overlooking the Hudson, backyard weddings on Long Island, church weddings in the Bronx and temple weddings in Queens, Buddhist weddings in Vermont, interfaith weddings in people's living rooms, and weddings at City Hall. The obvious and logical conclusion is that it's not all that hard to find a partner, for everyone in the world besides you, and the sub-conclusion is that there is something deeply and irreversibly wrong with you. This is further evidenced by the fact that you are almost never invited with a date. It doesn't occur to you that this is largely because you almost never have a boyfriend. What does occur to you is that everyone who knows you probably thinks you can't even get a date. This is on the growing list of Things Being Done to You. You believe that you should be invited with a date either way, whether you can get one or have one or don't want one at all. You have no idea who you would even bring, but every single time a fat white envelope arrives in the mailbox (and it's hard not to notice that they're getting bigger and fatter and more in-your-face than ever; undoubtedly the wedding industry is on the board of the Betsy-sabotaging conspiracy) without "and Guest" after "Betsy Crane," you can read the invisible calligraphy that reads instead "Who Has No One." What's crazy is that you like weddings, in theory, but lately the main thing on your mind, as one bride after another walks down the aisle, is that it isn't you.

You come in with no idea of what being a maid of honor entails. Nina's not really sure either. The wedding is mostly being planned by her future mother-in-law, who gives you a list: wedding-day duties include keeping track of Nina's wedding-related appointments, helping Nina get dressed the day of, and making sure she's calm and happy. But your primary task is to arrange and host the bridal shower. All of this turns out to cost about infinity more money than you have. You've been waiting tables on the Upper West Side since your summer on Fire Island. The dress Nina has picked out for you (from among the choices her mother-in-law has presented from Bloomingdale's) is absolutely gorgeous, a full-skirted Ralph Lauren, which Nina insists on paying for, which seems like it might be a good thing, because you have a few thousand dollars of credit card debt as it is. But this kind of generosity, where you are concerned, anyway, only leads to weirdness and misunderstanding. You are relieved for about a minute not to have to generate more debt, only to move directly into resentment. She has more money than you. She didn't even do anything to get that money, and now she's marrying more of it. She has no idea how hard it is for you, *it* being everything. You've been waiting tables for a couple of years now. She doesn't understand that gifts like this make you feel uneven, like she doesn't really know you, or worse, that she feels sorry for you. (You have no issue with feeling sorry for yourself, but the idea that others might pity you is an unbearable conundrum.) You don't want to understand that maybe she does understand and just doesn't have any better ideas about how to make you happy. So you try to pick a fight, which you regret almost immediately, because you can hear, as it comes out of your mouth, what it sounds like when you say *I appreciate it, I really do, but I don't think you get how shitty this makes me feel.* Nina, bless her heart, is inclined to try to understand, where it might serve you both better if she just told you to fuck off.

You insist on hosting the shower at your apartment, asking Nina to politely relay to her mother-in-law that she'd prefer a more intimate setting than the River Café. You still live in, and owe back rent on, your brownstone duplex, but it's always been a good place for a party. (That one time that guy almost fell backward off the front of the building trying to catch the beer he knocked off the roof, the one that accelerated like a missile and just missed hitting a pedestrian who turned out to be your downstairs neighbor: *Classic.*) Unfortunately, the mother-in-law insists on coming by to scope it out before the big event and gives you a list of things for the party that you didn't know you needed, like outdoor rugs for the roof garden and phone numbers for a desirable caterer and chair-and-table rental company. *You should probably carpet these stairs, too,* she says. Your indignation is growing, and as soon as she leaves, these numbers go right into the trash. You decorate the roof with your own Christmas lights and flowers from the deli and enlist me to help cook. I'll make a pasta salad and a salmon mousse and you'll bake cupcakes. But the whole shebang still costs about four hundred dollars that you don't have. Nina has boots that cost more than that.

All things considered, the shower is ostensibly a success. Nina's guests compliment you on the party, and the only one grumbling is the mother-in-law, who does not care one bit for the spiral staircase that leads to the roof (*Weren't you going to do something about this?*), nor the tattered AstroTurf she'd been hoping to cover with her fancy rugs (*What* is *this?*), nor the rusty folding chairs that were up there when you moved in (*Someone could cut themselves on this and get tetanus!*). Fortunately, one displeased person in a room is more than enough to confirm your inadequacy as a human, and even if the mother-in-law's face weren't betraying her at every turn, you have a sonar for that person, and a memory for nothing else.

That said, it turns out that sitting next to a bride-to-be, making a stupid-ass hat out of bows, and writing down a list of the thousand-dollar vases she's received and who gave them is the worst imaginable torture, an opportunity to review all the things you don't have, will probably never have. Right now you'd be happy with a toaster oven that doesn't give off sparks when you plug it in. If you could register for a list of things like that, you would. A Walkman that doesn't merely play but also rewinds. A typewriter that doesn't turn commas into apostrophes. Any one, single, properly functioning household item. In this moment, though, you would be satisfied with no less than the lifelong misery of everyone at this party. You would totally register for that.

—Uch.

—What?

—I'm not sure this draft is going any better than the one where I was frigid and had issues with my father.

—Why not?

—Well, now I'm self-pitying and resentful and totally unlikable, Mom.

—Is that not believable?

—No, it's believable.

—So what's the problem?

—I think you're still more interesting. Self-pity and resentment just aren't as interesting as excited, ambitious, and possibly insane.

—I'll overlook that for now, Betsy.

Ceremony

The best man escorts you down the aisle, drops you off to the right of the chuppah, which is covered entirely in pale pink peonies. (Nina's one big idea that got through, though the final shade was downgraded from hot pink.) There are some three hundred people at the temple; it's one of those weddings where half the guests are friends or business contacts of the parents, in this case, Nina's in-laws. Nina hadn't put up a fuss about it until her mother-in-law invited her manicurist, at which point Nina gently suggested she didn't want it to be that big a wedding (she hadn't wanted a big wedding at all), which was when the mother-in-law less gently explained that this was how things were done. (Nina had never understood this at all, but when she came to you to talk about it, your chosen strategy—which in your mind was something like tough love—had come out feeling a lot more like blame the victim: *Nina, you have to just tell her you want a small wedding and that's it. I can't. Of course you can. I really can't. Why not? I don't want to make her feel bad. Okay, but now you feel bad and it's your wedding. You have to speak up for yourself. I don't know, I can't start out my marriage having problems with my mother-in-law. But you* do *have problems with her. But she means well, you know?*)

The best man, Harm (*Harm?*), is a corporate lawyer, nice-looking if notably more conservative than your usual type, but he's single, and he's smiling down the aisle with you like it's his wedding, and all during the ceremony he smiles at you from the other side of the chuppah; he's got the wedding bug, and it's that *I could marry that girl* look, which you've seen a time or two before, that pretty much renders him altogether physically unattractive. After dinner he asks you to dance, then if you'd like to have dinner sometime, and you agree, mostly because it's a weak moment. You're moving into this headspace of *Maybe this is the best I'll ever do*, although usually this is a thought that comes with a mediocre or bad choice, and here in front of you is an attractive law partner who wears cologne and combs his hair. You're not looking for a poverty-stricken drug addict, but you are 100 percent certain that you will never fall in love with a guy like this. The kicker is that you feel altogether shitty about it. You should want a guy like this. Doesn't everyone? Time is running out. Right? Isn't it? But his name is *Harm*.

You lost track hours earlier of how much champagne you've had, but it's a lot, even though you're not falling over. Nina has failed to pay proper attention to you, instead bustling around to every table to greet each guest. When she takes a brief break to sit down for the toast, you tell her not to worry about saying hi to everyone again, that's what the receiving line was for. *Well, Mrs. D—— told me I have to say hello to each table. You don't even know half those people. Meanwhile I'm sitting here by myself like a lump.* Nina is far too kind to agree with you on that one, doesn't even think it, goes straight into problem-solving mode by pointing out how *Harm is obviously smitten and why not get to know him? He's not my type, Nina. But who is?* This is as stern as words ever get from Nina, but they're not even intended as such. She's asking from a genuine place, as though perhaps she might help you find him right now from among the guests here tonight. But you miss this completely. *I think I'm going to go home*, you say. *No, no, you can't, we haven't even cut the cake, plus I've been planning to toss the bouquet right to you!* All you can do is shake your head. If you stay, you'll cry, and you don't cry. Not for people to see. Now, of course, Nina is about to cry, so you tell her you're sorry, champagne doesn't agree with you and you should just call it a day.

Harm puts you in a taxi, calls the next day for the following Saturday night, as is supposed to be the rule; even though he is dying to go out with you as soon as he possibly can, he does everything by the book.

You hate that book. It's not even a book. When he calls, you mean to let the answering machine pick up, but knock the phone off the receiver by mistake. *Hello? Betsy?* you hear from the general area of the floor, so you pull the phone back up even though your head is throbbing.

Date night, he comes to pick you up for dinner bearing a bouquet of flowers that look like he yanked them right out of a Van Gogh. You don't have a vase because you don't get flowers. You have a slightly burnt coffeepot. He's wearing a navy blazer and khakis, you've got on jeans and an oversized sweater from the Gap. It's not like he's in formalwear and you're in a potato sack, but that's the effect. To him, because you're on the arty side, you're practically exotic; that only adds to it for him.

Harm orders a bottle of red wine with dinner, not your favorite, but it helps with the conversation, which dries up not long after where are you from, how many brothers and sisters do you have and such, and a second bottle is ordered before dinner is over, which makes him the tiniest bit more attractive, and the only reason you don't drink it all is that you figure if you leave some in the bottle he won't report back to Nina that you drank too much, which in truth is no danger at all, all he sees when he looks at you is the woman of his dreams. The booze allows you to let him kiss you, to think, Well, maybe he's not so bad, he likes you, give him a chance; you agree to go out again the next night for a movie; he picks you up again, tries to hold your hand in the movies; all you can think about is how to slip your hand out of his, how it's too soft and small in yours, almost like a child's hand, but not in a good way, just not right; you formulate an entire thesis in your head around why the feel of his hand is more than enough evidence that he's not the right guy, why didn't you get popcorn or candy so your hands would have something else to do, why did you agree to a second date, how are you going to break it off without hurting his feelings. You have never felt such immense relief as you do when he says he has a busy work week ahead, but that he should at least have time for drinks on Wednesday, and you agree to this because it's free drinks, and because the least you can do is tell him in person that you don't want to see him anymore. Maybe by Wednesday you'll be able to make up an excuse that sounds like a good enough reason besides his hands being too small. (That this shouldn't be a legitimate type of reason makes no sense; if a shirt or sweater were too small, you'd take it back, and no one would get upset about it. *I'm sorry, your hands just don't fit me. Oh, okay then. I might know someone the right size.*)

Harm tries to pick you up on Wednesday, but you insist on meeting at the All State, arriving early enough to have a pre-drink drink, which you hope will increase your courage but instead works to soften your judgment again; he looks at you so sweetly when he walks in, you want to like him, or a guy like him, you really do, things would be so much easier if you did, this guy would be so happy to support you financially, and you could just write or do whatever you decided you wanted to do next until you figured it out, or didn't. The All State is the perfect place for an ending. It's dark, grungy, you can get a big mug of beer, try to say nice things to make up for crushing his hope, and that will be the end of that. It doesn't go quite like that, of course, even though it's barely been more than a couple of weeks, his plan is to tell you he's falling for you. He's wanted to tell you since your first date, but hadn't wanted to scare you off, doesn't know that scared doesn't have anything to do with it for you, or at least that's what you think, anyway; you find it in you to bring up the subject, to say *I'm not looking to get serious*, which is an epic lie (His name is Harm. You can only figure it's short for Harmless. You just can't.), and he looks disappointed but says he's happy to take it slow, which you maybe could have anticipated, but you are committed to not taking it at all, and you say things like *You're such a sweet guy*, and he says things like *I could have seen us spending our lives together*, and he looks like he's trying hard not to cry, and you hate yourself. He offers to walk you home, he's crushed, knows he won't see you again, and you say no, it's only three blocks, though you don't mention that you want to stop at the deli for a bag of Milanos and more beer. Before turning away, you see in his eyes that he would have done about anything you'd wanted, tried to be about anything you'd wanted, if only you'd asked, and you are now entirely sure that you will be punished for this by forces unknown. You grab two bags of Milanos and a six-pack and finish all of it off at home. Alone. Again.

Smile

The oratorio is a huge success. You sew yourself a gorgeous gown for the occasion, a long column of puce satin with a chiffon overlay; you receive a standing ovation, you're swarmed afterward, sign a program for an eight-year-old girl, pose for photos with the other singers and the conductor, pull Dad into one of them, though that's a bit of an afterthought. He's brought a bouquet of roses—and he's not a flowers guy, he's a guy whose wife's friends occasionally remind him to act like a flowers guy—and roses are decidedly not in the budget but it's a special occasion. The feeling, absorbing all this attention, is unlike any you've had before. The applause and the audience on their feet move into you like a new power source, like you've just discovered solar energy. In the local paper the next day, you get a special mention as someone to watch, a bright new soprano on the horizon. The following week is a whirl, a buzz, magic, but the week after that is quite a bit different. The buzz is gone. And then you remember you're pregnant, for the first time in a week, and the first thought in your head is that this is a conflict.

You should be able to do both, have a baby and sing, why not, who said you couldn't? People have nannies. You don't have a budget for a nanny, you're on a professor's salary right now, but as your career gets going, you'll earn plenty in no time. You do want this baby, you're sure of it, pretty sure, granted the timing is suddenly not great, but it's too late now. So you'll just do both. Make a daily schedule and just make it work. Meanwhile, before the baby, you've got things to do. You've got a nursery to set up, which will need to be the best nursery ever. But in this era, you don't get to know whether it will be a boy or a girl, and you don't like yellow so you'll go with pale blue, you like blue, and you sort of hope it will be a boy, you aren't exactly sure why, though in remote parts of your brain where thoughts come not in words or sentences but hang around like smoke in a windowless room, there's a vague sense that raising a girl, for you, will be a challenge, though right now there's no time to give real attention to this, and if it does end up a girl you'll just add some pink accents later, a couple of pillows, switch out the curtains, easy enough. Audrey and Inge throw you a lovely baby shower. Pink-and-blue cupcakes with diaper pins on top, pink-and-blue ribbons everywhere, a pink-and-blue banner that says HELLO BABY hanging on the porch of Audrey's house to welcome you. Inge escorts you to a rocking chair with a big bow on it—that's from Dad—and you open boxes filled with stuffed animals, linens, rattles, books; the expected *ooh*s and *ah*s come from the group, but instead of building excitement—hooray, the blessed event is near! this is really happening!—when you feel a kick, instead of feeling the miracle of life or even placing a maternal hand to the belly, you are however briefly resentful, sure that this was a setup, that there was a conspiracy among your family and friends to steer you toward this path; but that's crazy, so you focus, focus, you were sure you wanted this, it's what every woman wants, and you want it too, but as you open more presents (carefully, saving the paper, always) and get to boxes of bottles and diapers, a picture emerges in your head of what those things are actually used for. Smile, Lois, just smile, your friends have done this lovely thing for you, they mean so well, they love you, and they have babies and toddlers, they're all still smiling, they're fine, you will be too, you're certain of it.

Cross-Country Problem Solving, Episode One

You decide that twenty-nine is too old to wait tables, so Victor gets you a job as a receptionist at the talent agency where he works. Oh, wait! I totally forgot that you moved to Los Angeles for a week. Let me go back. First, you decide to wait tables in another city.

—*Seriously, Mom?*
—*Well, you knew what I meant.*

So we throw a big going-away party at the restaurant. All your friends come for the send-off, and you and I pack up your stuff and put it in storage. Everything else gets shipped ahead; your old friend Jimmy from Fire Island has an extra room in his house in Laurel Canyon.

The night you get there, you and Jimmy catch up, and a couple of bottles of wine into this, it becomes a good idea to mess around. The next morning, not so much. How best to navigate this? Ah, yes, you will not get out of bed. You're in no hurry to drive anywhere anyway, and your head is a balloon filled with cement. Good enough. Until Jimmy brings you a breakfast sandwich from the deli down the road and says *Let's talk.* The cement in your head is preventing you from picking up any meaningful nuances in this *Let's talk*, but those are words you've never much cared for. You would love to know who the asshole was who first put those two words together. It makes talking seem like a terrible thing. Talking is a fantastic thing. You love talking. Until someone says *Let's talk.* And in this case, you have no idea if this *Let's talk* is going to be followed by *This is awkward* or *I've always really liked you and I'd like to see where this goes* or what, but you don't care, because you do not want to deal with either end of that range. You want to not remember what happened last night and start over. You came here to start over. Why do other people who drink have the good fortune to forget the shit that happened that they don't want to remember? You have had no such luck. What you've been lucky enough to forget, other people have reported back. Meanwhile, as you're mulling this over, Jimmy is still sitting on your bed and he does not look like he wants to talk about anything terrible, but today talking at all is not going to happen. *Can we talk later?* you ask. *I'm not feeling all that great. Sure, no problem*, he says, and kisses you on the head and leaves the sandwich, smiles before he closes the door behind him. He is adorable. He looks like a guy you should love.

The next morning, you listen carefully for Jimmy's footsteps and the sound of the front door locking before emerging from your room. This is as good a time as any to look for a job, so you drive over to Hollywood and walk around looking for Help Wanted signs, which is your best idea about how to do it, and you come across one restaurant with a sign in the window that says HOSTESS NEEDED (well, you come across a few signs, but this is the only one you deem suitable on this day; the distinctions might be microscopic to the average job-hunter, but the restaurant job you are seeking is one in which your hard work will be recognized, where there is a general and apparent good vibe, where the staff gets along, ideally one where you can wear whatever you want, but definitely not one that requires a uniform, or a terrible or embarrassing uniform, like a workplace sitcom with the usual cast of unlikely comrades—you, the arty one who doesn't have an art—but you're all in it together, all of this needing to be perceptible through a brief glance inside the restaurant); anyway, you haven't considered maybe putting on a skirt and some lipstick, you're wearing ripped jeans as usual, and the manager lets you fill out an application but it's obvious from the way she hands the application over without a pen that this isn't going to happen. You ask for a pen and the manager looks at you like you asked for a speedboat. Feeling like you've done enough for one day, you head back to the house, but it rains—pours, actually—and you've only just gotten your driver's license even though you're twenty-nine, and I get a hysterical phone call from you about rain, and how you just can't do it, and I tell you it's all fine, *It's not going to rain every day, Betsy, you'll get used to driving, give it time*, but you call back the next day when it's raining even harder, and there's no milk in the house and the closest store is a tiny market a mile down the steep hill where you live. You say *You don't get it, Mom, you can't even walk there, it's too steep, even if I rolled myself down the hill, I couldn't walk back up. You walk a mile easy every day in New York*, I say. *You can't walk anywhere here, Mom. Well, why didn't you think about that before you left?* I ask, and you say you just didn't. You call back the next day again, same thing, complaints about how driving is the worst, that the freedom of car ownership is obviously an epic myth perpetuated by the auto industry that for mysterious reasons has been swallowed whole by the entire country, and there's nothing here for you and you want to come home. I urge you to give it more time, though unbeknownst to me, you have already more or less made up your mind.

Meanwhile you're stuck in the house with Jimmy, whom you've been trying to avoid for days, to the point where he's knocking quietly on your door not knowing if you're even in there, asking if you need anything from the grocery store when he goes, because he knows the only food in the house is his. When you finally open the door to tell him *Yes, that would be great*, because you realize now that your existence here, were you to stay, would be limited to whatever might happen at home; you should just go ahead and grow long braids, claim your place as the Rapunzel of Laurel Canyon. Jimmy offers to help you get more comfortable behind the wheel, and mentions that he has a friend who knows about a waitressing job. You say *Thanks, maybe*, though at this point you're pretty sure he knows that none of these things are going to happen, and as such, thankfully, whatever it was he wanted to talk about can be put off for a few decades, until, hopefully, you will have gotten your shit together.

—So, do I do anything besides mess up relationships during this time?

—I don't know, do you?

— . . .

—Seems like you're kind of messing up everything during this time, no?

— . . .

—You remember not telling me much of anything about anything, right?

—That part you have right.

NYC, 1960

Before I'm born, you and Dad take a trip to New York City. Fred's parents have given you an extravagant weekend in the city as a pre-baby gift; they put you up at the Essex House and have arranged for orchestra seats for a performance of *Manon Lescaut* at the Met. You have a smart suit with three-quarter sleeves, which you can still wear if you let out the skirt just a bit, and you pick up a new pair of eight-button gloves to go with it. It's your first time in the city, and at the Metropolitan Opera, and you're giddy just thinking about it. Dad pulls the Buick up to the hotel on a Friday afternoon, not sure where to park; a valet offers to take care of it for two dollars, you and Dad look at each other wide-eyed, but since the trip is all expenses paid, you shrug and giggle and Dad takes out the suitcases and hands over the keys. The frisson of a lifestyle you wouldn't hate moves through you; it's physical. Another attendant comes for the suitcases; you haven't thought about how much to tip; you whisper to Dad *Twenty-five cents a bag maybe?* He says *Let's make it fifty to be safe*, handing over a dollar bill. Your eyes widen; under any other circumstances, handing out money like this would be unthinkable. You check in, and the bellhop escorts you to the elevator—operated by an elevator man!—then shows you to your room on the twenty-ninth floor, overlooking the park. You look out the window and put your gloved hands to your face like you're in a Doris Day movie. You need something to do, right this minute, with this energy in you.

—Okay, look, I'm stuck. There should probably be sex right here, but you understand why I don't want to imagine that, right?

—I imagined it when I was writing about you, Betsy.

—Not exactly.

—What do you mean? I've given you three sex scenes already.

—No, I've given myself three sex scenes as I imagined you would imagine them. But it's still me imagining me having sex, not me imagining you having sex. With my dad.

—Your father and I had sex, you know.

—I do know, because you told me many times. Can't I just summarize here, or skip over it? I don't like writing sex, period.

—You have to write the sex.

—No I don't. I don't have to do anything.

—All the great books have sex in them.

—That isn't true.

—I never heard of a book without sex.

—What?

—You can do whatever you want, but you may be missing an opportunity.

—I'll take that chance.

In summary: you and Dad have sex, and it's the best sex you've ever had. It's not like anything different happens, move-wise;

it's not like anything different ever happens. But whatever was already in your body makes this time totally different. It's the first time you realize you want more. Of everything.

—I'm going to eat a sandwich now and try to put this behind me.

The performance is spectacular. Renata Tebaldi is glorious, Richard Tucker is in top form, and you can feel their chemistry from your seat. You had heard their *Andrea Chénier* on the radio, which was riveting; hearing them together live is indescribable. You weep through half the performance, along with most of the audience. The Met orchestra is absolutely, divinely masterful. Tebaldi comes out for her bow, receives a standing ovation, wild *bravas* from the audience, roses are brought out, even Tucker bows to her.

Someday that will be you.

Wherein You Are Maybe Going to Be a Talent Agent

So you come back from Los Angeles after eleven days and move back in with us. Nobody's too happy about it, but because you are both depressed and humbled by this adventure in cross-country problem solving, we refrain from getting on your case about moving out, at least for the time being, and you find a new apartment soon enough, a one-bedroom on Eighty-Fifth and Riverside. It's one of those old buildings that doesn't have much to say from the outside (or from the lobby, or from any of the grim, mud-green hallways), twelve stories so they wouldn't have to worry about whether or not to have a thirteenth floor, neither prewar nor post-. It's not as nice as the brownstone you lived in on Seventy-Third, by a lot, but it's cheap enough that you don't have to take a roommate. You've reached the point where the money from waiting tables is hard to walk away from, but the tables themselves, not so much. You're just done, though you have no idea what's next. Victor introduces you to the lady from human resources at the talent agency where he works, hoping you can get some work there while you figure it out. You don't envision, from the get-go, that your destiny is to be a talent agent. You don't envision an office of any kind being your destiny. You thought you were going to be a writer, which you still mention occasionally; you even tell people you've been writing, like it's not something you've just been contemplating but something you actually do, which is true, though you admit you're nowhere near ready to let anyone read it. It's just not good enough. It's not that you've totally let go of the famous-writer fantasy, or even the published-writer fantasy; you say you're satisfied enough by the writing itself, though admittedly that's kind of a cop-out. It's not untrue that you enjoy writing. It's the level of satisfaction in writing for no one but yourself that's in question. Meanwhile, you have no health insurance, which at twenty-five seemed like nothing you would never need—*Why should I pay money for nothing* was once the totality of your big argument against it—but even three years later, when you learn how insurance works, and when your tiredness is hardly at elderly alert levels but ever-so-slightly hints that you may have need of medical care at some time or another, or like maybe it would be nice if you didn't have to go further into debt to go to the dentist, and it is also pointed out to you that sometimes insurance even covers mental health (although in this case it doesn't, which is a major oversight on the part of this talent agency, because the longer you remain in this job, the more you are certain that mental health care could be of great use to everyone employed there, especially you).

You're hired as a receptionist, and you're good at it. (A marginally bright twelve-year-old could also be good at it, you're sure, but whatever.) You're friendly, efficient, and well-liked. It's not a challenging job, but right now that's a plus. You have plenty of challenges outside work. You have nothing but challenges outside work, no additional challenges are needed, thanks. The receptionist on the seventeenth floor has been there for years and seems perfectly content, clocks in at eight, out at four, goes home to her fourteen-year-old Yorkshire terrier, has a sizeable pension at this point, and for the next few months as you settle in, this isn't unappealing. You're sitting down. You like sitting down. You like not being accused of serving regular instead of decaf, you like not being given a twenty-five-cent tip and spending the entire rest of the shift wishing you'd given the twenty-five-cent tipper back his quarter along with a *Norma Rae*–style speech about how hard you work and why doesn't he just put his quarter in his own piggy bank. You like not sleeping through the entire day and going to work at night and missing all the fun your friends are having going out to dinner and parties without you. You like meeting movie stars. Your movie star dating pool has expanded, and it's just fun telling people that you met Susan Dey, and that Captain Kangaroo (two of very few celebrities with the power to render you giddy) has an office down the hall. You like getting free passes to screenings and theater openings, and sometimes there's even a little time to write. All you need is a dog of your own.

You sleep with more actors. Look, you just do. I don't have to go into the details, but let's call it like it is. You work at a talent agency and you're young and you're a knockout—and you're not an actress, which is a plus for quite a few of these guys—and they're handsome and plentiful and this is a perk to take advantage of. Additionally, because you are so well-liked, every department in the place clamors to pull you off the reception desk and have you come work for them. Bored beyond belief after nine months on reception, you agree to take a "permanent" position as an agent's assistant. You are warned that it will be a boatload of work, that there will be overtime, that you will be expected to go to even more screenings and theater openings and parties, to take the calls of fragile actors and convince them that their agent is not dodging their calls even though that's exactly what she's doing. You are also told that if you do this well, you can move up the ladder in no time. This is not a draw. You see it as a drawback. You have a well-developed lack of interest in ladders. You are perilously close to needing that suit after all. You have no interest in representing people, some interest in being represented. You have some vague interest in the idea of security, though this is nebulous for you as a concept, something you're not sure can exist for you anyway, certainly not via any job you'd be interested in. If they could write "emotional security" into your benefits package, that might sweeten the offer. Why couldn't you become someone who desires only to do a job well and keep that job until retirement when they give you a Tiffany watch and wish you well? Isn't that still an honorable thing? Couldn't that be a satisfying thing? Does everyone have to want the same thing? Does everyone have to know exactly what they want? Is there a cutoff date for knowing what you want? And if you go beyond it, what then?

Unfortunately, once you accept one of these offers, these questions are moot at this particular desk. You become exhausted to the point of nervous breakdown, exhausted to the point of calling me crying about it, and I know by now that if you call me crying, it has to be bad, because this has happened maybe two times in the past, and the last one wasn't that long ago, when you were in LA. You say you don't think you can do it, this isn't what you want, though the question *What do you want?* is apparently not the right one, because you hesitate before you answer. *I want things to be easy*, you say. *Well, things aren't*, I say.

Still, you have just enough hope—just one small ember of hope in you that hasn't gone out yet—that somehow all of this, waiting tables, answering phones, dating actors, will add up to something meaningful someday.

You try this a few more times with a few more agents in different departments, and always end up back in reception, and this plays on repeat for four pretty miserable years.

Perks

Near the end of your time at the talent agency, you start to think about some type of teaching as a leading candidate for your next line of work. You don't know why this didn't occur to you sooner. You love kids. Your therapist encourages you to take the necessary steps: applications for grad school, GREs, things like this. This seems overly time-consuming; is this really what you want, enough to spend a few more years in school? You're supposed to study for the GREs, which in and of themselves seem irrelevant to the work you're looking to pursue. You think: You should study so you can study? Is that a commitment you can make for a lifetime, being a schoolteacher? Not likely. You were never a rest-of-your-life kind of person. You're a person whose longest commitment is to not owning a suit.

As good fortune has it, it comes to your attention at exactly the right time that child stars need education too, and you have a few contacts in this area who help you get a job as a location tutor, and in a matter of about a week after first realizing this (speed has always been your preferred method for making work choices), you get on a plane to Canada—and this time the job seems to be a good fit. The money is good, you're good at it (it helps that your student is in third grade, at which level you can still check the math and come up with correct answers), and the perks include nice hotels and meals, all expenses paid, a schoolroom trailer with a TV, a stocked fridge, and a sofa for naps, and still more movie stars to possibly date. Sometimes there's even a little downtime when you can write in your trailer.

For weeks, you flirt with the lead actor, who plays the father of your student. This escapes the notice of absolutely no one on set. He himself is currently best known for being newly divorced, two-days-ago newly, from an Academy Award–winning actress, this split currently on the cover of *People* magazine, and *The Star* and all the rest of those, covers with the fake tear down the middle and the box on the side with a paparazzi photo of the alleged other party with her head down. In this case, the gossip is that she may have she left him for someone more famous, which is technically true, if not the actual reason. Your lead actor has not yet worked this out for himself. Right now, any and all attention from attractive women is welcome, and on this set, in Toronto, you are at the top of that list. There may be other attractive women here, but you have positioned yourself in his line of sight, and the fact that you are not an actress is a major plus right now. He is smitten, and you are smitten, and this may not be a career, but it is a thing you could see yourself doing for the rest of your life, so that's something. Romantic words are said. Neither of you is thinking about the fact that he is so not over his ex-wife, though you spend some good time thinking about the fact that you are stepping in the shoes of America's current sex goddess. Drinking helps with that a good bit, though you haven't technically had full-on sex yet, as you have decided that though you like trailers for most purposes, and might even like a trailer for sex purposes if you were say, camping, but on a movie set, sex in a trailer is more like a storyline from the third sequel to *Valley of the Dolls*.

But what you have or haven't done in your movie star's trailer really doesn't matter when the second AD sees you coming out of it. Storylines will be cooked up, embellished, styled, reworked, revised, and retold by third cousins who were there, and these storylines will be gobbled up like the snacks from craft services. For reasons still unknown to you now, you are grateful that this gossip never makes it to the tabloids, like the way everyone knew Rock Hudson was gay but it didn't get printed until the end. You'll forever be known in the movie business as the woman who busted up that guy's marriage, but you'll be none the wiser.

—I'm not sure how this is helping my story at all. There's like one sentence about writing.

—In my mind you're just making notes for a tell-all memoir.

The Rest of Your Life

One night you're stumbling home from the P&G bar down the block when you trip over the curb and break your wrist for the third time—the same one, but again, when you wake up the next day with a giant purple paw in place of your hand, you're not really sure what happened. The guy you brought home last night, who isn't a total stranger but who is a good three or four friends away from you, tells you he doesn't know for sure either, but that you might want to think about getting some help with your drinking problem. You take great offense at this. He's the big drunk, obviously, and you tell him so. *I know,* he says, *that's how I know!* He says you should really go to AA. You *go to AA*, you say. *Ah, I've already been*, he says. You're thinking he's not the greatest advertisement for this program, but you give him the benefit of the doubt. *So you can drink and go to AA? No*, he says. *I don't go to meetings anymore. But it works, really. It's not magic. You should just go. No,* you *should just go,* you say to him, and point to the door.

But he's planted that stupid mustard seed, as they say, and you're pissed. First things first, the emergency room. The doctor asks how it happened and how much you had to drink; you don't have an answer to either question; he wraps your wrist in a cast, hands you a little card with a triangle in a circle, writes an address on it, says he goes to a noon meeting in the neighborhood when he can. *You should go there right now. It's five past noon now. You can be late.* He's cute. *Will there be other guys there who look like you? If I say yes, will you promise to go? Maybe. Okay, then yes.*

So you go. You go and you sit in the back of the room and listen to the speaker talk about almost killing someone in a DUI and still not getting sober and you think, Well, I haven't done anything like that, it's not too late to just slip right out with no one noticing, but then the speaker talks a little about what her life was like before she even started drinking, feeling hopeless and not smart and like her problems were so specific and different from anyone else's that there were solutions out there for everyone but her. Which seems very specifically how you've been feeling for what seems like ever. She goes on to say that drinking helped that some, until she started crashing cars, and that when she finally got sober, ten years ago, she found other people who showed her how to live without drinking. There is a lot of laughter in the room during her talk, none of which seems all that funny to you, but the laughter gives you a good feeling. You understand that there's a recognition.

At break time, they pass around a pan and make announcements. The person in charge asks if anyone is celebrating a sober anniversary. Several hands go up; they all take turns saying their names and how long they've been sober. Each person gets cheers, whether it is celebrating a sober anniversary of three months or three years. You are beginning to feel something, sitting here, you can't quite identify it because it's not something you've really felt before. Belonging? You haven't even talked to anyone yet. Weird. The person in charge asks if it's anyone's first AA meeting. Your hand goes up before your brain thinks better of it. *Fuck*. You're in AA forever now, obviously. You'll have to pay dues and pray to Jesus and fuck knows what else. The cheers in the room are louder than the ones for the other people celebrating. Well, okay, that's nice. The person next to you looks you dead in the eye, with a kind of warmth that's new to you. The person in charge says some words toward you after this, you're not sure what, you're a little overwhelmed, this morning you woke up thinking maybe a Bloody Mary would make things better, and now you're in AA for the rest of your life? You were never a rest-of-your-life kind of person. But you kind of are. When the meeting is over, the people to your left and right say something about happy destination roads and tell you if you're willing to do the work you can have an amazing life. This morning you woke up half drunk with a broken wrist and this afternoon you have ten new friends who take you to lunch and two or three of them are obviously weird and fucked-up but the rest of them are now your brothers and your sisters all over this land, in your life, forever, done.

—There's no one in charge of AA, Mom.
—Someone has to be in charge.
—No, there are no leaders, only trusted servants.
—That's not creepy or anything.
—It's not.
—Well, whatever. That's your big concern here?
—The rest of it works.

Cross-Country Problem Solving, Episodes Two and Three

A couple more years pass. You're still sober, but by now you've been unemployed for several months, so you begin to consider your options. You're not committed to staying in New York. You hear that a friend of a friend who's producing a new TV series in Los Angeles might maybe possibly be looking for a personal assistant. You're still not one for making advance plans. Your advance plan at this time is to start packing. You haven't forgotten about the driving issue, but it's been long enough by now that you've mustered up some small hope that you might be able to push through. You have learned thing one since then, if not thing two, so rather than shipping every last one of your possessions off to the city where you once resided for less than two weeks, you sublet your apartment, furnished, and leave New York with only a suitcase and a pile of books. What you don't do is schedule an interview before you get there, maybe consider interviewing over the phone. What you do is you just go. You can't think of a reason not to. Nothing is happening in New York. You'll figure out the driving thing when you get there. You're older and wiser now. It'll be different. You have friends in LA, you can ask for help if you need it, even though you probably won't. Ask. Or need it. Or ask. You fly to LA, interview with the friend of a friend; he gives you the job. It's only two days a week, but that's fine. You'll pay your dues, if not your rent; one thing at a time. Hollywood will for sure recognize your overall hilarity and promote you accordingly.

In exchange for performing tasks that are for the most part unrelated to writing sitcoms—the fetching of dry cleaning, the steeping of tea, the filing of folders, the paying of bills, the running of general errands—the big perk of the job is that Donny, your new boss, lets you sit in on the writers' room meetings. You are to be silent in these meetings or you will be banished, possibly in a way that involves public shaming. This is not, you discover, *The Dick Van Dyke Show.* It's not one of those writers' rooms you see on TV where everyone is laughing, riffing, trading sarcastic but good-natured jabs, effortlessly working together to make the comedy happen; it is one of those rooms where a couple of personalities have created an atmosphere less conducive to comedy than to insults, hurt feelings, tantrums, and slammed doors. It's tense. So you heed your boss's advice to speak only when spoken to, take notes, eat the free snacks, and brew tea when asked. One day, a heated argument transpires between the lead actress, who is allowed by contract to be in the writers' room even though she is no kind of writer, and one of the actual writers, who is telling her in no uncertain terms that what she thinks is funny is very clearly not funny. Her joke is dumb-blond based, which is bad enough, but the real problem is that it just doesn't make sense, not even after she explains it. *The brown bear has to explain to the light-brown bear what a milkshake is.* Silence. *The brown bear is smarter.* Silence. *Because it's brunette! God!* Silence. *It went to bear college! Come on.* It's like a bizarro riddle. Everyone is at a loss. One of the writers speaks up. *Do you watch this show? Fuck you, Jonah. Bear college isn't a thing. Yeah, I know, that's why it's funny. You picture it,* she says, *you picture bears at college, bears walking around, with bear books, playing bear Frisbee. It's funny. It's really not. It's hilarious! Bears at college! Doing things that bears don't do!* This goes on for some unendurable length of time, it might be only five minutes but it feels like a hundred; everyone tries to humor her until she leaves, but she won't, and you can think of no more excruciating way to spend five minutes. *This discussion is officially un*bear*able,* you say, to your surprise, out loud. The writers can't really stifle their laughter. It's not that funny, your mild pun; what is funny is that you, the newbie, have spoken up to the temperamental star, and she giggles too. She asks if you have any ideas for a bit that might make both parties happy, preferably a bit that has nothing to do with bears. Something kicks in, and you say you do before there's time to think better of it. *Okay, so the waitress has just put a milkshake down on your table. "Here's your margarita!" she says. You say to your date, "I know this is only our first date, but I hereby authorize you to euthanize me should I become unable to distinguish between a milkshake and a margarita. If I appear to exhibit pride upon identifying a milkshake as a margarita. Failing easy access to euthanasia, just bring a pitcher of margaritas. If you can be sure they're not milkshakes."* It's a bit long-winded and only modestly funny, but it succeeds in breaking the tension in the room, which bursts into relieved laughter. A heavily revised and edited version of your joke makes it into the episode. This is your entire career in sitcom writing. It's not that there couldn't be more from here; there could. It's just clear now that nothing about this endeavor has been enjoyable.

You're a couple grand deeper into debt than before you left, with one more résumé credit you don't really need. What you really want to do is write fiction. You can do that anywhere. New York is too expensive and you don't want to be there anyway. Clearly, it's time to move to Chicago. Just because it's the first I've heard of the idea doesn't make it surprising at this point. You will move and keep moving until you land in the right spot. This move happens with more or less the same amount of haste and suitcases as the last. Weirdly, I can tell just by the sound of your voice over the phone, about a week after you get there, that you're happier in Chicago. The way you gush about alleys and abandoned buildings sounds like you're describing Prague or Copenhagen. *It's my place, Mom. I'm glad, sweetheart. I know you needed to go. I can come visit.*

But I'm sick with cancer. You've decided you were a fiction writer the whole time, that you had to get the TV job to know this for sure. You come home to visit while I'm in the hospital and read me some scenes about me from your novel that are pretty funny, but you don't have any big plan about where to go from there. You say *I'm not about plans*, I say *Yeah, I got that*. You move from LA to Chicago to be a fiction writer and I get sick and this messes up your not-plans.

It's a wonder you don't start drinking again, and when you come to the hospital you try to argue with me while I'm hooked up to twenty kinds of machines and wires.

—You're seriously trying to say I started an argument with you when you were in the hospital?

—We had an argument. You stormed off. Can I finish?

—Yes, I can't wait.

There's an old lady in the bed next to me and she's rambling on and on about I don't know what, but she keeps talking even though the curtain between us is drawn. You and Victor are visiting and this lady's chatter about I-don't-know-what is making me nuts. *Lady!* I yell over. *Stop talking! The curtain is pulled! Mom,* you say. *Don't* Mom *me! This is my time with my visitors! That cunt is invading my privacy! Mom! Oh don't be all holier-than-thou, Betsy. Okay, I'm going. That's great. Walk off. I liked you better when you were still drinking!* You peer around the corner and whisper that you're so sorry to the lady before leaving the room.

—That's the argument I started. I said "Mom."

—You made me yell.

—I made you yell. You called an old lady with cancer a cunt.

—I didn't say it to her face.

All about the Baby

The next two years in Binghamton are all about the baby. You should have known. You sew the most precious clothes for the baby; later you make several sets of matching dresses for you, me, and my doll, one out of a darling red toile, another in pink with white rickrack trim, another from a tiny floral print. You genuinely enjoy having a girl and dressing her up and showing her off. (The doll alone gets a reversible raincoat, solid on one side, coordinating gingham on the reverse, not so much as a single stitch to be seen on either side. It's an engineering marvel.) You have not forgotten about singing, or New York City at all; even though you're an attentive new mother, even though it is a strong instinct in you, you vocalize when you can; why didn't you wait just a little longer to have kids? Don't some people do that? You still veer off, in your mind, baby in arms, to a life onstage, reviews in the *New York Times*, a high-rise apartment, a flash of someone with his arms around you who isn't Fred. You shake it off, that's not how it's supposed to go, but those flashes visit you daily, and when Dad gets a tenure-track job at LSU and moves us all to Baton Rouge, they become a constant presence for the next two years. Before the move, there's a brief discussion about how well it was going for you in Binghamton before the baby, that if you just wait until she's in nursery school and you have the time to get going on your performing career, it would be good to stay (though it could conceivably help your case if played right, you deliberately fail to mention how much closer Binghamton is to the city than Louisiana—one thing at a time, to ease him into the idea, seems the best way to go), but he's the breadwinner, and even if he's not the most conservative early-sixties *I'm the man* kind of guy, not by a lot, the reality is that he's generating the income and this is a job he can't turn down. You suspect he secretly wants to keep you from having a career, though he's said nothing to indicate as much; in fact, he's even mentioned that Baton Rouge and New Orleans are both cultured cities where you can develop your voice and pursue work. There will be moments, after I'm in nursery school, when this obsession sends you to your bed for extended naps; Dad knows nothing of this, as somehow you manage to get back up every afternoon and put an apron on over your full skirt and blouse (no heels until dinnertime, to heck with that) to make supper at five when he likes it, but you know that the only real solution is to pursue your career. You discuss this with him, he is still in favor of it, believes as you do that you have the talent, although he is less sure when you raise the idea of traveling to New York on your own for proper training and auditions. You convince him that you are sure you can make it all work, though you're not at all sure that you can make it all work, you aren't even sure if you can make some of it work, but he is convinced and that's all that matters right now and so you dip into your savings account and he sends you off on your first trip to New York.

Bigger

Your room at the Barbizon is tiny, but it has gloriously high ceilings with wood floors and crown moldings, and Grace Kelly once stayed there, maybe even in your room, and there's a heavenly skyline view, if you lean out the window a bit and look to the right. The hotel is filled with wide-eyed women just like you (though even by this age you are sure there is no one on earth just like you); over breakfast in the formal dining room, you make several new girlfriends, all as eager to forge their careers as you are, aspiring journalists and actresses and even a poet (about which you think—poet? You have no imagination for what that life would look like, post–Emily Dickinson). You observe that some of them have potential and drive, and others are entirely delusional about their prospects. One young woman you chat with, named Evelyn, wants to be a model, but she's not what you would call anything other than plain; compared with the beautiful, stylish women you've seen in the lobby or on the streets just since you arrived, this woman doesn't have a chance. Why don't people know this, that they don't have a chance, why not just accept it instead of holding out hope for some unattainable thing? It does not occur to you at this time that the city is also full of aspiring opera singers, several of them right here in the hotel, and that talent or not, your chances may or may not be better than anyone else's. You are certain that your spot is assured. Almost certain.

The opera director from Binghamton has recommended a vocal coach. You choose a pale-pink dotted Swiss blouse and your favorite wool gabardine skirt for your first lesson. Her name is Carolina, she's Cuban, sixty-something, with a cottony blond updo and a flair for the dramatic—you walk in and she says *Muy bonito! Come in, bonito!* offers a cup of tea, asks if you drink tea; you say *Occasionally*, she says *You must drink tea now and forever, every day, it is a must!* Everyone who meets Carolina falls a little bit in love with her and you are no exception.

Carolina sits you down on a sofa in her parlor before you sing, asks a million questions about everything: *Do you have a fam-ee-lee, where do you live, how do you practice, how do you take care of yourself, where have you sung before, what have you sung.* To say you're overwhelmed is an understatement; you have been told that Carolina is not guaranteed to take you on, so this is something of an audition, but you had thought all you'd have to do was sing; you weren't expecting an interview. Still, Carolina has a way of asking questions that indicates genuine interest; she nods, says *I see, I see*; you don't see, but it seems all right. *You will sing now*, she says. *First scales, like this: Lolololololo, Lalalalalalala, Lelelelelelele!*; you think she's simply having you warm up, but what she discovers through this process is that you have perfect pitch and four solid octaves. She nods, says *Wonderful, wonderful, very good*, finally asks to hear the aria you've prepared. You sing "Caro Nome" again because it's gone well in the past.

Ordinarily, Carolina has a game face for first auditions, a semi-ambiguous nod until the singer is finished. Many, many times, Carolina has said *Singing is not for you*, or *No, I am sorry, but you should think of something else to do.* (A warm and kind person, Carolina on these occasions will fix another cup of tea and sit down with the singer to hash out other interests and career directions to take.) Today, what Carolina says is *Lovely, lovely, lovely.* She's holding back because she knows a singer's ego, which she will neither stroke nor ignore, but she hears you reach the high C, a fifth octave, closes her eyes, keeps saying *Lovely, lovely, lovely,* and *I can help you. You have mistakes, but I can help you.* You are thrilled, in spite of the word "mistakes," only because it is offset by Carolina's unhidden enthusiasm. Carolina says *You must move here, it is no question that you will do this.* Your breath, which you usually have in ample reserve, is almost sucked out of you. Fred hasn't been at his job all that long; you weren't planning another move, that was just a little fantasy. You're just a girl from Muscatine, how will this happen? You don't know. It just will. You're bigger than Muscatine, bigger than Binghamton, bigger than Baton Rouge. Aren't you? You are.

Carolina schedules regular lessons for the rest of your time in New York. You don't even have an appointment calendar; she tells you to go get one. *Sometimes they give them out at the bank for free. Carry it always. You will have many appointments.* You race back to the Barbizon, scuffing your best flats without a care (you can touch that up later); you're dying to make a long-distance call to Fred to tell him the news, to outline a detailed plan for your entire future, but you've agreed not to call unless there's an emergency, long-distance is simply too expensive. So you sit down to write him a letter on the hotel stationery; three drafts later, you've got a version that seems reasonable, though when it reaches Dad, it's still shocking. Fortunately, by the time you return home, he's had some time to sit with it, and you reach a compromise: you will rebudget, you will go back and forth from New York every other month and see how that goes, and you will do this for a year.

But before you leave New York, something else unexpected comes up. Carolina, seeing your rapid improvement under her tutelage—you do everything she tells you to, practice as much as she dictates but no more (she knows you would be inclined to)—invites another student of hers, a tenor, to sing a duet with you. This goes as marvelously as she expected, though what she hadn't realized (or perhaps she had), was that there would be sparks between you and this handsome, also-married tenor. Carolina, married, divorced, married again, divorced again, married again, and now widowed at sixty with an *amante*, knows a thing or two about sparks, and she keeps you behind after the married tenor leaves and pats the sofa next to her, again. *I do not tell you to do this, my love. I do not tell you to do this, but I do not tell you not to do this. We cannot—must not—contain our passion. Our passion and our art are one thing, do you see? Discretion is everything, yes?* You try to interrupt Carolina several times during this; *Oh, I would never!* you insist (though you have imagined moments like this a time or two, harmless fantasies, weren't they?), but she shushes you, says *I don't say what will happen. I just say I know of this. Our hearts and bodies go where they will.*

Just a Letter

On a trip back east for a visit, you read me a letter to the editor you wrote that got printed in the *New York Times*. You are as elated as if you'd been proclaimed the next Virginia Woolf. *Someone published what I wrote*, you say. *I'm a published writer!* I nod; it was just a letter to the editor, though, granted, a funny one. Something about bagels. *Don't people publish letters to the editor all the time?* I ask. *How do you not get it?* you answer. *Someone read what I wrote and they saw something in it. Did you become a singer overnight? Hardly, Betsy. I busted my ass for years.* For a brief second you think I might key into your point, when Victor asks how much you got paid for it. *They don't pay for letters to the editor, Victor.* You're pretty sure he knew this before he asked. *If they don't pay then you're not really a writer. Everything isn't about money. Don't kid yourself. Well, it isn't for me. Yeah, I'm aware,* he says. *You have health insurance yet? You know I don't. Get back to me when your letters to the editor start offering major medical.* At this point, you look like you could haul off and punch him in the face, and if it had been my battle, I very well might have. Instead you tell him to fuck off.

—*You know I never would have told you or Victor to fuck off.*

—*Well, there's your problem.*

—You might be right about that.

—Anyway, you said you only wanted things that didn't happen.

—But this is not unlike something that did happen.

—So it could have happened, but didn't.

—Sure.

—Like all the other scenes so far.

—I guess what I'm saying is that the point of view gets blurry in these scenes. Because here, in this one, it's you, talking about me, sort of from my POV, even though you were actually there, as opposed to let's say a scene that we know didn't happen in any form.

—Now you're confusing me.

—It is *confusing.*

—How are you and I supposed to have any conflict if we're not in the same scene together? Someone has to write it. How do you have a mother-daughter story where the mother and the daughter are never together?

— . . .

Holiday Letter

Your father, on the other hand, is positively proud about your letter to the editor. *You're on your way!* he says. He buys you your first laptop computer to replace that clunky old desktop from the eighties. *You're going to need the best moving forward. You'll be on a book tour in no time! I have to actually finish writing a book first, Dad. Well that's why you need the laptop. Do you know that soon everything will be done on the computer? People are going to write letters onscreen, and send them instantly through their phones. It will be fantastic!* Your father has never had piles of money sitting around, and he and Jeannie do have other kids too, but they're always happy to help out when they can, and he could not be more excited to see your name in the paper. This is one of the top stories in his holiday letter this year, in the same paragraph as your sister's college graduation and your youngest brother's first son.

What didn't make the holiday letter at all: your father's heart attack.

—Interesting.

—Really? I guessed right?

—No, but he was in the hospital. A heart attack—that'll work. That sounds weird.

You drive out to Iowa City from Chicago several times a year now—it's just four hours door to door—so when Jeannie calls from the hospital with the news about Fred, you're able to get there later that same day without taking on any more credit card debt. The prognosis is good, assuming he changes his entire diet and currently non-existent exercise routine, but he'll stay in the hospital for a week for observation. Your father is a different kind of patient from me, he's a patient patient, he's a patient who doesn't hate the lukewarm beef broth or the pudding cups on his hospital tray (*Oh, these are delicious! Jeannie, can we get these at home?*), who's content to catch reruns of old Westerns on network TV and read the back copies of *Ramparts* magazine that have been piling up at home.

—Ramparts *hasn't existed since the seventies, Mom, but whatever, I guess.*

—But is it believable that he still has piles of them that he bookmarked in 1968 to read later?

—Yep. It sure is. Continue.

He would have never thought a thing of it if you hadn't made it there, but the fact that you did, and that you stayed the whole week, spent every day next to his bed watching those Westerns that actually put you both to sleep at times, sharing the extra pudding he got the nice nurse to bring, meant more to him than he could ever tell you. *You really didn't have to come, Betsy. Dad, I would never not come. Well, it was extra-special nice of you. You're a good daughter. I could improve. I don't think a poll of my parents would indicate that to be fact. You're a wonderful daughter, Betsy!* Jeannie says. *I fought with Mom when she was in the hospital. What? Oh, you're exaggerating. Not really.*

Lois Dies, Scenario One

So I die, and you're angry and sad and alone, and what comes home now is that you're single and childless and you have about five minutes to fix that.

—Why does it have to be fixed?

—Are you happy?

—That's not my point, Mom.

—I guess I have a couple of competing ideas for how it goes for you after this.

—You can say them both.

—That's not how stories work.

—Stories work any way you want them to work.

—All right, well you can figure it out later. Maybe you'll like one idea better than the other.

—Maybe I'll like them both. But I doubt "like" would be the word I'd choose here.

Okay, good. In that case, in scenario one, after I die, you decide there's no time to waste, so you sign up for a dating service and meet a nice man, Alan, who has some normal steady job with health insurance, which you need, and a nice house in the suburbs of Chicago. You get married and try to have a family right away, but you can't get pregnant, so you have one of those medical procedures they do now where sometimes you end up having multiples, what's that called, when they mix shit up in a petri dish—

—*In vitro fertilization.*

—you have that, and you have twin girls, beautiful twin girls. Before they're born you knit them sweaters; I remember you had done that a few times over the years for gifts, the sleeves were a bit odd, made some baby quilts too. You fix up an old dresser like I showed you I'd done once. You get caught up in that for a while; you love the girls, of course, but as they get bigger and throw twin tantrums, or you fail to connect with them in that rhapsodic kind of way you hear so much about, greatest thing ever, you don't know what love really means until you're a mom, blah blah blah, it's not even post-partum, it's post–worst decision you ever made, or you try to join one of those mommy groups only to discover that whatever joy there is in having children is utterly desiccated by talking about having children, that you maybe have a three-minute window before you want to yell that you don't give two shits about the details of a virtual stranger's labor, or the tenor of some baby's first burp, and from there it's a short hop to realizing that you were not thinking clearly, getting involved with a man named Alan, that you could last long with an Alan, and so you tell Alan he's better off without you and divorce the best thing that ever happened to you and leave the girls with him and move back to the city, but then you fall into a terrible depression since this makes you a horrible, horrible person. Eventually, though, you get a good therapist who prescribes meds, which is the other best thing that's ever happened to you, and you meet a new man, Eduardo, a chef, and you live happily ever after.

—Three hundred and ninety words. For the whole rest of my life after you die? I abandon my children in less than four hundred words?

—The kids are fine. I gave you a happy ending.

—A guy.

—Don't forget, there's another scenario too.

—I understand, but still. Married, divorced, married again, and that's it?

—What else do you want?

—Was getting married the end of your *story?*

—It was the best part of my story.

— . . .

—Okay, one of.

—I didn't have the sense that either of your marriages was so easy.

—Well, I *wasn't easy.*

—I won't argue with me-as-you saying that.

—It was better, though, yes. I needed to be married. But maybe you don't. Are you married?

—I'm just trying to say—married or not married, maybe more than three hundred and ninety words?

—I did say I had more than one idea.

Lois Dies, Scenario Two

In scenario two, after I die, you also decide there's no time to waste, but this time you focus on a career path. You still want to write, but don't have the drive to make it happen, so you stick with teaching, taking a job at a preschool that eventually earns you some good raises and a promotion to assistant director, which is fine, if not anything more than fine, and after a decade or two of dating with poor results, despondent about not having found the right person, you decide to give it up altogether and become celibate. The end.

—Oh, come on. That's a third as many words as the first scenario and in this one I'm alone and in a job I don't really love.

—Do you want to be married or don't you?

—I want you to imagine a life that I might really want and actually be able make happen. Loosely based on the information you already have.

—Just let me think about it for a while.

—Plus, do I not even grieve for you? I grieved for two sentences in scenario one and not at all in scenario two.

—I thought I covered it. But what is there to say about that?

—Are you kidding? People write entire novels about it.

—About grief? I wouldn't want to read that. Who'd want to read that?

—People. Me.

—But why?

—Mom, why do we read anything?

—To escape.

—That's only one reason. Not that I wouldn't mind doing that right this minute.

—That's my reason.

—Look, why do you suppose I wanted to be a writer?

—Because you were good at it.

—I was good at other things. As you know.

—I don't know what you want me to say.

—Mom. Didn't you ever read a book that made you feel . . . like someone who didn't even know you understood you?

—Pfff. No one in real life has ever really understood me. How could I possibly get that from a book?

Whale Rider

You've been combing the auditions in *Backstage* for years, finally decide to actually go to one, for the role of Graziella in the touring company of a Broadway revival of *West Side Story*, and after two callbacks you are given the part. It's your childhood dream come true, all these years later. You have been practicing your *ooo-ooo-ooobliooos* since you were nine. (You've been practicing all the parts, failing most noticeably while trying to sing them all simultaneously for the "Tonight" medley.) By the time you're done rehearsing in New York, you're already close with the cast, and by the end of the second week of the tour, in Kansas City, you're calling yourselves family. It is agreed that your real families are not nearly as much fun, and that they're messed up in similar ways, about which you talk late into the night on the bus to the next city. One dark night, six of you, high on pot brownies in the back of the bus, decide to stumble out to Cracker Barrel for munchies. All agree that Cracker Barrel high is the funniest thing that ever happened. You forget that Cracker Barrel is not someone's house party where you're invited to help yourself to whatever and grab a seat on the floor with several boxes of crackers and three types of cheddar, but this detail is overlooked until you decide to dance on top of a barrel—there seems no other reason for it to be there—at which time the police arrive, and you're arrested for trying to get them to dance on the barrel with you. Fortunately, your high lasts just long enough to hold you until morning, when you're released from jail, and after considering that you made it through this escapade without throwing up, you call it a win. Everyone should be arrested once. Box checked.

You are the newbie (though not the youngest by a lot) so the others make certain things known to you. One of them is that it isn't always like this. It is, as often, exactly unlike this. Diva behavior, bitchy queens, personality clashes—most of you have big ones, which on a tour bus means that there is almost literally not enough room to accommodate the magnitude of the sounds (vocal exercises that range from bizarre chicken squawks to simple scales sung by five different people in five different ways at five different intervals), and the things (hair accessories, undergarments, a drugstore's worth of products), everyone scheming to skirt the one-suitcase-per-person limit (people need options!), and the opinions (political, artistic, religious—remarkable, really, that there hasn't been a documented murder on a tour bus), and the assorted pre-performance rituals (prayers, meditations, chants, bells). But this doesn't concern you now, here in Tulsa or Omaha or Wichita; what concerns you now is your castmate who plays Anxious, who stops by your motel room at midnight with a bag of Krispy Kremes and a quart of milk from the gas station next door. You're about two months into the tour now; the nightly group hang has taken the predictable toll, and most of you over twenty-four are retiring a little earlier now, though you still get plenty of socializing done earlier in the day. No one misses who gets with whom, that's impossible, so you make your peace with it, and it is noted by all that you and Anxious are often in a corner by yourselves, and bets are taken as to when the sexy festivities will ensue; the girl playing Anybodys wins by picking the earliest time slot.

Anxious—he knows you. He says things to you no guy has said before; that he feels like he hit the lottery; wants to know where you would live, if you could live anywhere at all; if you'd be interested in quitting everything and sailing around the world with him and a couple of dogs, maybe make some kids; he has some ideas for kids' names, Adeline and Mabel and Billiam—which cracks you up, *Billiam?* you say, and he says *No one will make fun of our kids on our boat*—and you are more and more sure he's the one. You like this idea very much. *Let's do it*, you say. *Yeah?* he says, *Yeah*, you say.

So you and Anxious jump off the bus right that minute, laughing hysterically. You have no idea how one goes about buying a boat, but you've just hit Tampa, as good a place as any for that. You hitchhike to the nearest shore, giddy, thank the old couple who picked you up, jump out, ask some random guy where to buy a boat, he asks what kind of boat you're looking for, you say an easy one, you're new boat people, he says he's got one for you, takes you to a nearby boat dock and shows you a boat. *Mint Chris-Craft Roamer, 1965, sleeps ten. Practically drives itself.* You don't ask the price, or for any more details. *We'll take it*, you say. Naturally, it's perfect, room for the dogs and kids, so you jump on board, initiate the master bedroom, conceive. *Where should we go?* Anxious asks. You suggest going through the Panama Canal and then up to Alaska to ride some whales. He tries to explain that that may not be an option, but that you can go look at them; you say *Well you don't know, maybe we'll find some open-minded whales when we get there. All right. Whale-riding it is*. Your first stop: New Orleans. You get off the boat, eat beignets and pralines and listen to music on the street and dance in someone's funeral, but then you worry whether that may not be a hundred percent cool, so you dance out of it just as quickly; wandering New Orleans you find a little dog roaming around, one of those ones that's like a hairless Chihuahua but with a head of floppy hair in his face and ridiculous ears, ears that say *I belong to you guys*, and you pick him up and get him all checked out at the vet and name him Flavio and jump back on the boat and Flavio goes right to the front of the boat and perches himself on the bow like a little hood ornament, wind blowing his ears back like ear sails, like the power from his little ear sails could take you to wherever your destiny might be.

You discover that you're having twins, a boy and a girl, because why not, and when they're born they just pop out, it's not like my pregnancy at all, it's painless, like *shoop*, two beautiful babies, Adeline-Mabel and Billiam, done, next. You home-school Adeline-Mabel and Billiam, heavy focus on life experience and the arts, you were never all that good at math or science, but there's plenty of science out there on the boat, and you sing songs, play guitar, and then you reach Alaska and a whale swims up next to the boat to let you on for a ride and it's spectacular, whale-riding, you feel like this is what it all led up to, this whale ride, you, a giant mammal, the salt water, the sea air, the waves, the sky. The whale brings you back to the boat so you can pick up the rest of the family, Adeline-Mabel and Billiam and Anxious, Flavio in front, and you whale off into the sea and that's it, the end.

—That's good, Mom. Graziella doesn't actually sing in West Side Story, *but whatever, I guess.*

—Seems like that makes it the perfect part for someone who's scared to sing in public.

—Good point. FYI, though, you can't get high when you're in AA.

—You still have to go to that?

— . . .

Good Women

You return home to Baton Rouge energized and excited. You tell Dad every detail you can remember about the trip: the few sights you saw (*I went up in the Empire State Building! I went to Macy's and Gimbels! Oh, I've never seen such a thing as Macy's! Of course, the only thing I bought was a scarf on sale at Woolworth's*); every single word Carolina said about your singing (notable adjectives including *facile! bewitching! like molten silver!*); what you did with Audrey when she came to visit; your trip to the Automat (*Great fun! Food behind little doors!*); how you reunited with another friend who recently moved to the Upper West Side from Binghamton, a mezzo, who knows about an apartment you might share with her for the times when you return. Dad tries so hard to share your enthusiasm—he truly believes in your talent and is happy to see you so excited—but he feels this pulling you away from him, all of it, and that it's not in his power to hold on tight enough to keep you. A small part of you wishes he would, it would be so much easier, safer, but though you will travel back and forth for two whole years, you sense early on that you're putting off the inevitable. You continue to practice every day for hours, according to Carolina's instructions; you do fewer and fewer of the typical wife things, but you also do the typical mom things, make supper, more sewing, reading to me (though at one point you are displeased with what you feel is my overly dramatic interpretation of Mother Goose: *It's not an opera, Mommy. You don't make your voice go up unless there's an exclamation point. Do it like how Daddy does it, just normal*, I say, which provokes in you a desire to swat me on the behind that you thankfully resist). And you think about New York City, and what's there for you, always, every minute of every day, no matter what you're doing.

On the next trip to New York, you call the handsome married tenor from the pay phone down the hall at the Barbizon just as soon as you put your bags down. He was hoping you'd call. He wants to know if you can meet right away, but the Barbizon has a curfew, which is in about an hour. He doesn't live far, tells you to meet him at Schrafft's and he'll have you back home on the dot; you freshen up your lipstick and run right outside into the New York night and this is without a doubt the most thrilling moment ever, more thrilling than your wedding day, more thrilling than your first opera performance, more thrilling even than what happens next, though that is up there too. You dash to Schrafft's, a couple of blocks away, you're Holly Golightly in your kitten heels, New York belongs to you right now, and frankly, no less than owning an entire city in this way will ever be enough. Which will be a problem later, but right now is yours. Handsome married tenor says all the right things in the first five minutes, holds your hand under the counter, you talk about the last few weeks, but this is all just time-filling, you share a milkshake that doesn't get finished, he glances at his watch at five past ten, your curfew, you don't know it but he's done this utterly on purpose, and even if you did know, you would not care one whit, all cares about anything outside of now, this night, you and this man, simply do not exist.

In the morning, there are, of course, regrets. You play the evening over in your head: earlier it had felt like this was what life really is; there are still currents of it in your body, the city and the man; but right now all that's left is shame. You haven't forgotten what you learned in church and Sunday school, about good women and bad ones, or what was said when rumors went around Muscatine about the one or two loose women in town, and the payment due for this type of behavior (though the specifics of that were always vague to you, it seemed to have something to do with being spoiled for the right man); these weren't crimes, but it doesn't matter what the Christian punishment is, because you have now commenced the portion of your life in which you will punish yourself plenty. You try to call up Carolina's words, what were they, she had said this was okay, didn't she, you're sure of it, it doesn't feel okay today, but it will have to be okay, and thus ensues an endless amount of configuring in your head in which it is okay. It's happened in New York. A different, distant city. Your husband will never know. You've fibbed before, about a purchase here, a lateness there, and he never knew. It won't happen again. And it *won't* happen again, not with this man, not on this trip. You do not feel your very best, this morning, you did not get your beauty sleep, and you have a lesson later and you missed an extra hour you could have spent practicing this morning, and you want nothing, absolutely nothing to come between you and your future as an opera star, and you tell this man so. He claims he is crushed, that he would leave his wife and children for you; leaves messages upon messages at the Barbizon for you, flowers, gifts. You send the gifts back and are about to trash the flowers, but instead you give them to the girl at the desk. You don't want to look at them, but they're too pretty to toss.

—You're very good at this. I bet maybe you did become a writer after all.

—I'm noticing that it's extremely uncomfortable but also way easier for me to write as you than to write as you writing me.

—I don't know what to say about that. Are you blaming me again?

—You don't have to say anything about it. I don't blame you for anything.

—Hah! You don't blame me for ruining your life. Right.

—I might have, when I was twenty-five and miserable. But my life isn't ruined. There's nothing to blame anyone for.

Lois Dies, Scenario Three

All right, then. Your life isn't ruined. You grieve. You join a support group to talk about it. You tell the group that you had a complicated relationship with your difficult mother, but that you loved her, and you miss her. You wonder if you'll ever stop crying, and it takes time, but you do.

But now another year's gone by, and you still don't have much to show for yourself. You've stopped drinking, but haven't really started anything else. You teach at a preschool for seven dollars an hour, and you like the work, but it's demanding, and you could make more at Starbucks, where you'd also get the health insurance you still don't have. You want to be a writer, but don't have idea one about how to make money doing that, so you decide to use the money I left you to quit the preschool job and go back to school to get a writing degree. It might be a good idea to keep your job, but you've already established a pattern of kicking up dust behind you, so this isn't any different in that respect. You enroll at the University of Chicago. You've seen an Off-Broadway play, or whatever the equivalent of that is in Chicago, an Off-Michigan play, and it's weird and experimental but also inspiring, so you decide to study playwriting, which really seems to be your thing. Of course, the plays are all about you, or mostly about you, or about you and me and how I ruined your life, even if you insist I didn't, but they're also sort of experimental, like maybe I'm dead but return as a stray dog you can communicate with psychically; they're definitely funny, you were always funny, like your father, and you get some attention when your first play is put on at a prestigious Off-Broadway-equivalent Chicago theater, and you fall in love with the man who plays the stray dog version of your father, which is weird, but there it is. By this time you're forty, though, so it's basically too late for you to have children, but you discuss it with the stray dog man, and he doesn't believe in bringing children into the world anyway, though he would consider it for you even though he's one of these idealistic radical types who believes he'd ever see a world where that happened, zero population growth, so it's a big deal that he'd even consider it, and you would both certainly consider adoption, but together you just table the conversation indefinitely. Secretly—you'll never admit this to anyone—even though you like kids, and have always been good with them, you're not so sure you'd be a good mom anyway. You've lost your patience babysitting a time or two, and fear that any parenting style you might come up with would be a response to whatever you think I did wrong, like a lot of parents do, like maybe I did, maybe, which of course only fucks up their children differently.

You and the stray dog actor, his name is Leonardo—

—Hold up.

—What?

—I thought I was a novelist.

—Let's say you're both. People do more than one thing, don't they? I did.

—Sure. It's just that I was hoping to have a through-line here.

—Can't you go back to the TV chapter and revise again so that you write a play instead of a novel?

—I could. But that's kind of a pain in my ass.

—Practicing six hours a day was a pain in my ass.

—The thing is, novelist is so much closer to the truth.

—But how interesting is it?

— . . .

—I think playwriting has more dramatic potential. Also, isn't every other character in every book already a novelist? Or a journalist?

— . . .

—I'm right!

—You're not right, Mom, it's a very hyperbolic statement.

—You know there's some truth to it.

— . . .

—Okay, moving on, can you at least give my guy a regular name?

—What do you have against an Italian name?

—I don't have anything against them. I just think that's your preference, not mine. Plus, the most exotically named person I ever dated was Herschel.

—Oh, I remember him, he was very sexy, and his mother was a porn star.

—That's not actually true.

—She showed her tits.

—Can we get back to my fictional boyfriend's name?

—What would you like him to be named?

—I like the name of the person I'm with. If I'd written him into my life, I might have given him the name he actually has.

—You're with someone? Oh, sweetheart!

—Yes. I'm with someone.

—What's his name?

—His name is Ben.

—Benjamin! That's a really nice name!

—Just Ben. I mean, yes, Benjamin, but just Ben.

—I want to call him Benjamin. It's more actory-sounding. And it's not Italian.

—Fair enough.

—I'm really sorry I didn't get to meet him. He sounds wonderful.

—I haven't told you anything about him.

—I'm sure he's wonderful.

So you and Benjamin, the stray dog actor, who is also a director and writer, you get together and decide to form a theater company. You rent a space somewhere in Chicago, wherever it's cheap, some crummy location south of downtown. I don't know Chicago all that well outside the Loop. The first few years at the Betsy and Benjamin Theater Company are financially iffy, you pour a whole bunch of money into it that you don't have, but the two of you are hugely proud, and the notices are good, and you keep moving forward with it until you get a huge grant from the NEA or wherever—

—HAHAHAHAHAHAHAHA!

—that allows you to rehab the space and advertise properly and get larger audiences in.

—Is this your idea of a resolution for me?

—Yes. I thought you weren't about happy endings. This is happy-ish. It's a compromise.

—When did I say that?

—Maybe I'm just giving you what I wish you'd give me. I didn't have the happiest ending.

—I know. But I'm going for a sort of realism here. An imagined realism, anyway.

—Mmf.

Final Word

Just before you return to Baton Rouge, Carolina arranges for you to audition with New York City Opera. This audition does not get you into the company on the spot, but it goes well enough that Carolina reports back that they'll see you again in a year's time, and that now is the moment for you to move to New York and fully dedicate yourself to studying. It's a dazzling prospect, but you remind Carolina that you have a husband and a child. *Life gives us difficult choices*, Carolina says. You go back to the Barbizon that night, draft a letter. Many versions go into the trash. You should really fly home to tell Fred in person what you're planning, but you also know that if you do that, and if I start asking any questions about how long you're going to stay this time and if it will be forever, that you'll only end up postponing the inevitable. So you write your husband to say that you've decided to rent an apartment, and that you hope he'll reconsider coming to live in New York, though you've talked about this, and he's already said that he'd live almost anywhere but there. He's a small-town boy and Baton Rouge is plenty big enough for him. He writes a letter back to this effect, adding that he doesn't think New York City is any kind of place to raise a child, especially right now; reminding you, again, of his godforsaken perfect childhood in Mount Pleasant, telling you that he watches the *CBS Evening News*, that the crime rate has never been higher, and that he has strong reservations about the effect that will have on Betsy, her safety, and so on. You write back to say that the Upper West Side is perfectly safe, and that the public schools there are considered quite good, and that the culture that she'll have access to in New York is impossible to put a value on, and that you want more for me than you'd had in dullsville Muscatine for eighteen years, where the most stimulating topic of conversation was that nasty old grain smell. (Breathing it in was bad enough, talking about it day after day seemed like enough to drive anyone away forever.) After two more letters, Dad's done enough thinking about this for a while, and says he wants to wait to talk further until you return to Baton Rouge. When you get there, he tells you that Betsy is going to stay put and that's his final word on the subject, and you accept this for now, because he is the man; but "final word" gets stuck in your head, and you promise yourself right then that yours will be the *final* final word.

But for now you leave me behind with him, delaying, again, the conversation that is coming. You do keep returning to Baton Rouge, though a little less often, and two years later, when you are accepted into the company at New York City Opera, you write another letter, this time asking for a divorce, and managing to convince Dad to bring me to you rather than him forcing you to come down one last time to collect me. *Children need their mothers*, you tell him. Dad is as angry as Dad ever gets, which is to say that some vague but recognizably unpleasant feeling that some other person might recognize as anger stirs within him, an odd, unfamiliar rush of heat in his hands and feet, though he appears to have no need to explore it further. He's been my primary caregiver for the last three years, and all evidence shows that I'm well adjusted, bright, and happy in Louisiana with Dad, and he tries to remind you of this as calmly as he can, but he already senses that he's losing, and he can physically feel his anger as it deflates into something like sorrow, which is also not a feeling he wishes to experience, and so he rather abruptly stops talking, and from here forward, almost no dialogue will ensue between the two of you that doesn't serve some practical purpose. He knows I've missed you, and since the conventional wisdom at this time is that kids go with moms, with little consideration given to other details of care, you say *This is happening, Fred, you can bring her or I will*, and he relents and brings me to New York, and leaves shortly after. And almost as soon as he's gone, it flashes through your mind that this was a terrible decision, that you *should* have left me with him, that I *had* been well cared for, and that if you had done that, you'd be free from the huge responsibility you now face, to provide for a child with the minimal income provided by the opera company. But these are not thoughts you like, these are not things mothers think, so you redirect. Best to put it outside you. You and Dad haven't discussed money yet, you'll do this by mail as well, and during the separation, until a legal agreement is reached, he'll send thirty-two dollars a month for my food and clothing, which to your mind is a small fraction of what is needed, and to his mind and calculations is exactly what is already being spent, and so therefore should be sufficient.

And there's another little shift here, inside you, a little shift where it feels, physically, like the amount of air in your lungs is now just over capacity, that someone's inside your head with a flail, that if you were to loosen your jaw, which is currently clenched as though wired shut, packs of rabid hyenas would fly out. To say that these feelings and thoughts are a shock is not strong enough, and at first you simply shake, not knowing what to do with it, but soon enough you understand that it has to come out, you are sure that if you let it out it will be gone, and so you turn to me, because I am the one who is there, and you do manage not to scream—you can see that I am still only a six-year-old, just as I was the day before—but you say, with an intensity that I know means you are screaming in your mind, *Your father is not who you think he is!*

Why *Does* Your Mother Have So Many Problems?

Your theater company thrives. You have a big hit with a show called *Why Does My Mother Have So Many Problems?*

An excerpt:

The set consists of three bare walls and a small, worn floral sofa in the center with an ancient standing lamp on one side. Suspended from the rafters in front of the two side walls, facing each other, are two massive frames. The frame on the left features a Chuck Close–sized portrait of me; the frame on the right holds a mirror. Ben is seated on the sofa, reading; Betsy is stage left, looking into the mirror.

BETSY: I've been thinking of redecorating.
BEN: (*takes a beat*) I think that's a really good idea.
BETSY: What do you think about a sectional sofa?
BEN *looks up at the audience, deadpan.*
BETSY: (*still looking deeply into the mirror, which of course reflects both herself and the portrait of her mother*) My mother has so many problems.

That guy who did *Titanic* buys the rights to make it into a movie. There's talk of Julia Roberts playing me; ludicrous, but I guess Catherine Deneuve wouldn't be able to play young me.

Either way, the movie never comes to be. Still, it doesn't matter, the movie rights buy you and Benjamin a beautiful house on the lake with a view of the Chicago skyline.

—Mom, surely you know that James Cameron is not going to buy the rights to an absurdist play.

—Absurdist? Who's James Cameron? Do you want a lake house or not?

—Okay, yes, sure, why not.

You're way too old to have kids of your own now, so you adopt a fourteen-year-old girl, Maritza, but you're in way over your head on that one. You would have done better to take home a boy. Ordinary fourteen-year-old girls are tough, and this one's been in foster care for too long; thankfully she's not on drugs, like a lot of them, but she's got more than enough on her plate without that, she's just pissed at the world, and the world has given her reason to be; you do whatever possible to help her, send her to an excellent private school, ask her what she's interested in, with the idea that you'll help nurture those interests, but right now she's interested in one thing, a sixteen-year-old boy. This is an area of expertise, an area you're sure you could help her with—you were fourteen once, you know this and that about boys—but you're not getting through to her, because she's fourteen. *You don't understand, old lady!* she screams. *I don't know what it was like back when you were fourteen or if you were ever really fourteen but you have no idea what it's like, old lady.* She only calls you "old lady," refuses to call you by your name, and "Mom" will never be an option; this was the first thing she told you when she walked through the door and so far she's sticking to it.

You cry to Benjamin about this every night. Maritza's right. *What was I thinking?* you sob, *she's half Puerto Rican and half black and half Portuguese and what do I know about any of that? I should have thought about all that! I thought we could just love her!* He's very sweet. He doesn't have too many ideas about what to do, either, but he promises you'll get through it together, swears that all she needs is time and patience; she's been horribly neglected and god knows what else for years; she has no reason to think we're any different from anyone else. *But we are, aren't we?* you ask him, and he says *Sure we are, of course we are*, but you're not totally sure, maybe you're fundamentally part of the problem, that you're part of the universe that allowed this to happen to her in the first place, and he's not totally sure either, but you wonder what you could do to change that, not just with Maritza but maybe at the theater, initiate some community arts programs, get underserved kids involved in some way.

—This is getting a little closer, Mom, but I think there's a missed opportunity here. I think your story is still more interesting than mine.

—And whose fault is that?

—Why does something always have to be someone's fault?

—How could anything not be someone's fault?

—You're missing my point.

—Can't some things just be what they are?

—What?

—Look, I can't help it if you think I'm more interesting than you. But honestly, Betsy, would you ever have wanted to be inside my head?

—I feel a little bit like I'm inside your head now, which is why I'm only writing this about an hour at a time.

—Right, and you don't know the half of it.

It's 1968!

New York is harder than you thought it would be. You're not sorry you decided to come, not one bit, but you hadn't given much thought to the single mom thing, to the single thing. The single thing is not your thing, and it never was your thing, and so you head into dating as full-on as you do everything else. You meet several more men through Carolina, a few more through other friends. Not one man who meets you isn't interested. That is never the problem. All men who meet you are interested. But you need only one, ideally one who is everything Fred isn't. So after a number of uninspiring dates you settle on Stan, a nice Jewish man, an attorney at an entertainment law firm, works in the city, lives in a big stone house in Westchester. He's got two sons, my age and younger, thankfully they have a mother already, one they live with. You and Stan spend a great deal of time together; he's not the first person you sleep with after the split, but he is the first to sleep over, and you're not quite sure how to handle this. You're not ready for is-this-my-new-daddy-type questions. So you have him leave before I get up in the morning; this goes on for a good while. Stan is gaga for you. He doesn't spill the L word too soon, doesn't want to scare you off, but this forty-two-year-old man with gray in his eyebrows can barely hold it in, says he's sure now that light didn't exist before you, tells you to pick out any star in the sky you fancy and he'll make it yours, that you are the most captivating creature he's ever laid eyes on and that he can't imagine what he did right to get to be with you, but that he is grateful. Fred never said thing one like that; he was kind, but his compliments were mild, like the fluff from a dandelion; *Dinner was delicious!* about a pork chop you laid in a pan and salted, *Mommy's such a good seamstress!* about the woolen coat you made for me. Without a doubt, he found you exceptionally beautiful, he just wasn't inclined to say it out loud very often. But Stan's boyish admiration isn't quite on the mark either; it's harder to hear about your *immeasurable beauty* than you imagined; turns out it's nearly unbearable because you know it isn't true. Or worse, even if it is true now, you know that one day you'll be old and wrinkled and measurably less beautiful, and you care, and you're going to hell for it. Around the five-month mark, you're stripping the bed to do laundry and discover, written in red Magic Marker on your pillow, STAN LOVES LOIS inside a big red heart. It's meant to be a romantic surprise, of course, but what it really is, is the sign you needed to be sure that Lois does not love Stan. Making matters worse, you are in no financial position to throw out a perfectly good pillow, which is exactly what you'd do if you could. Some nerve he has, not thinking of that. You turn it over and put a new pillowcase right on it and that's the end of that. You will break it off tonight, and Stan will be crushed, but soon enough he'll find another woman to put on a pedestal and then divorce again, though he doesn't know this now. And it's no concern of yours.

So now you're a single gal again, but you have a new girlfriend, Peggy, the mother of my friend Liz from school, and you and Peggy make a little connection when you pick me up from a playdate at her house, and Peggy suggests that next time Betsy comes over you should stay and hang out with her. Peggy sees something in you, buried under your buttoned-to-the-top blouse and full skirt, and wants to help you uncover it. The following week, Peggy brings you into her bedroom and closes the door, tells us kids to knock if we want to come in. She asks if you've ever *done grass*. You hesitate—mowing the lawn is the first thing that comes into your mind—and when you do clue in and say no, you feel like she may as well have asked if you've ever had sex with a woman, and you're a tiny bit afraid that might be next. But it isn't. So you share a joint with Peggy, she shows you how to do it, and soon you're relaxed and floppy and giggly, you'd do this 24/7 if you could accomplish anything this way, but you imagine having to take a voice lesson on marijuana and picture yourself rolling on the floor, peeing your underwear. You admire Peggy's flowy Mexican blouse; she looks comfortable in it and in what's under it. She takes it right off and tells you to put it on; you do so. You giggle; she tells you to keep it, throws on a paint-splattered, stretched-out T-shirt that was on the floor by her bed. Peggy is an artist. She tells you stories of some of the men she's been with since her own divorce—*Nothing special*, she says, *but quite a few amazing lovers in there*. Peggy sees the curiosity on your face, gets that you haven't fully worked out the sleeping-with-people-you-aren't-married-to thing, in spite of having a go at it when you actually were married. *It's 1968!* she says, smiling. You know what year it is, but you don't know what her point is, and she sees that. *You're a modern single woman. You're in New York City. It's your time. You can do what you want now and not feel shitty about it! I had a three-way once on peyote!* You don't know what peyote is, you think it might be a type of bedsheet, but you do know you're barely ready for another two-way. *I mean, it wasn't all that great, honestly. You can skip that, in my opinion. But there are lots of men out there. Why limit yourself?*

Your mind is effectively blown. This is not what you were taught. You set your hair with rollers, and you will do this forever and always. Women wear slips under their dresses; they go on proper dates until proposals are made; they maybe, maybe work part-time until they become with child. What could you have been thinking, leaving all that behind? This way has not been quite what you imagined, though that didn't go far beyond Grande Dame. You hoped to be so celebrated that you're given a name, like Sutherland's "La Stupenda," or Callas's "La Divina," or even just be referred to by your last name, like Caballé. Not yet. And this blouse is *so* comfortable. Stupid slips. *Right on!* you say. Okay, too much. You and Peggy fall on top of each other laughing.

Lois Dies (What Scenario Are We up To?)

Okay, I think I have it this time, Betsy. Scenario four—or is it five?

You're not a kid anymore. You've stopped drinking, but that's about it. You go to the AA meetings. You're still single. You're broke. I die, you grieve, now you're in your mid-thirties. You've given it a go as a writer, but it wasn't what you wanted after all. You decide it's now time to pursue your life's dream of becoming a Broadway star. As you see it, now that your mother the singer is dead, you no longer have to use that dimmer switch anymore; that's not really true, but you hope. You still have stage fright, which is the reason you say you never pursued it—it was hard enough for you to sing for the singing coach—so you contact a woman who specializes in stuff like that, and she works with you for a year, breathing exercises and guided meditations and the like. Some of it is flat-out silly. She tells you to picture yourself on a stage that faces an ocean; the ocean is your audience, the ocean doesn't judge you, the ocean only wants you to succeed. You have always loved the ocean, but right now you're picturing tsunamis instead of gentle, encouraging waves; this can't possibly help, and you tell the coach so. She says just keep doing it, it's not magic, and so you do, you don't have much to lose, and one day an audition comes up that you don't say no to, for a supporting part in a new musical. You were already on the old side to make a start in this field when you went to the coach in the first place, but this part is tailor-made for you, exactly your age, a spinster character, the kind with glasses and a bun that comes down at some point when she meets a nice man. You get the part. I could give you a year's worth of auditions like this, so you know what it's really like for most people—how it stinks when you get feedback like *You're not ready* or *Do you have anything else* or *Have you ever* or *Would you be willing to dye your hair/get a nose job/do a nude scene* or sometimes even just *Thank you*, which may as well be them saying *You may now go jump off the Chrysler Building.*

Their primary concern is that you're too old, but your talent is undeniable, and they decide unanimously to hire you, and you're flattered, although you're not at all sure you should have taken this on. You are, now that you're here, decidedly *not* sure. It should be said that it was never that you didn't know you could sing, and sing well. That has nothing to do with the fear, which returns in the form of that swelling ocean, on this actual stage, as you're receiving actual praise from actual people, and you see in front of you an enormous Hokusai wave coming down over the house seats, over the casting people, over the orchestra pit, hanging right down over your head.

—But Mom, a bunch of scenes back I quit my singing career to jump on a boat and make babies. Why do I keep trying to audition for things?

—Weren't you the one who said this story was nonlinear?

— . . .

—Is that storyline resolved for you, in real life?

— . . .

The Services

The Pill is increasingly popular, but after weighing your options, you land on the diaphragm and decide to stick. It's a messy pain in the ass that makes you certain a man invented it, but the phrase "weight gain" was enough to cross the Pill off the list of choices. It's not like you're out sleeping around anyway, you've always been a one-man woman, but by now there's been a series of ones, you dumped the last one just a few days ago, and having another child right now is not under consideration. The child you already have is only in second grade, but you've spent the last year wondering why elementary school couldn't go nine to five. Nine to seven. Thirty. That would leave time for bath, book, and bed. Quality time. Perfect.

Your monthly time has never been anything other than an alert, something to set a clock by. You've been marking a special calendar (kept in your nightstand drawer, a tiny one picked up for free at the pharmacy) since just before you got married; you never had a sex talk with Grandma, exactly, no more than the beginning of a talk about *relations* when you were eighteen and yes, still a virgin, though you were aware of how the parts went together, enough to tell her she didn't need to say more, to her great relief. And of course it wasn't long after this that Dad came into the picture, and the day after your engagement, Grandma suggested that you start marking your calendar, thinking less of prevention than of planning.

Double-checking the calendar, this year's with the unfortunate image of a top-hatted Baby New Year on it, you see that your monthly time was due yesterday. Surely everyone is late once in a while, yet signs indicate otherwise this time. You haven't felt so much as one cramp thus far, and you've never had a period yet without at least one day beforehand when murder seemed comprehensible.

Three days go by. Still no cramps or twinges of any kind, nor so much as a drop of blood. On the fourth day, you make an appointment with a gynecologist, but they can't get you in until the seventh day, at which time you are given a test and told that they'll call with the results in a week to ten days. You refrain from noting that you're now already a week late, and that in a week or ten days you expect to be sure one way or another, extremely clear on what the results will say. But denial can be an intoxicating lover. There could be some good medical reason you haven't gotten your period. Maybe you just need to eat better. Maybe you have some minor medical condition. Could be a million explanations, really.

The eight days that follow have extra hours in them. There is no possible way that these eight days have not gotten progressively longer, twenty-five hours at first, you could have slept through that and not noticed, but it feels like thirty hours on the second and forty on the third and so on, until, on the last day, looking at the clock, you see that the second hand is clearly moving in increments of a minute at a time. Finally a nurse from the doctor's office calls and makes an appointment for you to come in for your results.

The doctor says *Congratulations*; you burst into tears. You get up to leave. He asks if you don't want to go ahead and schedule a series of appointments. All you can do is shake your head and go.

You're pregnant and single and you earned about four thousand dollars last year. You couldn't afford another child even if you did think you wanted one; nor is it an option to announce your single motherhood to the world. The world still hasn't forgiven Ingrid Bergman for getting pregnant out of wedlock, you don't imagine they'll be easier on you—not that you could ever tell your mother, or father, or best friend, and definitely not Stan, who effing did this to you. That guy would freaking beg you to marry him. Putting the baby up for adoption is the only option, and that's going to fuck up your next six months pretty royally. Maybe, for the first few months, you can say you've gained a little weight if anyone asks. Your career has hardly even begun. You've failed.

Another few days of crying go by before you remember a conversation with that woman Evelyn, the aspiring model you'd met at the Barbizon. She'd couched it in language you hadn't really understood at the time, or at least, hadn't wanted to. Evelyn had spoken frankly about not wanting kids, said that she took care to make sure that didn't happen because she knew what her options were if she were to find herself pregnant. That was more or less the extent of it, but you recall being struck at the time by the tone of what she was saying, that there was a vague implication that there might be options you weren't aware of, even if they weren't terribly desirable.

You call Evelyn immediately, leave a message with her answering service to call at her earliest convenience. When she calls back later that evening, you catch up briefly before telling her the real reason for the call. She gives you an address in Queens. You've never been to Queens. You ask for a phone number. Evelyn says *There is no phone number. What kind of doctor's office doesn't have a phone?* you ask. *It's not exactly a doctor's office. There's a doctor.* Every lick of good sense in you says this can't be right. *This is how it is*, Evelyn says.

You study your subway map, tell me you'll be out for a few hours, that the babysitter will take me to the park; you take the IRT to almost the end of the 7 line, which takes nearly two hours. You've got a paperback book, a romance, but it's hard to focus. You might have considered that romance wouldn't take your mind off things today. Everyone on the subway looks like they need things taken off their minds. You get out of the subway in an unfamiliar land, notice a deli outside the subway stop called Flushing Foods. Flushing? Honestly? That seems like a cruel joke. You find your way to the address Evelyn gave you. It's a nondescript two-story residential building on a side street. You enter into a waiting area that was once a living room, walls lined with wooden folding chairs, not so much as a tattered magazine or a sad clown painting to look at. One of the women waiting points to a clipboard on the wall, tells you to put your first name at the bottom of the list. You sit down on one of the chairs, feel a splinter pulling at your skirt. The mood in the room is a level of somber that's new to you. Almost every woman here is alone, silent. A couple of them are crying, a couple of them look terrified. One looks to be about sixteen, the rest around your age, women of every imaginable kind. One by one they are escorted into another room; the waiting room fills with still more young women. Two hours in, an unshaven man in a lab coat comes out and calls your name. Why didn't he shave? This strikes you as the worst impression a doctor could make—until you are taken into the back room, which looks like someplace a kidnapping victim would be held. One wheeled stool for the doctor with a rip in the vinyl, one table for the patient, one small sink, one metal tray with one long, sharp-looking metal instrument. The unshaven guy—is he even a doctor?—asks you a few questions. *Are you married. How many sexual partners have you had. How often do you have sex. Have you ever been pregnant before. Is this your first* procedure. No, but this is your first time hearing the word "procedure" used in such an ominous way. You spy blood in the sink. There will be no proceeding here. You leave. You'll sooner have another baby.

You call Evelyn back, describe what you've just been through, she says she's *real sorry* you had to go through that, *can only imagine*, says she may know one more person who has a contact, she'll call back later with a number. *Tell them you're calling about their special services*, Evelyn says when she calls back. Nothing about this seems special to you.

You do as instructed and receive an address for a clinic in the West Village. The clinic is not marked as such; it's on the ground floor of a brownstone that looks like any other residential brownstone. Four other women are waiting, looking as nervous as you do. One of them is visibly pregnant. A receptionist hands you a card to fill out with relevant medical information, again asking for only your first name. Previous pregnancies—2, Miscarriages—1, Major illnesses—0. Emergency contact—none. You hand this back to the receptionist; she glances at it, hands it right back. *You have to put an emergency contact.* You look at her—doesn't she know why you haven't filled that out? She does. *You have to put someone on there or you can't get the services.* The services. Now they're not even special anymore. You put down Audrey's number and pray to god it's never needed. In your heart you know Audrey would be nothing but discreet and gentle about it, but this is a secret that will go down with you.

The receptionist escorts you to the back; this time, thank heavens, the doctor's office looks like a doctor's office. *You're in good hands*, she says. The doctor is female, introduces herself as Joan. You've never met a female doctor before, though it's not news to you that they exist. Your eyes start filling up as soon as she extends her hand. Maybe *she's* not really a doctor. Why didn't you ask anyone before you came here? You are the queen of asking questions. Dr. Joan hands you a tissue, puts an arm on your shoulder, gestures to the table with the stirrups, explains the procedure step by step, asks if you have any questions before she begins. You shake your head, *I guess not*. Dr. Joan senses that you're still not sure about any of this. *If this were legal, Lois*, she says, *it would be the same procedure. I'm a licensed obstetrician, even though I am listed as not currently practicing. Some women aren't so lucky*.

Lucky.

Out through the Hole

Your career is progressing steadily. You have now played both Musetta and Mimi at New York City Opera, and have been invited to perform with several other orchestras and opera companies, mostly around the Midwest: Cincinnati, Ann Arbor, Milwaukee. You receive standing ovations wherever you go, reviews never less than stellar. ("Her coloratura in 'Sempre libera' compares with Sutherland," "A compelling and magnetic Tosca, with a dark weight to even her highest notes." One review took note of your flawless phrasing, but you knew it wasn't flawless at all the night they'd come. You'd done it much better in dress, but even that hadn't been perfect. They should have just given you a bad review. "Her phrasing was good, but not without flaws, like her very self.") By anyone else's standards, this might be considered a successful career, but for you it's not enough. Your dreams are bigger. The Metropolitan Opera is right across the plaza from City Opera, yet it seems inexplicably far away. You've auditioned there to polite nods, unreadable smiles, limp handshakes, and little feedback from your manager. He tries to reassure you by saying that they went with *that mediocre So-and-so*, again, but this doesn't help, both because of the mediocrity and because So-and-so is the same bitch who stole the last job from you. At this point, a polite nod for you is the equivalent of a blazingly bad review, whether or not that's true, so you simply work harder. There's always room to improve, though it frankly enrages you that you aren't being recognized. You double down with Carolina, an extra lesson per week that isn't in your budget—but even Carolina reminds you of the importance of rest. *Equal measures, my darling, equal measures!* She says *Practice as usual but no more, take sleep, take lovers.*

You remember what Peggy said, too. You ask if she has any friends to fix you up with. She invites you to an art opening. You've been to museums, but never to a gallery opening—so exciting! You envision handsome art collectors in tailor-made suits, men with penthouse apartments on Fifth Avenue. You once saw Jackie O on the street; you could look just as chic as her with an oil magnate on your arm. You pick out a black cocktail dress, simple but sophisticated. Pearls? No pearls. The gold circle pin mother gave you? That's not it either. A printed scarf, black and white silk, with a tiny bit of red. You knot it around your neck, move the bow to the side. Perfect. You meet Peggy at her place; she's wearing faded bell-bottom jeans, a loose white top, a long necklace with some kind of a crystal pendant at the end, long, straight blond hair parted in the middle. Maybe you got the date wrong? *Not the date, just the outfit*, Peggy says with a warm smile. She pulls you inside, opens up her closet, rifles through, grabs a pair of flared white jeans, a bright yellow crocheted top with bell sleeves, leaves the scarf. *But it doesn't match!* you say. Peggy laughs, says *Matching is overrated*, looks at you again. Getting there, but not quite right. Peggy takes a brush to your hair, flips the ends up at the bottom. It's still a bit too *done* for where she's taking you, but it'll do. You look in the mirror, heartbeat speeding up. You've always considered yourself fashion-conscious; why doesn't this feel quite like you? You feel exposed, though you're basically as covered as ever, in these loose-fitting clothes that aren't yours, but Peggy has the solution for that, of course: one hit off a joint and you'll be good to go.

You giggle together on the subway downtown. There's a Miss Subways card above your head—real New York glamour. You left the house looking like that, but that seems like ten years ago now. An hour later you hardly know who you are anymore, you've said the word "fuck" out loud, twice, and it felt good, you feel like you're in a book about a carefree single gal in New York on a string of innocuous big-city adventures. The buzz from the marijuana is gone by the time you get there, but you have a sort of natural buzz now. You get off the train in a part of town you've never been to before, is it the East Village? You're not sure, but people are out and about, people of just about every variety but the ones you left uptown, scruffy, dirty, drunk, on drugs, young, old, black, white, Spanish, Chinese and what have you, guys with ponytails!—criminals, you're sure, they must be, so you're glad you're with Peggy, who's holding your hand. Peggy whisks you into what seems like a randomly chosen storefront, the window of which is filled with what looks like a big heap of trash, stuff you'd see in a junk pile, rusted things, old newspapers, broken toy parts, empty milk containers, and bottles of Wild Irish Rose. You take your eyes off the trash pile before you're quite done figuring it out, to see a room full of people, practically body to body, drinking things, smoking things, laughing, dancing—they dance at gallery openings?—and across the room, on the far wall, a hole, a large, raw-edged circular hole that leads directly outside; a woman in a mini dress is standing in it, moving to the music, smoking. You have never seen, could never have imagined, a scene like this, do not know what you're doing here. Peggy kisses several people on the cheek, makes introductions, at one point hugs a slouchy beanpole of woman with the stringiest, greasiest hair you've ever seen; did her parents not tell her to stand up straight, take a bath?; stringy-haired woman walks away, Peggy says *That's Patti Smith, she's amazing, you guys would totally groove on each other*; you nod, that's the first and last time you'll hear that name, and you and Patti will do no further grooving. You can barely manage the intensity of the grooving happening as it is.

Deeper into the crush of people in the gallery, Peggy introduces you to the "artist." You have absolutely no idea what to say, you aren't even yet sure where the art is, or what the art is, though your gut tells you that "beautiful"—about the only word in your art lexicon—isn't right. Everything is better when he kisses your hand, and he takes you away from Peggy and out through the hole in the back of the room. You sit together on a pile of bricks in the empty lot behind the building, and you tell him you're embarrassed to say you don't get it, this isn't the kind of art you saw in Europe ten years ago, and he laughs, says *I find your honesty and your figure delightful*, and he happily explains what's happening in contemporary art right now, and it's fascinating, what he has to say about it, though you're not at all convinced yet that what is happening here is in any way art. But this man could be Marcello Mastroianni's double: thick, wavy dark hair, intense brown eyes that never leave your gaze. He doesn't ask you too many questions, and right now that's just fine. He takes you for a walk down the street. Should he be leaving his own show? He waves it off. *They don't need me. They'll still be there at dawn.* He takes you to a café, buys you espressos, tells you more about himself and his art and his life, takes you in a taxi back to his massive loft in yet another part of downtown you've never seen, lays you down on his bed, and does things to you in the first five minutes that make the entire evening suddenly seem like foreplay (things neither Fred nor you knew were things), and he's only getting started.

When the Sound Comes Out

Your starring Broadway debut is a musical based on a movie based on a comic book about a shy accountant by day, crime-fighter by night. The dress rehearsals go well, but this is not just a supporting part in a tour, it's a whole different thing, and you break out in hives the day before opening night. Fortunately, the makeup crew has seen this before and they can make it so the audience won't notice a single mark, even if it leaves you feeling like you're wearing a flesh-colored ski mask. Every night, it feels like a realistic possibility that you'll throw up before you walk out onto the stage, or possibly once you're center stage, as the curtains are coming up. You wonder if your mom ever felt like this. You wonder if you'll make it through the run. The reviews call you "a natural" and "a captivating new talent," but it's the one that uses the phrase "slightly stiff" that will stick with you forever, even though the complete sentence is "Although Ms. Crane is slightly stiff on the stage, hers is a talent that hasn't been seen since Streisand debuted." Again: you are compared to your childhood idol, favorably, but for weeks afterward, still wounded, you introduce yourself to new people by saying *Hi, I'm Elizabeth Crane, I'm slightly stiff*, sparking more confusion than laughter, and thank god, after the sixth time, Nina says *You have to stop saying that.* Further, your efforts to remedy your slight stiffness only compound the problem. Your consciousness of a single charge of stiffness only makes you stiffer. The show is looking like it could be a hit, you've got an extension in your contract if it does, but in the dressing room you consider going back to waiting tables. That wasn't so bad, was it? It didn't make you want to throw up. Why did you ever think you wanted to do this? Oh, right, because when the sound comes out of you, when you get it just right, it's like it's not even you, it belongs to a power greater than yourself, which is an enjoyable feeling, given your ongoing doubt about such things, and that part of it is good and reassuring, though it lasts only as long as the sound itself. For you, the applause is nice only on an intellectual level. It would suck if there were none, and you assume it's genuine, but it isn't a thing that keeps you going. In between sounds, you sometimes aren't sure what it is that keeps you going. But you've had it in your head since we went to see *Godspell* when you were in third grade; you played that record until it was practically transparent and sang those songs over and over at full volume whether the record was playing or not. (Subject matter of said musical probably not relevant, unless you want to spend time discussing coincidences and/or serendipity and/or fate, though it's fairly clear, given your equal enthusiasm, at that age, for the musicals *Funny Girl*, *West Side Story*, *Oklahoma!*, and *Hair*, that your responses were strictly melody-based.)

All these years later, after you work far enough through some shit so that you can actually perform, it still gets you only so far; you're doing it, but you're still massively uncomfortable; you decide to go to therapy. But therapy takes time, so let's just say that before the show's run is over, a bunch of stuff comes up in therapy that you hadn't been dealing with as regards your mother. Your therapist gently suggests that your mother may have discouraged you from being a singer. *But why would someone who was willing to sacrifice everything to become an artist not want to encourage her own child to become an artist? Why, if you're going to make a point of saying that your own parents did these things wrong, would you then go do those exact same things? Why do you think, Betsy? I don't know. I know what she told me, that it was too hard, and she wanted something easier for me. Is it possible that she believed that? I guess, but I think there's more to it. Okay, so what's the more, do you think? I think the more is obvious. Maybe, maybe not, but I want you to say it. Well, maybe I was competition for her. Say more about that. Ugh, do I have to? No, you don't have to. You could keep struggling. Fine. I think it's possible that she felt she had enough competition out in the world and didn't want any more right in her own house. I think it's possible that she had me and then spent the rest of her life wishing she hadn't. And how does that make you feel? Nauseous.*

—I actually do feel nauseous right now.

—Nauseated.

— . . .

—You're a writer, don't you want it to be right?

— . . .

—Anyway, that's probably psychosomatic.

—Either way, I am having a physical feeling in my intestines, the kind that portends throwing up.

—It'll pass. I'll send you some Reiki.

—Reiki from the beyond. Interesting.

—It's a thing.

—Is it.

—Weirdly, I feel a little better already.

—That's the Reiki!

Anyway. So you're in therapy, and you recognize these things that have been holding you back and making you want to throw up every night, and you even make some progress, and that first show comes to an end but you've gotten only excellent notices, and you're asked to join the touring revival of *Godspell*, of all things—why not?—no audition, and you're still single, and you've wanted to leave New York since forever—and so a year on the road, in a supporting role, is a perfect opportunity. Your last tour was an amazing experience, with some wonderful benefits: the camaraderie among the cast, a new lover, a sense of having a place and a purpose, even a transitory one. You begin to allow yourself to enjoy the applause as much as the music, though it's not sustenance for you in the way it was for me.

La Bella Donna

Artist Marcello Mastroianni comes and goes. It's a whirl of a week. He flies you to Barcelona, where he has another opening. He pronounces it *Barthelona*, which sounds positively absurd until you hear a number of actual Spaniards pronounce it this way, after which you will pronounce it this way forevermore. It's hard not to compare this trip to Spain with your last, more than ten years ago. The first time, everything was new: your marriage, art, the world. This is new too, there's a sensual charge to it; your skin feels like a penny in your mouth, and the world itself seems altogether changed, and it feels harder to reach that sense of promise you had back then. Is it just the difference between being nineteen and thirty? How could a person feel simultaneously so alive and so full of dread? Marcello's Barcelona show is closer to what you imagined: a gallery with actual doors, art you can identify as such (even if it's still probably not what you'd call *your thing*), with an added flurry of attention on him, photographers, acolytes, women younger than you—when did that moment happen? You're barely into your thirties, not a line on your skin, but these women seem to have been born in groups of threes and fours, long-legged, effortless European beauties, style you can't grasp; born muses they are, would that you could be one too, someone free of what exists in you, someone who could exist simply as an inspiration for the art of another, a type of well for another to draw from whatever he might. There are those, like Marcello, who would happily offer you this as a permanent post, yet it is not your calling. Marcello pays these muses-in-waiting no mind, though it's impossible not to notice the amount of attention they lavish on him, the exact reverse of the ratio you aspire to. You have more than a few jealous bones, though in this case you're not sure jealousy is exactly what's at play.

You stay at the Majestic Hotel (silk fringe ties on the heavy brocade drapes, full-size bath soaps scented like lilies of the valley!—you like this a great deal), and he orders room service, which comes with champagne. This part of the trip is all about your wishes. You and Marcello spend the rest of the weekend in bed. For a second, this bed, with its incredible sheets and carts of covered food and its Marcello, could be the ideal place to stay forever. You're not a big drinker; one glass of champagne is more than enough to make you forget you were once a genteel young lady from Muscatine, one whose parents have no capacity to imagine a universe where people do other than get married and stay that way; you only wish the champagne would help it stay forgotten the next day. You are not so much hung over as just no longer buzzed. You fly back to New York with a suitcase weighed down with Majestic Hotel letterpress note cards and a half-dozen bars of soap you pilfered from the maids' cart when they weren't looking; nothing wrong with that, it's paid for. Bouquets of roses come to your door, some exotic breed with blooms the size of grapefruits, but despite the romantic notes pinned to them, you waste no time before breaking it off. Marcello treats you well, but you're not interested in holding his spotlight, which is about all he asks in return. Audrey thinks you're crazy, though she'd never say as much to you; it sounds like a dream to her, she's a full-time nurse with four kids, you let it slip though that you "almost" envy Audrey, which she's too nice to ever call you out on. You go on to say that she got a winner in Jack; she laughs and says *Sure, I got lucky, but it's still not all rainbows and kittens. I have three boys and a teenage girl. With boobs. Big boobs.* You tell her you're not ready to think about teenage girls and their boobs; she tells you not to worry, it'll happen whether or not you think about it. Audrey knows that all you want is for her to tell you whatever might make you feel good in any given moment, so she says sure, she understands that's not quite what you're looking for, though secretly she does wish for some real thing that might make life easier for you. Her fear, and yours too, is that there may be no such thing, though Audrey is slightly more optimistic about this than you are. Audrey has a gentleness to her voice and a perpetual look in her eye that shows she was born to give care, seemingly just for you, though she has compassion to spare, and so when she asks directly what might help most, you say *I don't know, and if I did there probably wouldn't be a big enough supply of it anyway.*

You try a few singles bars with Peggy, and meet two or three men who by contrast make Dad seem like Cary Grant, dullards mostly, a long parade of businessmen types, blurring together to form one massive dullard, always enamored of you, always by and large unimaginative in bed, and adding these boring notches doesn't help your feelings about yourself any.

A few more years pass with the dullard collective while you continue your studies, performing when jobs arise. Carolina arranges an audition for you with an agent from a more powerful outfit. You had not expected dissatisfaction with your career so soon, have not wanted to complain about it, but in confiding to Carolina she agrees that you have made great vocal progress and that she has someone for you to meet. She mentions nothing about how handsome—not to mention young—he is, and you're glad she doesn't. You prepare for the audition as though you'll be meeting yet another closeted fifty-year-old music rep, and so when Victor Silvestri, a handsome, affable twenty-eight-year-old comes in, your eyes brighten just a little. His brighten a lot. You sing "Una voce poco fa" to which he responds with laughter, bold, jubilant laughter—he can't stop looking at Carolina, who knows him and knows what it means, but for you this is a first. The closeted types tend to nod and smile, if you're lucky. (You come to believe that you could have a dozen octaves and the voice of a seraph but what you're sure these guys want is a tenor fresh out of college willing to carry their umbrellas and make themselves available for any darker whims. This is a belief you will hold until your last days, and your future husband will not disabuse you of it.) You're pretty sure he isn't laughing at how bad you were, but it's an unusual response to say the least. He says he can have a contract ready for you tomorrow and would you like to sign it over dinner? Some quick math: eager + agent + Italian + handsome = everything you're looking for, all in one.

You have a sense that the black cocktail dress you almost wore to the weird gallery opening might work for this one, and you're right. He's wearing his suit and tie from work. He picks you up at home, greets you with a kiss on both cheeks, takes you to dinner at Abruzzi, a dimly lit place on West Fifty-Sixth Street where he's friendly with the owner, the kind of joint with old-man waiters who've been there forever. Tony, the owner, himself from Abruzzi, asks if you'd like some tomatoes and basil from his garden, it's that kind of place (or it is for Victor).

Tony doesn't wait for an answer—*Vito, slice up some of the tomatoes with basil, a little olive oil, a little mozzarella for Signor Silvestri.* Vito brings this out in about ninety seconds, and it is the most delicious-tasting tomato ever. Tony says he has a *Fantastic vitello, how does that sound?* and you nod, even though you don't know what vitello is, Victor says *Terrific,* and you close your menus and Tony says *Enjoy your evening with* la bella donna. *La bella donna!* You know what that means. That could be your diva name. Victor opens the conversation by saying *Let's get business out of the way first.* He leans in, changes the tone of his voice. *You're a tremendous talent. You have something special. And it doesn't hurt that you're a knockout. I have big plans for your career. We'll put together a huge promotional packet; I've got a great photographer for new head shots. I also represent several conductors who will go ape-shit for you. And I can have you on the road before the end of the year.* This is more than you could have hoped for and you say so. *Good,* he says. *Business done. Now tell me everything about you.* So you tell him you married young, got divorced, have a nine-year-old daughter, beautiful, bright, and well behaved, news of which doesn't cause him to flinch one small bit even though he's not yet thirty and only weeks ago moved into his first apartment. When he asks why your marriage didn't work out, you try not to say anything bad about Fred on the first date, so he says *Something must have been wrong with that guy to let you go.* You learn that his family is from the Bronx, *Typical Italians, a little nutso, but good to the core,* lots of musicians in the family, grew up with classical in the house always. You tell him you grew up with Benny Goodman. *He's good too,* he says, and the next thing you know he's asking if you'd ever want to get married again, you tell him you think so, he asks what June looks like for you. You giggle. It's way too soon, but you can kind of see it.

Stick

By the end of your first week together, Victor stops asking you to marry him and simply tells you instead.

By the end of your first month together, he's broken the lease on his midtown bachelor pad that he never really lived in and moved into our apartment on West End Avenue.

By the end of your second month together, you say yes, by the end of your third month he's going to parent-teacher meetings with you, you've had three high-decibel arguments, and by the end of your fifth month together, you are married.

It takes a while to figure out why, of all your suitors, this one. It may be nothing more than his timing. You've been in New York for the better part of five years, which is about three years beyond your original timeline for becoming a world-renowned opera star and meeting a good man. He's handsome, sure. He knows music; you have things to talk about. He wants to help your career, that's a huge plus, but that's not the whole of it. He's not the first to fall madly in love with you, not the first to propose, and he's not a whole bunch of other things too. He's not uncertain, about anything, and to your mind that is possibly his greatest asset. You are certain of few things, and rely heavily on the certainty of others. And he is as certain of you as he's ever been of anything, which is good, because that is the thing about which you are least certain, and you hope to god his certainty about you will make up the difference. And as much as anything, he's not Fred.

New York has been, at times, exciting beyond your ability to handle it. You've also barely made your rent more than a few times, even though your rent is still about as cheap as it gets. You don't mind pinching pennies, but you're growing tired of store-brand everything, and there's not always time to let down the hems on Betsy's dresses when she grows two inches in a week—it would be nice, once in a while, to send them to a tailor. And let's face it: you're thirty-four. It's 1971 and you're thirty-four—almost thirty-five—and that's not ancient but this is a weird era for you. It doesn't feel like yours. It's confusing. War protests, race riots, *moon landings*? *Women's lib?* It doesn't seem bad in theory, you might never have made it out of Iowa without it, but still. If you'd been born even ten years earlier, you might have gotten stuck with a Fred for your entire life, but all of this—hippies and free love (you live only two hours from Woodstock, but hear little of it)—you did your best to try on a version of that, only to find that wasn't you either. Love is never free. Not to mention that there's all kinds of holy hell happening around the world that you don't understand the half of and couldn't handle if you did. There's plenty of holy hell happening inside your own head. You want some stability. You had thought you might be a star by now and you aren't. You hope that Victor will help turn that around; in opera, you're not over the hill yet at all—look at Sutherland, Tebaldi, Price—and you know, you *know*, that you are better than ever and could be better still. But you have doubts on top of doubts, about your career prospects, about yourself as a human fit for the world, epic, wide-ranging doubts—and this new man has not a one. This is something you can only marginally comprehend, that a person could be so utterly doubtless, but Victor Silvestri is a man who knows what he knows. He knows music, he knows talent, he knows what he loves (you, in absurd amounts, to the point where he sees your flaws as assets), he knows what's right and what's wrong without doubt, ever, and though you have been known to state many and varied and sometimes even conflicting opinions as though you have no doubt, really, you don't know anything without doubt, and you suppose that it would be nice—more than nice, a relief—to have someone in the house whose doubt couldn't blow down the entire building with one heavy sigh. And you do like him; he's sexy, he's steady, he's a good father figure, he takes care of you, and you know now that you are a person who likes being taken care of. Who needs being taken care of. "Taken care of" here meaning being there with an unassailable point of view and a steady paycheck, and perhaps even just being around for those times when pouring out a bowl of cereal for your kid before school is more than you can manage by yourself.

It's a June wedding. You should have been a June bride the first time; that was probably mistake number one. (You will never admit that being nineteen was mistake number one; you will claim forever and always that you knew exactly what you were doing.) This time, you have engagements on the books to rehearse for, so you have the dresses made for you: yours, Audrey's, and mine (though you have to do a bit of alteration work on mine because I've gone and grown, again, since the measurements were taken); you plan this shindig with two months' notice.

You learn the extent to which Victor's mother is perpetually late; today, two hours. This would be unacceptable on most occasions, save for some horrific circumstances not involving simply getting dressed and made up, and today, it's just under bring-me-a-straightjacket level. She's *in* the wedding. You could go ahead without her, but after an exchange of heated messages between your dressing room at the church and the anteroom where Victor and his best man are waiting (your messages leave your room heated—*Tell Victor she has ten minutes to show up or I'm leaving*—but they're delivered by Audrey's husband, Jack, with enough of a wink that Victor remains calm, and thank Christ his mother shows up before you have to make good on that. There's no time to shift back into joyful-wedding-day mode before walking down the aisle, but Audrey whispers in your ear that it's all going to be fine, and Audrey invented the reassuring tone of voice, and on your way down the aisle, on your father's arm for the second time (thinking: Why in creation did we decide to do it this way? Why such a big deal, again? Why not City Hall?), you give your groom the death glare from the aisle, which only causes him to stifle his trademark loud and high-pitched laugh, over how much he loves you for and in spite of your death glare—which, in turn, reminds you why you decided not to split.

At the reception, some relative of Victor's in a polyester suit wants to dance with me and won't take no for an answer until I'm near tears. I turn to you and whisper *I don't want to*, you say *It's fine, Betsy, that's Victor's uncle, he's all right.* I'm insistent; I try to make you look at my face so that Victor doesn't see. *Mommy, pleeeeeze, I don't want to.* You'd already given me instructions, prior to the wedding, to be an especially good girl today, but I have already established a zero-tolerance policy for creepiness that has served me well to date. You call Victor over to mediate with Uncle Whosis.

—Hold on, Betsy, what kind of creepiness are we talking about here, exactly?

—It was 1971 in New York City. The creepiness levels were at an all-time high.

—Did something happen to you?

—No. Things just happened. And/also things could have happened to me, but didn't.

—Why didn't you tell me?

—You had other things on your mind.

— . . .

Victor comes over and says *Maybe later, Silvio,* and escorts me back to my table to sit with my friend Miriam, but now I'm all worked up and demand to sit next to you, and you relent, because though it doesn't happen often, I am sobbing loudly and you are not having any more of that on your wedding day. You try to squeeze an extra chair between Grandma and Grandpa, but I remain firm that my seat must be next to yours. You remain firm that I must keep my shit together for the rest of the reception, and we reach an accord.

You don't know, of course, that your doubts about this choice of spouse will remain after the hubbub of the first year. In your honeymoon suite in Mexico, you have your first real shouting match—a preview of the future—when Victor takes off his ring to go swimming and the room is burglarized while you're gone. *Why did you take it off in the first place? I didn't want it to slip off. You can't take it off ever! I can do what I like. No you can't, we just took vows! I didn't vow not to take off my ring. I knew this was a fucking mistake! Calm down, Lois, it's just a piece of jewelry, it's replaceable. No, it's not! It's the one I put on your finger and now it's gone! I'm going down to the bar until you calm down. Oh, no, you are not! If you do, then don't come back!*

Victor does come back, of course, but now you're too tired to get back into it, and he tells you how sexy you are, and the honeymoon makeup sex helps you deny that this incident could in any way bode for your future together as Mr. and Mrs. Silvestri.

You have big auditions and a calendar that's almost as full as it can be with singing engagements spread all the way into 1974. You don't anticipate that someone with absolute conviction in his own opinions might infuriate you at times. How does he know what Mayor Lindsay should do to solve the financial crisis, or that he can buy a stupid two-door LeBaron if he wants because *We'll always have plenty of cash* and *You can't take it with you. In that car I can't take anything with me, Victor. Then we'll get two cars,* he says. *We're not keeping two cars in Manhattan, Victor! Calm down, Lois, everything is fine. How do you know that, how do you know what you're going to think about something, anything, everything, a year from now? Because I do, Lois.*

With Victor, you're able to dine out, meet powerful people, perform with some of the big stars of the day, send Betsy to private school, buy real, whole milk instead of powdered, don't have to have some weird braless girl living rent-free in your apartment as a so-called babysitter when you leave town for jobs, because Victor will be there. You're more resigned to being married than convinced that any one man will ever be perfect for you. Victor's fun and he's funny and he knows how to please you and this one will stick. You'll deal with the arguments; they'll probably stop anyway. You've decided. Stick. (He already knew this, but you believe that you decided it; you're both right.)

Your Problems Are All in Your Head

You and Victor have been married for five years now. You love him, in your way; he adores you, still, always. You fight, loudly, sometimes every day. You always, always believe that each fight will be the last, though evidence over time suggests otherwise. Notably, in one of these fights, the kitchen telephone gets ripped off the wall on New Year's Eve.

—I think it was Christmas Eve, Betsy.

—Okay, it doesn't matter.

—So you say. It could matter.

—It could for sure, but it doesn't.

—But it could.

—But it doesn't.

—I will win. Just let it happen.

— . . .

—Sometimes I'm not sure who's talking.

—Sometimes that doesn't matter either.

—That's ridiculous.

—It's not.

Victor walks toward the door, opens it to leave, all the neighbors can now hear, without a doubt. *I'm not going to that party if that bitch Bernadette is going to be there! She's harmless, Lois! So you say! I see the way she looks at you! You're crazy, Lois. Bernadette is my mother's friend. You dated her in high school, Victor! She shouldn't be friends with your mother anymore! It's sick! I can't control my mother. Well, there's your problem. But that's not news.* Victor buzzes the elevator, slams the door, comes back a couple hours later, apologizes, but also tells you that you make up things to worry about. *I know*, you say, even though you don't, really. The following day, New Year's Day, all is well. You and Victor stay in bed all day, reading the paper, eating cold cuts, and watching *The Gang That Couldn't Shoot Straight* on channel nine. You think about Fred, how the two of you never argued; for a moment you think of him fondly, for the first time since the divorce. The whirl of those early years with Fred, the better years, had never really been about Fred. This, with Victor, is love. Sometimes you fight, that's all.

You still make love as often and as intensely as you fight. You're now forty. Thanks to him, your music calendar is always booked three years ahead. Your voice is richer, more powerful than ever, your reviews always raves. You have performed opposite all the greats, sung all the roles you've coveted (Gilda, Lucia, Tosca, Queen of the Night), performed with all the major orchestras (Philadelphia, Chicago, Caracas), all the major opera companies and concert halls (La Scala, Covent Garden), and maestros (Ozawa, Mehta, Chailly, Muti). But the thrills are briefer and briefer, and now the crashes are harder. Post–standing ovation, post–dressing room visits, they come hard and fast, but as soon as you're in the taxi they're replaced with an empty space; you're entirely hollow, and no amount of love from your husband—and he has a lot to give—keeps it filled. It is sink-ing in that you may never have a recording career, though you will never fully comprehend why. Over many a supper, you and Victor discuss the possible reasons, all of which have to do with the nefarious business of classical music and those who run it. *That cunty R—— won't hire me because I'm better than her. And she's got that weasel D—— at her side making sure it doesn't happen anywhere else.* You will claim, for all of your days, that there are compromises you are unwilling to make—that there's a classical casting couch you are unwilling to lie down on, and that this is the sole reason that you have never recorded. Your self-doubt resides elsewhere and calcifies until it's not even doubt anymore. You are certain that everything else about you is bad. You're definitely not the best person. You're not the prettiest, you're not the thinnest, you're not the smartest, you're not the *-est* anything, except when it comes to singing. You do know how talented you are. This may be the only thing about you that you know is truly good.

You are not fooling yourself about that, either—you are a gifted musician and still in your prime, as far as singing goes, so you haven't given up yet. You'll never give up. It's all you have. And so when you get pregnant, in your forty-first year, this is not the good news that it might be at some other time, some right time. You and Victor discuss it. You choose not to mention the services from back in the day. You don't much want to remember that yourself. Victor tells you that he wants whatever you want. It's true-ish, but there's an ever-so-slight speck of melancholy in his eyes that betrays the earnest tone of his voice when he says it. You know he hopes that you want to have a baby, his baby. But your silence says what needs to be said. It's not that you don't wish you could give that to him, but you do both know, you really do know that if not this baby, no baby.

You've made the right decision, you're sure, but you've failed, again. It's time for therapy. You will fix yourself.

Therapy does not result in fixing yourself. You push forward with it; it seems like a good outlet for your screams and tears, though one hour a week hardly covers your screaming and crying needs. You are sure that everything is about your father and your husband, who you are coming to see doesn't understand you, not that anyone ever could. *Well, then, why are you here? I don't know.* You really don't know. You want it to work. You do. You don't think you're keeping secrets, or that you're unwilling to do the work. But therapy plus time seems to change exactly nothing. You think it might be worse if you couldn't go somewhere and scream once a week with impunity, but there seems to be no notable cumulative effect. Victor says *Therapy is bullshit; it's for weak people. I am weak! What are you talking about, Lois, you're the strongest person I know. You never back away from a fight. I don't think you understand what strong and weak mean. Are you crazy? Maybe, yes, I think so. There's nothing wrong with you, Lois, you just have to think differently. That's kind of the end idea behind therapy. Why pay seventy bucks an hour to do that? Because it's not that easy. Sure it is. It doesn't work like that, Victor! Tell me when you ever in your life decided to think differently and then just thought differently? I never had to, Lois, I already think the right way in the first place. Ha! So you say. So I know. So we're back to, we should all think like you. Things would be a lot easier for you*—and *me. Ha! You don't even try to understand me! I understand more about you than you do,* Victor says. *You don't know shit. I know, your daddy didn't get you a pony, boo-hoo. You're an asshole. Leave me the fuck alone. Suit yourself.*

Victor has other phrases for occasions like this: *Get over it. Tough titties. Guess you're SOL.* Yes, you tell the therapist, he is supportive in his way: you have no doubt of his big love for you; he is expressive both verbally and demonstratively; and he tells you often that everything is really okay, he doesn't know why you don't know that, you have no problems. *Your problems are in your head,* he'll say, which doesn't help, even if he says it in the sweetest tone, like *Honey, don't you see, all you have to do is realize that you've been making all this up, and then you won't have any problems?* You see now that you agree, on this problems-in-your-head idea. But you need him. He has something you don't have. And you're not going back to being single again. That is not for you. Unfortunately this therapist, and the next three who follow, are missing some vital information that could actually help. They miss it, and you don't exactly offer it. There are times when you believe, genuinely believe, that the outside world is conspiring to make your life more difficult, that this isn't just a feeling but a real thing—whether it's drivers who cut you off in traffic, or taxis with their on-duty lights clearly on who don't pick you up even though you're practically standing in the middle of the fucking street with your arm up, or snowstorms when you need to go out for groceries—that, in essence, anything that doesn't go smoothly for you is the work of some malevolent force determined to hold you back because you deserve no more than you already have. You don't offer any of this information in therapy, because you know the world is a hostile place for everyone, but most especially for you. That's not something that can be treated. It's what is.

—*Christ, I wish I could do some of this over.*

—*That's a phenomenal idea.*

Sister Daughter

So let's say we're sisters.

—We aren't sisters.

—Yeah, I know. Let me finish.

Let's say we're sisters, and I'm fourteen and you're seventeen and we live on a houseboat at the Seventy-Ninth Street Boat Basin and it's 1975. Our parents are dead.

—I don't see how this is an improvement, Betsy. Or a story about us, for that matter.

—Because I'll still be like me and you'll still be like you.

—Our parents are dead? That sounds grim. And don't you think we'd be completely different people if our parents were dead?

—Our parents are all dead. Did you or did you not want to live at the boat basin in 1975?

—I suppose I did.

—I'm making that happen for you.

We're sisters. I'm fourteen and I'm an aspiring writer, which right now means mostly that I read all the time and once in a while I work on my novella about my half-sister/half-squirrel who lives under the dining room table, and you're seventeen and you're an aspiring—

—Wait. Let me be something different for a change. An interior decorator.

—Sure thing, Mom.

—you're an aspiring interior decorator, which means mostly that you redecorate our room all the time without ever consulting me about it first, and we live on a houseboat, and our parents are dead. They went to Zabar's to get us some black and white cookies and died on their way home through the park, murdered by drug-addicted muggers.

—Jesus, Betsy, that's a terrible story. That's a do-worse.

—The parks were rough back then.

—That doesn't mean you have to write about it. Who wants to read about that? Couldn't our parents die of something nice?

—That's not really a thing.

—Just try it for me.

Okay, we live on a houseboat and our parents are dead, they were much older parents who adopted us later in life, and they were wonderful, loving parents who encouraged us to do everything we wanted in life, and they died peacefully of old age in their sleep in their twin beds holding hands. Their last words were *Life has been perfect and we love you girls more than all the world and there's a key to our safe deposit box in the wall behind the life vests that has our will and plenty of money for you girls to get through high school and go to college.*

—Well, that's nicer, I guess, but now it's just not believable.

—Yes, and it's also not terribly interesting.

—I've had plenty of interesting for one lifetime. I could spit interesting.

—Mom, seriously, just let me tell the story how I want to tell it right now.

—Fine.

The funeral is a bleak affair. This is not one of those sad-beautiful celebrations of life with occasional chuckles, this is a *let's get this over with as quickly as possible* in a small chapel in the basement of the Baptist church on Broadway and Seventy-Ninth. We're not even Baptist. We don't have a lot of relatives in New York, they're mostly all back in Iowa or in other parts of the country. A couple of them make excuses about coming because it's too far, too painful, too everything. So it's about six friends of our parents' from the boat basin and Nina, everyone sobbing, plus a minister who didn't know either of them and calls our mother Louisa instead of Lois. *Louisa and Fred were a remarkable couple.*

—Hold up there, sister daughter. Lois and Fred, really?

—Well, I could have gone with Edna and Walter, but it was harder to imagine them ever moving to New York for any reason whatsoever.

—What if Daddy got a job with the New York Times*?*

—That's a pretty liberal paper. Almost as unbelievable as you being your own mom.

—Good point.

The minister continues. *When their young daughter Lois suggested they live on a houseboat, the first thing Fred and Louisa said was "All hands on deck!" They saw an opportunity for the experience of a lifetime, and they went for it. Louisa and Fred had left their small-town*

Iowa life behind for New York City as soon as they graduated college, but this was a whole new opportunity. Yes, it ended badly. Very badly. He shakes his head and takes a long pause.

Jesus, you lean over and say to me, *what the fuck is wrong with this guy? I don't know,* I say, *but I feel like throwing a tomato at him, like they do in old movies about a bad play.* We both giggle. He glares at us. You glare back harder, with your neck extended in front of you. He doesn't notice.

But they raised two beautiful girls, Lois and—he tries to glance down at his notes surreptitiously, fails—*Betsy, and gave them a foundation and community in this quirky little riverside neighborhood. We pray that their souls are at eternal rest.*

—Betsy, this is some weird, dark shit.

—Have you read my stuff before?

—Not since about 1993. But I remember thinking what I did read was really cute.

—Cute.

—I'm giving you a compliment.

—No, you know what, it probably was *cute. My concern here is that this, too, is leaning to the cute side.*

—It has murder and orphans. What is cute here?

—Black and white cookies, houseboats. I don't know. It might be twee.

—I don't know what that means.

The first thing you do after the funeral is raid the liquor cabinet. *It's time for cocktails!* you say. *I don't want to drink, Lois. The kids who drink at my school are a bunch of assholes. That's what drinking is! I like being in control of myself. Well, that's not one of your choices today, Betsy. Pick your poison,* you say, opening the door to the liquor cabinet. I say *I'm not sure I want anything that's in there. Unless you see something that tastes like a milkshake.* You push some bottles around, say *You might like this*, hold up a bottle of something that says "coconut" on the label. *I hate coconut, Lois, you know that. Oh, wah, I forgot something about you. Relax. I know!* I say. *I want a Martini and Rossi on the rocks, like Angie Dickinson. I don't think we have that, Betsy. How about this?* You hold up a bottle of Boone's Farm apple wine. *Oh, that looks good!* I imagine it will taste like apple juice, take a big swig, almost spit it out. *It tastes like if apple juice was made of gasoline. It tastes like what apple juice would taste like if it were made of gasoline. Oh, whatever, Lois. Do you want to be a writer or not? Yes. All right, then, straighten up that grammar and let's get drinking. You have to start slow. Booze is an acquired taste. I don't know what that means. It means you have to learn to like it. No, I mean, I understand the idea, I'm just saying it makes no sense to me. If you don't like something, can't you just not like it? Sure, Betsy. But there are some tastes that you realize are good once you get used to them. Like anchovies. Anchovies are the best! Right, but some people think they're disgusting. Okay, but they don't have to eat them. It's just about trying new things more than once before you go saying you don't like them. The reason it applies so well to booze versus other things is that booze gets you drunk. So it's totally worth it. Sip it. You'll see.*

I take a small sip, let it slide down, nod. Better than the first big gulp, yes. Take another, another, another. *Yeah, okay,* I say. *Okay. Yeah, okay.* Another another. I slide down into the built-in bench sofa and everything slips away, my algebra test, the shaggy-haired boy who hasn't noticed me, my bossy older sister, our dead parents. *Kind of the greatest thing ever, am I right? So far it's up there. But I haven't been alive that long. I didn't know you were a drinker, Lois. There's a lot you don't know.* If I weren't half-drunk I might comment on that, but the urn with Mom and

Dad's ashes has caught my eye and I'm distracted. I open the lid and look inside. It's a little unsteady in my hands as I take it off the kitchen table. *Christ, Betsy, be careful! I just want to see what it looks like. They. It. They.* I have an urge to plunge my hand into it. I open the twist tie on the plastic bag inside to get a better look. My vision is blurry, and it's dark in there, but it looks like sand. When you get up to go to the bathroom, I sink my hand in halfway up to my elbow. It seems like the exact right thing to do. It feels cool and satisfying. It feels like if Mom and Dad were the beach. Nothing about this seems weird to me.

You come back into the cabin and see me with my hand in the urn and my eyes closed. *Oh my god, Betsy, are you fucking nuts? What the fuck is wrong with you? Give me that!* I hold the urn to my body more closely, push you away with the other hand. *We should scatter those in the river*, you say. *It's morbid to keep an old urn around. No!* I say. *We're keeping them. We're keeping them. Okay, we'll talk about this later. We're keeping them! We'll talk about it later. WE'RE KEEPING THEM.* You roll your eyes, I'm clearly out of my mind with grief or with drink or possibly both, so you try to shift gears. *I think we should take this thing for a ride. Oh my god, Lois, that's an amazing idea. Where should we go? The beach*, I say. *I want to go live at the beach. I like the mountains*, you say.

We try to think of places with beaches and mountains and settle on Seattle. *For Christ's sake, please take your hand out of the urn now.*

—Betsy, there are so many things wrong with this. This isn't better, it's just different.

—It's sisters on a sailing adventure! I moved you to the mountains!

—A houseboat is not a sailing boat.

—It can be if we want it to be.

—Also, I feel like this is pretty obviously you blaming me for your drinking problem.

—It's not. I was thinking about how I wish I'd started drinking a little sooner so that maybe I could have quit a little sooner.

—You don't wish you'd just never drank at all?

—Nope.

—Huh.

So we set out for Seattle. It takes almost two years. We're almost there when we run into some trouble in Mexico, because I studied French and your Spanish is—

—For shit, I know, Betsy.

—I was just going to say you struggled with it.

—It's fine, my Spanish is *for shit.*

So when I get arrested for prostitution (really just drunk and disorderly, but I'd gotten my tube skirt and my tube top mixed up, so basically I had made an extremely short dress out of my shirt), and I'm sure that I'm facing life in a Rosarito Beach prison, it takes a while before you're able to understand that I understood wrong and that all they want is about six thousand pesos for their trouble. *Should have just left you there. Very funny. You owe me six thousand pesos. I have no idea how much that is. Neither do I.*

—I should have probably mentioned something sooner, Betsy. I never really thought through the houseboat thing, I just wanted something that was as different as I could think of from Muscatine, Iowa.

—That's okay, I never really think through anything.

—. . .

—I'm kidding! Sort of.

Respectable Living

Five years pass. You have still not made a recording. You gave up a lot of things—and you should have been rewarded, but you weren't. You're not ready to give up, not yet; you've been making a respectable living for years now; few singers get to this level, ever. It could still happen, your voice is still glorious, but you're growing tired of the effort. You like paperback novels and doing needlepoint and you don't at all mind having a few weeks off between jobs. You've spent parts of summers in New Hampshire since I was in high school, have often considered taking the entire summer off to go up there and sit on the deck, look at the mountains, read, sew. But let's not kid ourselves. Relaxation is not an area in which you excel, and doing anything with less than excellence is not for you. You're all for a good long bubble bath or a half glass of wine now and again, but sitting around for a week with nothing to show for yourself in the end is for lazy asses. In late May you head up for the summer—Victor will take some long weekends and part of August—and it's about four days into sitting on the deck reading and looking at the mountains when the black flies start to bite, and for whatever reason, you taste really good to the black flies, and the bug zapper doesn't help, the coils don't help, and no amount of Off! helps prevent the black flies from chomping on you and covering you with golf ball–sized welts. This black fly-biting coincides, though, with your growing a bit itchy in another way, which is to say that sitting on the deck for four days reading and looking at the mountains turns out to be the maximum sitting-still period for you, though you don't realize it in that way; what you do realize is that you should build a screened porch on the other side of the house, which will obviously and once and for all solve the black fly problem. So you run to town, buy a book on building stuff, find a design for a porch, run to the lumberyard, ask where people rent bigger tools and supplies. The people at the hardware store laugh when you tell them what you're planning, that no, you're not picking this up for your husband. But you're not insulted. This is no different from reupholstering a chair, you tell them; you simply follow directions.

It doesn't occur to you to be insulted. You're not a feminist. Or, more accurately, you think you're not a feminist. You spend next to no time thinking about feminism. When you think of what a feminist is, you think of unattractive women with hairy armpits holding signs in the streets and feeling sorry for themselves. Your response to life is, in essence, a response to the word "no." It doesn't occur to you that this is in any way feminist—that your desire for a career, for something other than the domestic life that 1957 thought you were supposed to have, has anything to do with this—or even that you're doing something for your daughter (much less her generation) in this way, not even in an I'm-just-trying-to-feed-her way (because you still think that's the father's job). You want what you want, that's all. And right now you want a screen porch. So you build a screen porch. There's some building and taking apart, because there are parts that aren't perfect; some nails go in angled a tiny bit wide and the floorboards are off by a fraction of a centimeter that even a top-notch carpenter would be happy with, and it's to be expected that that's part of the process, same as everything else. You'll do it and undo it until it's right. Two weeks later, you have a marvelous screen porch; you get some lounge chairs, a table, it's adorable. But your body is killing you, so you decide to splurge on a massage. It's forty-five dollars for an hour and a half, way cheaper than in New York, still a huge splurge, but just this once you spring for a massage, and it's transcendent, and you can see now that this should be a legitimate business expense for you, given the amount of stress you have to endure. What's more, you make a connection with the masseuse. She asks a number of questions pre-massage: she's a firm believer in the mind-body connection, wants to know not only what hurts but where you "hold things" in your body, a mind-blowing idea for you, but one that rings as true as anything you've ever heard. So you tell her. You say you hold them in your neck and shoulders and in your fingers and in your chest and sometimes your back and in your skull. *My calves are fabulous*, you say. *Utterly empty of things. Ha!*

Afterward, she makes suggestions. There's a bookshop in town that specializes in spiritual books; she recommends some titles. She mentions that she's learning Reiki, explains what that is, and if you're interested in being a guinea pig, she needs practice. The spiritual bookshop might be the loveliest place you've ever been. The gray-haired woman behind the counter is positively lit up, and the room smells divine with handmade candles and scented oils and lotions. You sample scents and browse books and by the time you head to the counter you've racked up a hundred and nineteen dollars' worth of merchandise. A shitload of money, but that's all right. It's an investment in yourself.

You gobble up the books like you're eating M&Ms, highlighting passages in different colors. With a ruler. Is there another way to do it? You consume books by Leo Buscaglia, Shakti Gawain, John Bradshaw, Wayne Dyer, M. Scott Peck, Shirley MacLaine. You call Audrey to talk about it. She's read a few of the same books; some of them have helped her, too. *Shirley was a little too out there for me*, Audrey says, with some hesitation. You laugh, you know it's true, but you can't help think that some trauma from a horrible past life could explain a lot about this one, because you still haven't come up with anything conclusive, trauma-wise. *What did you think of the Louise Hay? That kind of blew my mind. I mean, under "high blood pressure" it says, "Longstanding emotional problems unresolved!" That is totally Victor! And under "arthritis" it says it relates to feeling unloved!* Audrey's a nurse. She has a spiritual life, but she believes in modern medicine. *I don't think you gave yourself arthritis, Lois. But what if I did?* You'd never given any thought to a mind-body connection prior to this, but now all your aches and pains make sense. No wonder you bruise so easily. You haven't just been bruised literally, you've been bruised figuratively too. Your world is now cracking open with possibility. Finally. There are affirmations for this. You have found something here.

Celeste, the masseuse/Reiki student, is thoughtful in explaining her practice and gentle in her touch, often not even touching but simply hovering her hands over parts of your body that she *feels drawn to.* You can feel the energy and heat from her hands going directly into you; you are sure that evil cells are breaking up and dissipating with each passing second. Never having done anything less than full-bore, you tell Celeste after one Reiki session that you feel better already and ask where you can take the training yourself. It feels like this is something you could do that would be useful to people, something that could help mitigate the worldwide conspiracy against you. Of course, you could never give up music, but you do feel you're on to something here. A year later you're a Reiki master. Even your skeptical daughter has to admit she feels better after you treat her minor aches and pains. You take on a few clients, referrals from the center where you took the training, an overworked waitress, an elderly woman, a couple of AIDS patients. They, like everyone, adore you. You're moving in the right direction, you're sure now, though you're still depressed, and you haven't—won't—give up singing, although you're somewhat choosier about accepting dates now. You won't go back to Memphis to work with that cocksucker J——, won't go back to Stuttgart if they put you up in that shit hotel where they sassed you about using your coil to boil water after you spent good money on an adapter, won't go back to Houston unless you get an apology from the conductor about the way he let that no-name whore muscle you out of an aria that should have been yours, you won't you won't you won't. Victor is disappointed that you're turning down jobs, especially in pursuit of this hippy-dippy voodoo stuff; when he sees you wearing crystals around your neck or smudging the house with sage, he puts on a baby voice to ask *how your widdle magic is coming along*, and you're disappointed that he doesn't get it, though you're not surprised. He's never really gotten you. He loves you and takes care of you, and you thought that would be enough.

One day you wake up and you almost, almost wish you hadn't. You don't exactly know where this came from, it's a new feeling, and it's frightening. Best to stay in bed. You tell

Victor you're tired, you're just going to take it easy today; he doesn't think anything of it. You don't call Audrey, and you let the dog pee on wee-wee pads in the house—nothing new—but you almost forget to feed him until he comes up to you whining, nearly an hour after feeding time. This is somewhat alarming, so after you feed the dog, you set the clock to wake you for his dinnertime and go back to bed. You can't read, can't even focus on the TV, though you leave it on; the shades are still drawn from the night before. Victor is concerned when he comes home, but for now he's still buying the story you're selling about not feeling well, even though the description of your symptoms is vague. *I don't know, just ecch-y*, you say, he cracks up at your made-up word. He giggles and asks if you want him to call the doctor about your ecchi-ness. *No*, you tell him, *I'll be fine. I just need some rest.*

This goes on for the better part of a week. You're frankly baffled by it, because you haven't been crying; you know what crying means, at least. Right now, what you are is vacant. That's not technically a feeling, but it seems like all the parts of you that care about anything have turned in their keys and checked out. You have no energy for or interest in anything, and no matter how shitty you've felt in the past, you've always been motivated to whip up a new concert gown or screen porch as needed. Right now, zero. Victor finally insists on taking you to the doctor, so you make an appointment, but the doctor can't find anything wrong with you; he prescribes Valium, but that only makes you feel worse; still, you put it in the big plastic bag with the rest of the stash of pills you keep on hand—and you call the doctor back and tell him you didn't respond well to the Valium and he prescribes something else and that something else perks you right up. You'd be more than happy if there were a pill for what you have, and there might be, and it's not for lack of trying; two of your shrinks have prescribed things that don't work and sometimes made things worse. You've been saving all these pills in your Ziploc for years now—Xanax, Percocet, and so on—some make you drowsy, some make you feel nothing at all, which you're discovering is no improvement—but who knows when something might come in handy, whether it's a pill or a set of pearl buttons from a blouse that's out of style. Betsy might need it sometime. Waste not, want not. Bonus, you lose five pounds, that's always good, so by the end of the week, you're not so much good as new as you've just *gotten through* whatever that was and now it's over.

You Can Always Help It

When I call home from college as scheduled one Sunday afternoon, Victor answers and tells me that you took a last-minute job covering for someone in Santa Fe who got pneumonia, that you'll be gone for six weeks. In fact, you're in a psych ward on the other side of town.

—*Hm.*

—*No? Never happened? I didn't really think it did, I just wondered if maybe it should have.*

—*Well, let's leave it there then.*

Unbeknownst to me, and anyone else, you've had what you're calling *a spell* and Victor and your best friend are calling one week of crying followed by three weeks of staying in bed. Somehow he gets you to agree to check yourself in. He's tried everything he can to help you, and he is still no fan of psychiatry of any kind, but he's worried enough now to force you to do something. He tries to help you throw stuff in a suitcase, but he has no idea how to pack. *I won't go at all if you don't let me do it myself, Victor. You're not going to the Ritz-Carlton*, he says; you say *Just go away!* and neatly fold three cashmere turtlenecks from the outlet mall, a couple of nice pairs of slacks, a pair of jeans, plenty of undies and warm socks, nightgowns, perfume, a Robert Ludlum paperback, jewelry, scents, toiletries, meds, an afghan you're half finished with, and a petit point of a pastoral scene that Grandma had given you to finish because the stitches were too small for her to see anymore.

When you get there, you're barely inside the automatic doors when they take your suitcase away. Later, it gets returned minus your meds, your dental floss, your hot rollers, your crochet hook, your yarn, your stork-handle mini-scissors, your tweezers, your Rive Gauche and your Paris, and the notepaper you took from the Broadmoor in 1975. *Christ*, you tell Victor when he calls, *what do they think I'm going to do with any of that stuff? I'm going to look like the Wicked Witch of the West in a few days if they don't give me my hot rollers back. I can't burn myself to death with a hot roller.* He laughs and says you couldn't look like a witch if you had a pointy hat and six moles on your nose.

The next morning, a nurse comes by to return your notepaper. You ask why they took it in the first place; the nurse says something snarky along the lines of *The staff knows what they're doing and maybe you're here because you don't.*

You have never been one to take kindly to sass, but you're still dopey from whatever it was they made you take before lights-out last night. *I have rights* is all you can get out of your mouth, which feels like it's full of flour, which is too bad, because you're sure that if you could add "Missy" to the end of the sentence she'd know who she was dealing with. You point to your head, to indicate that you've got a wicked headache; you've got just the right thing in your bag of meds for that but you're done with words right now. You scribble on the paper she just handed you, capital letters, *HEADACHE*, show it to her. She shakes her head and walks out.

After breakfast, your head is still pounding, but at least you can get a few words out. The people at your table include one quiet old lady (hard to imagine what she could have done wrong besides get old), a young girl with bandages on her wrists, and a woman, a bit younger than you, attractive, early twenties, so of course you can't begin to guess why she's there.

You're so pretty. What are you doing here?

Young woman laughs at this, says she wishes that were her ticket to anything good. You don't understand. She says she'd been having hallucinations and got violent with her boyfriend because she thought he was a feral pig. She laughs saying it; you do too.

That's a very specific hallucination, you tell her.

Well, he is cuter than some of the other pigs, she says. *My name's Annie.*

Lois.

You're now best friends.

After breakfast you meet with your assigned psychiatrist. You can't quite get a bead on her; she's expressionless, asks some of the routine questions you've been asked before. You've been to all kinds of shrinks by this point, had various diagnoses—chronic depression, atypical depression, generalized anxiety disorder, borderline disorder (what a load of bullshit that was, you've known borderlines, that is *not* your problem)—but none of the shrinks or their bullshit diagnoses made any difference. Why should it be any different this time? A significant part of the problem is that you don't tell them everything. You don't mention that, like Annie, you've seen some weird things, too; you tell yourself that you just shouldn't have had that glass of wine with the pill you took that time, or that you were just tired. You don't tell them thing one about the rages, although they all get glimpses of your anger, but you don't tell them what it's like inside your body, like hot lava, like an actual substance in you that has got to come out when it gets in there or it will melt you from the inside out. You don't tell them this, because what causes them always seems justified, the rages, the unfairnesses of life perpetrated entirely upon you, you are sure, by evil guiding forces; starving children in Africa have nothing on you. If these things were different you'd be just fine.

Group therapy is a joke. You know enough about psychology, having been to therapy before and read any number of books by Carl Jung, Rollo May, Viktor Frankl, that you can tell putting this bunch of loonies together will not help a one of them. You can't randomly toss together a pile of barely functioning people and expect anything productive to come out of it. In your group alone, there's a young mother with severe postpartum depression; a full-blown narcissist (no help to anyone); a lady who spits every five minutes (you don't know what her problem is, but you have asked repeatedly to have her removed or fucking muzzled, because that is disgusting and unsanitary); a woman who claims to have the voice of Art Fleming in her head; a couple of alcoholics; and a junkie. The narcissist accuses you of being a narcissist, which is hilarious; the junkie and one of the alcoholics think you're an addict, though you've noticed that they say that about everyone. You have a bit of compassion for the postpartum mom, but she alternates between crying and staring blankly into the middle distance, and not once in all the weeks you spend here does anyone besides Annie say anything insightful. You walk out together and sit down for coffee with her in the atrium by the lunch room. *What bugs me is just how inexact it all seems*, Annie says. *Like, with all of the advancements they've made in modern medicine, they still have to try sixteen things in case maybe one will work. Plus, their other genius idea is to throw a bunch of whack-jobs in a room together? Ha! Well said. You're how old? Twenty-four.* Annie tells you she's been arrested three times on domestic violence charges. *I only ever punched him, but still. I don't know how not to, when I get to that place. He probably deserved it*, you say. Your own rage is nonviolent, but it's not unimaginable to you. *He really didn't*, she says. Something about her reminds you of your daughter, though it's not anything she's saying, and not the way she's saying it. She doesn't even look like Betsy—in fact, she's tiny, and her voice makes her sound like a sexy Muppet—but you feel something deep for Annie, though you're not sure what it is. Holy crap, you feel something.

The staff continues to go through your drawers every day, no matter how many times you tell them you're all out of crochet hooks to murder anyone with. (This is not amusing to them, and it only prolongs your supervised probationary period with the one crochet hook they'll allow.) They give you meds that make you slightly too drowsy to argue with anyone, but otherwise do nothing to turn you into a regular person, whatever that is. Someone who thinks only nice things, maybe.

A million years later, on the return of your petit point (during supervised free time only) you suppress a joke about how they must have figured out how many times you'd have to stab someone with a petit point needle before any real damage was done.

In one of your last appointments with the shrink, you learn the one thing from your entire stay that is of any little use: that sometimes there's a cross-diagnosis—that a patient has a little bit of this, a little bit of that—and that when that's the case, it's difficult to treat with success. *Well then what the fuck am I supposed to do?* you ask, and she screws up her mouth in an *I'm sorry for what I'm about to say* kind of fashion, and says *You take the meds we give you and you stay vigilant and you come back here whenever you need to.* But you're not coming back here if you can help it. Which you can. You can always help it.

Social Work Because Why Not

You join a Unitarian church in the neighborhood. Your belief in a higher power (if not your faith) has been restored by all of your recent research (that is, your growing library of spiritual and self-help books), and though you've always placed a percentage of the blame for your problems on having been forced to go to church as a child, you hear about this church and its more open-minded beliefs, and in no short time you make friends and become actively involved, serving soup on Sundays, passing the basket, even singing in the choir. (Although everyone else is almost insufferably off key, you singing at full voice doesn't help, but church choir isn't the place for that, though once in a while you can't help yourself.) But you could always do more to help. When you're helping, you feel just a little more purposeful in the world; your mind is redirected away from you and toward others, and even though you still come home with all kinds of judgments about those others you've been helping—over dinner you tell Victor you don't know why the poor people can't all just go work at McDonald's (a part of you truly does not see that there might be a larger picture, though you vaguely want to) and he for sure doesn't either, though he is sure that their race, whatever race it might be that isn't his own, has something to do with it, that all their race wants is handouts, and you wonder how you married your father, when you were so sure that the sexy, cosmopolitan, jovial big-city man you took vows with was his natural opposite. Victor has clients of all races, religions, genders, and sexual orientations, your home is open to all races, as you had vowed it would be when you grew up (though you never did find out what became of Ginny), and Victor always welcomes everyone to his home happily, with genuine warmth. So it's just confusing. You don't openly disagree with him; you aren't even really sure if what he's saying makes sense. It still feels like you should do more to make up for the conflict about it in your brain, and in talking to Audrey she asks if you might be interested in social work, and suggests the program at NYU, and the fall you turn fifty you're enrolled.

When your mind is active, it's always a good thing. Your plan is to take two years off from opera to devote to your studies, though you'll still practice an hour or two a day, for when you go back to it. For those two years, you study diligently—you were always an A student, but the kind who worked hard for it. Victor and I help quiz you when there are tests, but mostly it's papers, so many papers and so much thinking and so much studying, some of which even helps illuminate some of the larger social causes and conditions you wondered about, going at least a small way toward explaining why "they" can't all solve their problems with minimum-wage jobs. At no time, though, do you connect any dots between what you are learning and your own personal story; your father caused your problems, sometimes Victor causes your problems, and what obviously needs fixing is them.

The summer after you graduate, you schedule a face-lift (even though your husband begs you not to), because you can see where in two years your jowls will be to your knees. You know looks matter—Victor implied as much on your first date—and in the fall you're offered a part-time job at a hospital in Yonkers, in part, you are certain, because you now look ten years younger.

You practice social work for several years, take only the best singing jobs that come along, turn down concerts with great orchestras but shitty conductors, or oratorios opposite that fat egotist P——. You decide it's time to exercise, as the doctors suggest; as with anything you do, there's no doing it halfway. You buy a half-dozen exercise tapes and work out for a couple hours each day, lose twenty-five pounds in six months, none of which needed losing. You've had some smaller weight fluctuations before, but because of your height and your carriage, until now it's been imperceptible to anyone but you. This weight loss is not imperceptible. People worry. Plus, you've always chewed your fingernails, but now you bite and pick at the skin on your heels and fingers relentlessly, unconsciously, until they bleed, like if you can just get down to the bone, something will be discovered, like if you could chew down to the bad core of you, you might finally dig it out. There's almost no thumbnail left at all on your left hand; you've had Band-Aids on it for a month. No one will see it, but you know, and it seems like it should be no big deal—a habit, everyone has them—but it's also a deep shame. Audrey and Victor and I all beg you to stop, stop exercising, stop chewing, stop worrying. Part of you has no idea what's wrong anymore; you still know that *you're* wrong, but it seems outside of you, or it's easier to think so, and so as sad as you are, you're also angry. Victor doesn't understand you. He never has. He loves you but he doesn't know you, not the way you want, anyway. If he really understood you, you wouldn't feel this way.

You fantasize about leaving. This ultimately sends you back to bed again, so you stay. You stay, you get a new therapist and a new wrong diagnosis and a new prescription that doesn't work.

And then Mother dies. Daddy had died ten years earlier; you hadn't been too set back by that. You remembered some of the good things about him, but mostly the less good, and you were busy with your career then. You cried, a little, at his funeral, though "grief" for someone you never felt close to is a funny word. It's more like *There goes the Daddy I never really had, so long, see you later, I'll think about something else now and keep wondering why I rage randomly when that time comes.* You felt worse for your mother's loss than for your own, but she's always been pretty stoic. She shed some tears when her husband died, a corner of a delicate cotton hanky's worth, but she knew how life worked, someone had to go first, and after Daddy died, Mother spent her last ten years traveling with her sister, visiting you and your own sister more often, and those years were good for her. You adored your mother. You'd never been close in the sense that you told her everything; in fact, you always gave her a carefully curated presentation of yourself and your life. She knew of no real problems, you believed. Even with your divorce, which to her was about the worst possible thing that could happen, in time you made her see that it was necessary, convinced her that I was just fine, bright and well adjusted, which you sort of seemed to believe, that your career was bringing you everything you wanted, and that when you met Victor (she was smitten with him from the first, blushing at his *colorful* stories and covering her mouth as if every last bit of her propriety would escape if she laughed too hard) you really did have it all.

But your mother dying is different. It's too much not to have her in the world, information-sharing or not. She was nothing if not steady. Why didn't you get any of that? Your father may have been opinionated, but he was still generally imperturbable. And Marjorie's not like you either. There's no history of hysteria in your family; why you? Just knowing Mother was in the world helped a little—that such steady kindness existed, somewhere. Does your daughter have some of that quality? Maybe. But a mom's a mom. A daughter never stops needing a mom. That you are also someone's mom is not a thought that follows. This is about you.

A few days after the funeral, before heading back east, you go to her grave for one last good-bye. You sit down on the yet-unsettled soil, pull a couple weeds from the edge; time passes, you don't know how much, but at some point you find yourself ripping the grass from the earth, hoping to pull her out. Back home you cry for about a month straight, spend most of the following month in bed. Again.

—I think we should have more scenes together.

—I've written some short stories about us before. I also might write a memoir someday. I didn't want to overlap too much.

—Some people might think this *is a memoir.*

—It's so not *a memoir.*

—It's not so *not a memoir, Betsy. It's* mostly *not a memoir.*

—It is in no way a memoir, Mom.

—Okay, so especially if it's not a memoir, couldn't we just do our own thing here?

—I did just whale off into the sunset.

—Right. So we could do anything together, couldn't we?

—I took us on a houseboat ride a few chapters back.

—That was a bleak tale.

—Okay, well, what would you like us to do, Mom?

—I don't have any particular ideas.

—I've always wanted to time-travel. I'd like to go to 1961. I want to see what life was like when I got here.

—Uch. I don't think I want to go there again.

—I do.

—Why would you want to go to difficult times?

—I just want to go to interesting times.

—I want to go to times that don't hurt.

In Which We Go to Parsons Because It's Not a Memoir

Okay. So it's 1961. Let's try being sisters again, a year apart this time, very close. You can be the older sister again. There's no Marjorie. She was never born. We've just graduated from college. You went to Parsons against the wishes of Mother and Daddy (your parents are our parents this time); we were both supposed to go to a state school to get husbands, but we both dreamed of being world-famous couturiers like Coco Chanel, so I follow you to Parsons and we share a big two-bedroom apartment in London Terrace because you can do that at this time. *It's Deco, Mother! Absolutely fabulous! There's a swimming pool! Tell Daddy that Babe Ruth once dressed up as Santa for the annual Christmas party!* But Mother and Daddy are beyond freaked out that we're on our own in New York City, and Mother keeps sending letters begging us to come back to Iowa, telling us there are so many nice young men right at home, at church, sons of friends who work at banks and insurance companies, and we tell them not to worry, there are men here who aren't criminals, and we didn't come here to meet men anyway, and we're happy and well, and more and more women are working now, and we like it. After college we get jobs in the garment district, you as a seamstress and me answering phones, but at night we come home and sketch and gossip (my boss is a creep, has been *doing it* with his secretary, has patted my bottom more than once); we design clothes for a modern working woman, separates, slim skirt suits, simple dresses with an eye to detail, seaming, covered buttons, pockets, always pockets—that will be our trademark! We create a small line to begin: one suit, three blouses, a skirt, a cardigan in three different colors (with a narrow satin ribbon trim around the neckline), one cocktail dress (with a satin ribbon and small bow under the bust, to match the cardigan), and we take it around to the department stores. We point out all the special details—the quality of the fabric, the different ways the pieces can work together, ways to take the pieces from day to night—and we are turned down, store after store, no Saks, no Bergdorf's, no Bonwit's, no Macy's, no Gimbels. The good news is that Alexander's offers us a deal, but only for the suit, and it's a much smaller offer than we hoped for, but now we're in a pickle, because it's barely enough to cover our electric bill. But we shake on it, and on the 1 train we try to hide our disappointment that we didn't become famous designers overnight. *Maybe we* should *just go home and get husbands*, you say.

—I don't understand, why, Betsy, if you're making this all up, it all has to be so hard. Why couldn't we just go to New York and become successful fashion designers and meet wonderful men and live in penthouses with maids?

—That's not a story. That's not what a story is.

—I thought a story could be whatever you wanted it to be.

—Think of it this way: The notes in an aria aren't random. They follow an order. Imagine how awful it would sound if you tried to sing from a score that someone had put through a shredder and then taped

back together. There are still some basic principles that make a song something you might ever want to listen to. I might also point out that you sing some of the saddest songs in existence.

—Yeah, which is one more reason why I don't want to read sad stories.

—Look, if there aren't some bits of conflict, the results are likely to be boring, or meaningless, or very, very short.

—But there are happy stories in the world. Heartwarming stories.

—I'm not big into heartwarming. When I'm done you can write your happy story for us.

—Okay, then, I will!

—What if we were to go back to that time Ginny came over to your house and Grandpa was a racist jerk?

—Mmf. Won't that mess with the time-space continuum or something?

—What do you know about the time-space continuum?

—I read things.

—I haven't figured out the science of that fiction just yet, but I'm pretty sure the time-space continuum will be just fine.

The Wedding of Chappy and Althea

One day, you bring your friend Ginny home for a playdate after school. You're having the best time: your dolls are best friends, and they're having a doll wedding where your teddy bear is the groom because nobody has any boy dolls. Ginny's doll Althea is the bride, with a veil made of a scrap of tulle and a piece of ribbon trim from our mom's sewing basket. Chappy the teddy bear is wearing a black ribbon around his neck for a bow tie. Your doll Patty Ann is the maid of honor. *Dum, dum da dum,* you sing together. You walk Althea to the altar and stand her face-to-face with Chappy. A naked baby doll is jumped in for the minister because you forgot about the minister until just now. Ginny makes the baby doll have a deep voice. *We are gathered here today to bring together Althea and Chappy in holy matrimony. Chappy, do you promise to take this doll, Althea, to be your lawfully wedded wife, to have and to hold in— Wait, I don't think that's right, it's not "to have and hold* in*"— Sure it is, so you don't let the sickness out— To have and hold in, sickness and health, richer and poorer, until death do you part? I don't think that makes all-the-way sense. Just say I do. I do,* you say for Chappy, trying to sound like a bear who talks. *Althea, do you promise to take this teddy bear to be your dear husband, to have and to hold in sickness* *and health, richer and poorer, until death do you part? I do,* Ginny says for Althea. You both burst into giggles. *You may now kiss the bride!* Ginny says, and you both mash the doll and the teddy bear together, completely cracking yourselves up, and this is when Daddy comes in.

He gives the scene a good long stare. His face is perfectly still, but his eye sockets may as well have flames shooting out of them. You have no idea why, though Ginny has an idea. He leaves the room and goes downstairs to get our mother, who's sewing in the den while I'm doing homework. *Get that colored girl out of here,* he says. Mother hustles upstairs and I follow on her heels, crying *Mom, Mom, don't do it.* She says *Shush, Betsy.* I say *Mom, Mom, don't let Daddy do this,* and she says *He's the man of the house,* and I say *Uch!* and I run back downstairs to find Daddy smoking out in the backyard, and I say *Daddy, Ginny is a person just like you,* and he says *You are asking for big trouble, young lady,* and I say *I don't care! I am here from the future! We have an African American president!* and he says *What the hell is "African American"?* And I say *It means black, negro, colored! We have a colored president! There are two little colored girls in the White House! I'm going to wash your mouth out with soap just for thinking such a thing!* And I say *I don't care! The future is here!* This is when everybody comes downstairs, Mother holding Ginny's hand, you right behind, and Mother is extremely worried that the neighbors might hear, what with this happening outside, and she says *Walter! Betsy! Please!* and I say *No!* and Ginny really does want to go home now, and you are rather unsure about this whole scene, and I yell loud enough for the neighbors three houses down to hear *A racist lives here! A racist lives here!* and this is when I get a hand to the face, but I say *Go ahead and hit me! I don't care!* You're crying now, Ginny's crying now, saying *I want my mama.* Mother wipes Ginny's eyes gently with a hanky from her pocket, says *Okay dear, we're going to get you home now.* They leave; Daddy tells us we're both grounded until we graduate from high school; that's when I say *Fuck you, I'm going back to the twenty-first century.* Daddy actually laughs in my face. *You just got yourself grounded* until *the twenty-first century, Betsy.*

Later that night, when we're tucked into bed, you tell me I'm crazy. *What were you thinking, Betsy, everything is worse now,* and I say *No it isn't, it's better*; you say *You got grounded forever!* And I say *We spoke up. We spoke up.* You say *You spoke up*, and I say *We spoke up. We're a team.*

—I have something I want to do next.

—What's that?

—I want to go to your wedding.

—That would be nice. It was an awesome day.

—So you are married!

—Yes, Mom, I'm married. Didn't we already cover that?

—It's getting a little blurry for me, what's real and what isn't.

—Well, let's just try it.

Betsy's Wedding

You always said you wanted a beach wedding, so you plan a ceremony on the beach on Fire Island, and the Solomons are kind enough to host a backyard reception. Everyone you want to be there is there. I make your dress, of course. I'm not sure what's in style right now, so let's keep it simple, it's at the beach. You don't want to look like some dumbass in a ball gown on the beach, you want to go sort of bohemian. Off-white with an empire waist, maybe a slim brocade ribbon under the bust with the ends hanging down, a flowy chiffon skirt, with off-the-shoulder straps, almost like a cap sleeve. A flutter sleeve. Very Juliet. It's a perfect New York September day, not a cloud on the entire East Coast. Your friends gather on the beach; there's an aisle made from two rows of beach glass on either side, leading to a driftwood archway decorated with all kinds of white flowers. Ben is at the end of it, with his father and best friend next to him. Nina is your maid of honor, of course. I'm a bridesmaid, because we're sisters, but it's informal so we're just standing there on your side. Everyone is happy.

—That's nice, Mom. Ben's parents are actually long gone.

—Oh no!

—I guess this confirms that you aren't all out there somewhere having a big after-party.

—No, I wish. Well, I'm sorry for Ben.

—Yeah. He's okay. But I'm sure he'll be happy to have his dad there too.

Fred walks you down the aisle. He is, of course, beaming.

You say your vows; your old friend Bob has gotten ordained just so he can perform your ceremony. People cry and laugh; they know you're a good couple. I sob and sob, more than a sister might, ordinarily, to the point where some of the guests are wondering what's wrong with me and are maybe thinking it's because I'm still single and not because I'm both your sister and your mom and I'm so happy to see you so in love. Everyone walks back up to the house, which is where I unfortunately have to deal with the fact that Victor is now married to that awful Bernadette, and because I'm your sister I can't just say *I knew it!* I have to keep acting like we're sisters, which I guess means that Fred is my father too, which is a little weird. (Am I my own mother? Too much to process at once. Let's pretend Fred's second wife is my mom.) At the reception, Fred/Dad takes me aside and tells me how lucky he is to have two such special daughters. He believes he's had a whole lifetime of knowing me, and that that version of me is someone he would say such a thing to. I want to ask him a bunch of questions, basic ones, like *What exactly do you know about me?*—which is, of course, absurd, something you might say to a stranger you were suspicious of—but I don't have to, because he immediately tells me about a camping trip we took when we were kids in the seventies, and our mom was away (ha!), and how different you and I were: you were happy with a Tab in a hammock with your nose in a book, and I wanted to do everything that could be done, go fishing, paddle a canoe. He told me I even asked about hunting, which is hilarious to even think about, me with a gun, not to mention him with a gun (*We skipped that*, he says), and of course, hearing this, I knew he'd have been just as happy to sit in a camp chair with you and read too. No question you were his kid. Me, anybody's guess how far back my odd string of DNA came from. But in his version of history, he took me to do all those things, and you were not happy about having to go along, didn't know why you couldn't stay back at the tent. *Because you're nine*, he said, so you brought your book into the canoe and we fought; I was pissed that you were sitting in the boat like a lump, and I didn't know why you were allowed to just do that, and he says that he told me *You girls are both the best daughters around, but you're two different people, and there's no one thing that's going to make everybody happy besides roasting marshmallows, and we can't do that all day, so if she wants to read a book in a canoe that's fine with me, and if you want to spend all day swimming in the lake, that's fine with me too.* Of course, he also made sure there was time for you to read, and told me it wouldn't hurt me to read a book either, and after the sun went down we told the silliest ghost stories around the campfire that we could think up, about ghosts who come back and do nice things, like make delicious lobster eggs benedict before you wake up, and then when no one in the family takes credit for it you're a little spooked because where would you get the lobster in Iowa anyway, and you happen to notice that there are no lobster shells or eggshells in the trash, there's nothing in the trash at all, and you say *Well, you or Mom could have taken the trash out*, and you say *Mom never takes the trash out*, and you laugh because it's true. The truth is, seeing Fred all these years later, in this way, is weirdly nice. I'm many decades older than I was when we were married, and here I am in the body of a forty-year-old, and I mean, yes, I have had sex with that old man, but he doesn't know that.

—*He probably was a really good father to you.*

—*He was, Mom.*

But getting back to that awful Bernadette. I chat with Victor during the cocktail hour, and of course, just the way Fred thinks I'm his daughter, Victor thinks I'm his stepdaughter; we haven't seen each other in some years, not so much a falling out as maybe a predictable drift after a late remarriage. He doesn't know I'm the dead love of his life. Bernadette's shoving pigs in the blanket in her mouth; she's a rather crude eater, I have to say, and she looks god-awful, not that she was ever all that attractive but now she's got her hair dyed dark black, she could use an eye job, and her dress is 100 percent polyester if it's 1 percent, and it's been hanging in her closet since 1982. She excuses herself to go to the bathroom. I ask Victor if he's happy. He says *Sure, you know me*, I say *I mean, with Bernadette.* He tells me it's a different kind of relationship after you lose your wife. *She takes care of me instead of the other way around. Yeah, but do you love her like you loved . . . Mom?* I ask. *I love her,* he says, but I can tell it's not in that way that means someone is head over heels. *So not like you loved Mom?* I ask. *It's just different. She's a different person. So, different, but also not just as great*, I say, and he looks at me like he knows what I want him to say, except I know he doesn't, he says *Sweetheart, what do you want me to say?* and I tell him *I want you to say that you loved me the best*, and he says *What?* and I realize how that might have sounded, so I say *I want you to say that you loved Mom the best*, and he says *I'm not going to say that*, and I say *Well,*

I can tell the difference when you look at her, and he says *You don't know everything,* and I say *I know more than you think,* and I walk away, and I know he knows I'm right.

—*Does that make you feel better, being right?*

—*Kind of.*

—*We've still got some super-weird blendy point-of-view science here. Maybe we're inventing a new genre. POV-sci.*

Betsy's Wedding #2

Okay, so here's my real wedding, with you thrown in. You're not my sister in this scenario, you're the plain old mother of the bride, as it should be. Not that there's anything plain or old about you. Are you back from the dead? Okay, yes. You're back from the dead. But not in a zombie way. You've just risen. But not in a Jesus way either. Let's say it's like you went on a death vacation and then came back.

You show up at my house the night before, because in the afterlife when people get married there's a notification system for dead parents, who are then given a day pass to come back. Most of the time, the parents opt not to totally freak out their kids and possibly all of the guests as well. After I recover from this shock myself, I introduce you to Ben. We sit down with a cup of tea; he's now wondering where *his* mom is, but we can probably assume that his mom was one of the many who opted not to freak people out. You look around the room, and seeing all the traces of you—afghans, photos, furniture, little needlepoints—you get misty. Ben says *I've heard a lot about you*, and you laugh, *I can only imagine*, you say, and he says he can see now where Betsy gets her beauty from, and you smile at me, you can tell he's a good one. He thinks I'm beautiful. Maybe all you need to know. We catch you up on some of the other major developments. I've published my first book. *Am I in it? Yes, Mom, you're in it.* Ben says *The common response to news like this is "Congratulations." Oh, well, yes, that goes without saying. No it doesn't,* he says. *You're actually supposed to say it. It's okay, honey,* I say. *How were the reviews?* you ask. *Seriously?* Ben says. *The reviews were good,* I say. *Well, that's wonderful,* you say. *What if they were bad?* Ben asks. *There's usually a grain of truth in them,* you say. *Honey, don't,* I say. *There's no point. No, I want to know, what if they were bad? I'll tell you what if,* you say. *I only ever got one really bad one in my entire career: the Kansas City paper said I overshadowed the tenor in my death scene in* Bohème, *but Christ, what a bunch of bullshit that was. I took it down, I'm supposed to be dying of consumption, but that guy couldn't have sung his way out of his own ball sack. But what if, Mom, what if, I felt confident enough about the work that I wasn't concerned about the reviews? You may have thought that, but if you didn't get any bad reviews you wouldn't know what it would be like. Most people get bad reviews at one time or another. So I shouldn't be a writer because I might get a bad review? If someone told you before you started that you might get a bad review someday, would you not have become a singer? That makes no sense, Betsy. Right, Mom, it makes no sense.*

You may end up being just as surprised as everyone else tomorrow, I say. *I suppose that's true. Victor's remarried. I knew he would be. That's as it should be. Okay, good.* I go to fix up the guest room, and while I'm gone, you tell Ben you had your doubts about whether I'd ever get over my issues with my dad enough to have a healthy relationship. He laughs; he's not going to take that bait, even though he's heard another side of that story a few times. *She's good at it,* is all Ben says, but when he says it, you get it, and you guys have a little moment.

In theory, you don't want to upstage my wedding day, you just want to be there like any mother of the bride. But you're you, and there's no way around the fact that you're you *and* you're dead, and that's likely now to be what everyone remembers about this day. So you agree to watch the ceremony from the bedroom window so that Ben and I can at least have our ceremony be about us. When I come back from the hairdresser's ready to lose it about the overly fancy updo they've given me, you help me loosen it up a bit, make it more daytime-y; it's a big improvement. Your eyes start to fill up. *Cut that out, Mom! You'll make me mess up my makeup. I can't help it. My little girl. You can be a big fat pain in my ass, Mom, but I'm glad you're here*, I say. *Better than a pain in your big fat ass, ha! I wouldn't have missed it.*

The ceremony is in our backyard on Noble Street in Chicago. The trees are decorated with garlands I made from paper and string; I sewed the skirts for the bridesmaids and the ring pillow myself. My dress . . . you made my dress. It's the bridesmaid's dress you made me when I was a bridesmaid in that all-white wedding in the eighties. We got that brocade fabric on Thirty-Seventh Street; you left the seams extra wide in case I ever needed to let it out and wear it again. I had a designer help me update it by taking off the sleeves and making straps and a kind of a mini-train; I'd kept the leftover fabric. You, for reasons that shouldn't mystify me as they do, are wearing a heavily sequined Bob Mackie gown you got at the afterlife Loehmann's. *It was a bit much. I had to take off some of the sequins*, you say. I try to picture this dress before you worked on it, because it's still as flashy as a fireworks display. *I was never a big Loehmann's fan, but my other option was Forever 21. Did you come from hell?* I ask. *No one really says*, you say. My stepbrothers walk my bridesmaids down the aisle: Nina, my sister Susan, and another friend who did all the flowers. We got them from Trader Joe's and she arranged them in mismatched thrift-store vases I picked up for a quarter or fifty cents each, wrapped with tulle.

—Why doesn't the flower friend have a name?

—That's another story. We haven't spoken for a few years.

—Why not? What did she do?

—Why would you assume it was something she did?

—Okay, what did you do?

—Mom, it's too long a story. I wasn't completely honest with her.

—About what?

—Lots of things. I spent years telling her things I thought she wanted to hear so she'd stay my friend. I mean, not lies. Agreeing with her when I didn't. That kind of thing.

—Why would you do that?

—. . .

—I just don't see what this has to do with me.

—I know.

—You can tell me.

—The shortest possible version is that one day, after many years of friendship, I came to feel that I was dealing with her in a way that was not unlike how I had dealt with you.

—Well, I'm sure it was her fault.

—I'm trying to take responsibility for my part, Mom. There were two people involved, yes. That's all I'll say.

—I knew it.

—Mom, it's just a whole other extremely complicated, unresolved story.

—So maybe you should cut her out of this scene altogether.

—I probably should. I was trying to keep the day as real as I could under the circumstances.

—YOU SAID THIS WASN'T A MEMOIR.

Two of Ben's friends from Michigan, Anne and Chafe, have a ridiculously awesome four-year-old, Ruby; she's the flower girl—I made her dress too (on the big side, I learned that from you, told myself this way she could wear it again)—and my step-brother Rob's boys Matt and Tom are the ring bearers. Ben's at the altar with his brother Fritz, Chafe, and his other old friends from Kalamazoo, Dann and Tim. Victor walks me down the stairs, because Dad's too wobbly with Parkinson's now, though he's able to take over for the short walk from there to the tree we've decorated to stand under, and he got a new suit and a bright blue tie for the occasion. His joyful smile could light the tree at Rockefeller Center; he's found a bit of a kindred spirit in Ben. Dad has always been proud of his artier side, and he's tickled to have a son-in-law who is genuinely interested in his old woodcuts. Our friends play music as we walk down the aisle; from the altar, Ben and I look on as Anne sings a Nick Drake song, "Northern Sky" (*"Been a long time that I'm waiting . . ."*), with Chafe on guitar, they chose it themselves, it makes me cry; it's a perfect day. We've asked our friends and family to speak as the spirit moves them. Jeannie reads a poem; Ben's sister gives a tribute to their parents, sure they would have been so happy to see this day. Bob talks about the old days when we were friends and we were both miserable and single and how happy he is to see what my life has become.

Meanwhile, upstairs in the house, you've started reading my book. You skim the first story after a couple of pages, confused by the style, and flip through looking for "Mom" or "Mother" until you land on the one that's about the year after your death. You've lost track of time and missed half the ceremony because you've been reading the story about you, and just as Bob is wrapping up, you poke your head out the window waving the book in your hand and yell *Mood-oriented? Mood-oriented?*

Everyone turns to look up at the window. Three people faint: two of our pregnant friends and your sister. I give you a dead stare, which is, no surprise, entirely ineffective, and a wave back into the window doesn't help either. Quite a few of the guests have no idea who you are, which I thank god for—friends we met after you were already gone, Ben's family. Many of the guests have seen pictures, of course, but nobody seems to be going straight to *Mother of the bride, returned from the dead.* Nina whispers to me *I've got this,* hurries back upstairs to pull you inside the window. *What does that mean, "mood-oriented"? That I have moods? That I'm moody? The whole world thinks I'm moody now?* Nina gently pulls you back inside. *Nobody thinks that, Lois, everyone loves you and misses you. Come on inside now.*

At this point, after the guests recover from their fainting spells, there's a pause, a pause so literal and long it's almost like a freeze-frame. All remaining heads are staring up at the window, even though you're now inside. Finally Ben's sister stands up, because no one else has and someone has to. *Okay, everyone. Here's what's going on.* Amy calmly explains the deal about the day pass. Everyone listens silently; it seems impossible to believe, but Amy adds *You saw her. If it weren't true, what would the alternative be? Betsy and Ben decided to have some weird lookalike of her mom show up to freak everyone out?* She further explains that the reason she knows this is that her own mother had come to her wedding. *What?* Ben says. *Mom came to your wedding but not to mine? I was there, Amy, I didn't see her. She stayed inside. Didn't she want to talk to me? No, it wasn't that, I'm sure. . . .* Ben looks thoroughly crushed. *I was the first one to get married, and I was her daughter, and . . . it's possible she thought better of it after the last time. Mom loved you so much, Ben. You know that. Let's try to have a good day. I'm sure there are plenty of people here who are happy to see Lois.*

I know I'm glad to get the chance to meet her. Ben and I look at each other. I whisper *I'm sorry.*

But a chain of events has been set in motion, and now every single guest who got married after the death of a parent is wondering why theirs hadn't shown up for their wedding. Several guests immediately get out their cell phones to call siblings. *Was Dad at your wedding? Yes. Why did he come to your wedding and not mine? I was her favorite. That's not the right answer! Was Mom at your wedding? Yes. Why didn't you tell me? I didn't want you to feel bad. But I feel bad now! Was Mom at your wedding? Are you insane? Was she? Was she? Dad was at your wedding, wasn't he? What are you talking about? I just found out that dead parents of brides and grooms get to come to their wedding. You're off your meds again. It's true! Don't try to tell me Dad didn't come to your wedding! It would have been just like him, Daddy's girl. Did Mom come to your wedding? Mom was dead when I got married. What are you talking about? I'm at a wedding, there's a dead mom here. Can you hear yourself? Don't lie to me! You've always been a liar! I'm not lying! You dated my ex-boyfriend for a year behind my back! That was eighteen years ago! I'm just saying you're a liar! Fine, she came! I knew it! Did Mom come to your wedding? Yeah. What? Did Dad come to your wedding? Yes. Mom mom mom dad dad dad wedding wedding wedding yes yes yes yes yes yes why didn't you tell me I hate you I hate you I hate you!*

Seventeen guests depart without saying good-bye, before the actual vows have been taken.

I remain standing there with my eyes open wide and my jaw locked shut for fear of what might escape. This is when Ben steps up to the plate.

Hey! he yells. *Everyone stop! Hey! Everyone! Everyone shut up!*

The remaining guests fall silent and look toward the altar. The groom is yelling.

Betsy and I are getting married right now. Who wants to stay and see that happen?

All who aren't seated return to their seats.

You and Nina peek back out the window. *I authorize you to cover her mouth if you have to!* I yell up. The guests laugh loudly, a welcome break in the tension.

Ben and I say the vows we wrote for each other. Our friend the minister asks everyone who approves of this union to shout *Yes!* and a resounding and enthusiastic *Yes!* comes forth.

The reception is down the block in Pulaski Park; you walk there with your sister, who's still crying. Marjorie was never a weepy one, but she's beyond overwhelmed to have a chance to see you again. She asks if you're back for good; you explain again about the wedding deal, that this is pretty much it. *So, not even if there are grandkids?* Marjorie asks; you say you hadn't asked about that, but that you were told this was a one-time thing. *And Betsy's too old to have kids now. People have other options,* Marjorie says dryly. *What about if she gets divorced and remarried?* Marjorie asks, and you say *Jesus, Marjorie, I don't want to think about that, if she waited until she was forty to get married, hopefully she's learned a thing or two,* and Marjorie says *Okay, touchy*, and the old pull to get into it with her comes up, but just as you're about respond, you both crack up. *I know you didn't kill Whitey*, you say, feeling an opening. *I'm a lot of things, Lois, but I'm not a dog killer. I know, Marjorie. It was that nasty Mrs. Snatchface down the street. Mrs. Stackchase! I should have known*, Marjorie says. *She's paying now*, you say. *But I always knew it wasn't you anyway.*

Marjorie asks if you've met Fern yet. *Who's Fern?* you ask, and your sister points across the room to a blond woman who's clinging tightly to Victor. You look over and reserve judgment for now. *Well, it was to be expected, Marjorie.* This is when your dear old friends Inge and Dan come over to greet you. Inge is fighting tears too, until she sees you looking at Fern. *Oh well,* she says in her sweet German accent, *she's all right. He's been ill, a bit, she takes care of him. Ill? Ya*, Inge says, *a stroke, cancer. Not long after you . . . he's better now. You should go say hi. I'm sure he's waiting.*

Inge squeezes your hand; you take a deep breath, walk across the room. Victor has tears in his eyes, like everyone else, but that doesn't make it any less awkward, and he almost has to peel Fern off his arm to give you a hug. He introduces her, she says *I've heard a lot about you*, in a thick Staten Island accent, sort of a monotone; you don't know yet that this flat tone is her only tone, the point is that it seems potent. It's an absence of tone functioning as tone. The truth is, Victor hasn't talked that much about you; he's told her he loved you and that you were a brilliant singer, but "complicated" is about the extent of the rest of it. It's in the past, and he's never been one to linger there. And you're sharp, if somewhat paranoid, and you're not altogether off in perceiving something in Fern's toneless tone, though what that is has yet to reveal itself. Fern's phone rings in her purse; she says it's her mother calling her back. *Ma. Yeah. Yeah listen, Ma, why do you think Pop didn't come to the wedding? No I haven't been drinking, Ma, it's a goddamn booze-free wedding, but I'm going to run to a deli to get some right now*, you hear as she walks away. You and Victor stare at each other for a bit; it's hard to know how to open the conversation. *Hey, how's that new wife working out?* isn't quite right, though that's what you want to know. *She seems . . .* you say, having no idea how to finish the sentence. You were reaching for something along the lines of *nice*, but it's not coming out of your mouth. *She's a good person*, Victor says. What you don't know is that he says this a lot. *Betsy's not— I hoped maybe they'd be friends, but . . . I think Betsy just can't get past her not being you.* You can imagine that there might be a shred of truth to this, and also that it's far from the full story. *Maybe you should give Betsy more credit than that. What's that supposed to mean? I'm saying maybe she has some reason to think this woman isn't right for you. Betsy doesn't know her. I've tried. We've had Betsy to the house. Wait, what house? The house, our house. You mean* my *house? Sweetheart, where did you imagine I would live? I imagined you'd live in a new house! Who would want to live in my house? It's a nice house, why* wouldn't *we want to live there? Because it's creepy! You're crazy. It's where I live. Did she redecorate? No, sweetheart, we haven't redecorated. Look, I'm about to retire and we'll probably move to South Carolina, there doesn't seem any point in moving now. Does she wear my jewelry? No! Of course not. Betsy has your jewelry, just like we agreed on. Good. She had the nerve to ask me for the old dining room table and chairs, though. My mother's table and chairs? Yeah, we use it. No you don't, we always kept that folded up. Yes, it's folded, it has picture frames on it. It's supposed to be Betsy's—you can't put picture frames somewhere else? That table is supposed to be hers after I die. But you're not using it. I'm not having this conversation. It was wrong of her to ask. Give her the table! I see crazy is still an issue in the afterlife. Fuck off, Victor! That was my mother's!*

All of the wedding guests can hear what's going on. Marjorie comes over to try to calm you down. *Lois. I can't begin to guess what this might be like for you. No, you can't,* you say. *Lois,* Marjorie says again, *listen. We don't really like her either. She isn't you. You're right. Don't you suppose that might have been exactly why he chose her? I can't begin to guess why he chose her. I know, that's what I'm trying to tell you. He had his big love. He's a guy. They don't do well on their own.* You muster a snuffle that represents a laugh. *He was the one who took care of* me, *though. Yes, he did, but he was heartbroken to lose you, and Fern showed up on the right day when he was tired enough of crying. Yeah, what, a month later?* you ask, and Marjorie laughs and says *Roughly, yes, but he was heartbroken and lonely and she was there and she was the opposite of you and that was what he thought he needed.* Your sister is slowly breaking through. *But she's using my stuff. Yeah, that stinks.*

—I'm not sure this scene is doing what I want it to, Mom. I feel like I'm just having you say things I think.

—Maybe we think some of the same things.

— . . .

—Can we go to the future now?

—That's gonna be weird.

—It's weird now.

—Let's wrap this weirdness up first.

At the bride and groom's table, you have a chance to talk to Dad and his wife. It's not the first time you've seen Dad since the divorce, but it's been a good number of years, and though he and Jeannie have been married for decades, you've never met her. You offer Fred a hug; his illness has now aged him to the point where there are barely traces of the man you remember, but the sparkle in his green eyes is still there and it's hard to call up the limitless anger you once had toward him. *Betsy's missed you so much,* Jeannie says, the kindness in her voice settling into you. All you've got is a sad smile of gratitude. *She thinks I'm mood-oriented.* Jeannie is too polite to know how to comment on that, but I'm not. *Mom, let it go. Did you bother reading the part of the story where I cry for a year? No. Hm.* You turn to me and whisper *It's too bad Jeannie didn't meet Fred first. Nobody's sorry things worked out the way they did, Mom. I caused him a lot of pain. Yeah, you did.*

But he recovered. I have a sister. Jeannie has three sons. I wouldn't exist at all. Well, maybe that would have been for the best. What? No, I just mean, whoever you might have been would have had a more normal childhood, a more normal life. I should have probably never had you. Mom! So you're sorry you had me. What if I said I was? Are you? No! You just said you shouldn't have had me. I said probably. So you're not sure. That's what probably means, yes. So probably I shouldn't have been born. That's not what I meant. It's fine that you were born. Fine? It's great that you were born, really, it's great. Great? It's the greatest thing in the history of great things that happened to me. Honestly. Honestly? Yes, Betsy. Why won't you say what you meant? I don't want to. C'mon. I'm dead. Can't you just cut me some slack? I've cut you plenty of slack. I misspoke. That's all. I'm not sorry you were born.

—I feel like I'm losing control of this narrative.

—I don't know what you just said.

Honey, I'm sorry. Of course I'm glad you were born. I only meant that I wish I could have given you a more normal upbringing. You could have, you just didn't want to. Okay, well, maybe not normal, exactly, I did love that our life was—even in poverty, it seemed extraordinary to me. Yes, sometimes a little too extraordinary. I guess if I could change anything I might have wanted things to be like they were, but less . . . sad. You kiss me on the head. *But look at you. You've done better without me. Mom. You were there for thirty-seven years of my life. There is no me without you. That's a good thing. Or—it's a complicated thing that's also a good thing.* You nod, pull a crumpled tissue from your beaded sleeve to wipe your eyes. *Oooow! I scratched myself in the face.*

Colorado

You're now sixty. How the hell did that happen? Sixty is old. Victor tells you that you're as beautiful as ever; one glance in the mirror tells you he's out of his mind to think so, and you are certainly glad you avoided the sun your entire life, but sixty is sixty and you were a young woman only moments ago. You never thought about what sixty would be like. It feels close to over. You're tired now, *all* the time. Which makes your brain start to do what it does, again. If you have another twenty years, what do you want for that? You try to picture yourself like your mother after sixty, a tight gray perm, senior cruises to Alaska. Haven't you traveled enough? Would you really want to do anything like getting on a boat you can't get off, just to spend two weeks playing shuffleboard with a bunch of old people? No. What you would like is to get the hell out of New York City and be with someone who understands you. You will never be Callas-level famous, it's finally clear. You haven't made peace with it, but you know it's true. New York has taken its toll. So you live in a nice apartment in the Schwab House, with a view of the river and your long-awaited second bathroom. You want out. You've always loved Colorado. Your high school friend lives there, she's always wanted you to come, has a guest house you can rent. Done. Within the space of about a month, you go from turning sixty to telling Victor you want a separation and packing up a U-Haul with furniture and driving yourself to Boulder. You have no idea what this looks like to everyone else. You try to explain your reasons to me, that it's all Victor's fault, and that he doesn't even try to understand you. *He's not the person you think he is. Hm, where have I heard that before?* I say, you say *What are you talking about?* I say *Never mind.*

Colorado lasts six weeks. Long enough to unload your truck, hang curtains and pictures (well, who are we kidding, that part is accomplished in about three days), make a sweet little home in your carriage house apartment with a deck above a stream in the woods. It's peaceful, which only serves to make you understand clearly now that there is no peace for you. Attempting a task as basic as ordering telephone service results in full-on screaming at an automated voice system until your throat hurts, which in turn magnifies your existing self-hatred for possibly damaging the only good thing you have to offer. You do some writing, a life review to date, pluses and minuses and in-betweens (not many of those). You are able to get the briefest glimpse of what it looks like from the outside. You've sung with La Scala. You've been married nearly twenty-five years to a man who adores you; you've traveled the world, raised a beautiful daughter. These are things to be happy about. You have had your joys, but you have never really known peace. Still, a few things come into focus. Your brain doesn't work quite right, you know this now, though you still haven't pinpointed the whys or hows. You're beyond tired. Physically, mentally, spiritually. You want to rest everything. And you realize, here in Colorado, that that's been available to you all along back east. So you tearfully ask Victor to take you back. There was never any question that he would. You ask if you can move to New Jersey, though; you can't live in the city anymore. You call Betsy and tell her. She seems surprised, but weirdly relieved.

Jersey

You and Victor buy a beautiful four-bedroom house in Upper Montclair with a big front yard and a big backyard. Why didn't you do this sooner? You have a guest room, an office, a sewing room. You spend three months decorating, allowing yourself to buy some new living room furniture for the first time in twenty years. (Victor would have done this years ago; you saw no reason to spend the money when you were fully capable of reupholstering sofas and chairs.) You celebrate your twenty-fifth anniversary together with a backyard party. He buys you a puppy. At the end of these three months, with no new projects yet begun, you're restless again. What the fuck is wrong with you? Victor asks if you want to take a couple of engagements that come in, you say sure, get back to practicing. He drives you into the city for a lesson; you get your foot stuck in your purse straps, on the floor of the car, and fall out onto the sidewalk, breaking your hip. You're pissed. You've taken vitamins for decades to prevent this; fuck those snake-oil-selling con artists. Everything is X-rayed, hip-replacement surgery is scheduled, but there's more news as well.

The worst news. Cancer. Of the lungs. Lung cancer. What? Yes. As soon as you've recovered from the hip surgery, you will have another surgery to remove the cancerous part of your left lung. You respond to this news with silence, at first; Victor holds off from discussing it until all three of us are gathered in the kitchen in Montclair. Your first thought is blank. Your second thought: That asshole just ruined my new kitchen. Your third thought: I spent an entire lifetime not smoking. I made not smoking an active thing. That's not easy to do. Your fourth thought comes out of your mouth: *Hold on. Victor. The doctor discussed this with you before he talked to me, Victor? That's* wildly *unethical. I can't even . . . I knew as soon as they called that it was bad news, Lois. I persuaded them to tell me the results over the phone. I thought it would be better if I told you.* The rest of your thoughts blur together into what is commonly recognized as shock. You don't cry for another day or two. You can't understand why everyone else isn't crying, though; it doesn't occur to you that they don't want to upset you any more than you already are. You believe in expressing all feelings at all times, though this has never been a successful practice for you insofar as your feeling-expression resulting in any real change. Victor says that the doctors have given him some percentage chance of full recovery. The number doesn't fully land, but you're sure it's above 50, and that's enough for now. You can work with that. You'll think about it later.

In post-op, the doctors report that they had to take two-thirds of your lung but that they've gotten everything, that you'll have a full recovery. Your lungs, from years of singing, are impressive, the doctors say; the amount of lung removed still leaves you with more lung than most people have before the operation, so essentially you're at everyone else's square one. Something to be proud of. You made a little guest room for cancer in these lungs, great. The doctors strongly suggest a rigorous course of treatment as a matter of prevention, and Victor is also in favor of this, but as soon as they outline your treatment options, you know you're not going to have any of them. You have done your research, of course. You are a person who asks questions and demands answers, and when you don't like the first ones given, you go looking for ones you do. There are no guarantees. You learn the phrase "cut, poison, and burn," and you've already been cut so you'll skip the rest of that torture, thanks. You've brought this on yourself with your broken brain; maybe you can get rid of it if you can learn how to think better. You can say affirmations. You can affirm the hell out of this godforsaken disease. You don't want to lose your hair; you don't want to spend any more days in bed than you already do. You have things to do. You've got an engagement with the Virginia Symphony next spring. Victor is fully prepared to cancel that on your behalf; you say *Oh no you don't.* You don't want anybody in the business knowing about this. You've already been vocalizing, and right now you sound like shit, but your shit is ten times better than whoever they'll replace you with. Plus if you can sing a concert that will obviously mean you're fine.

So you practice. You double down on lessons, double up on your lung rehab exercises, learn compensation techniques. It takes a little more out of you than it has in the past, and by the end of this time, before the concert, you're not at all where you've been before. There's a different tone to your voice, and there's less power, but there's no less art. You receive the usual standing ovations and rave reviews in the local papers. Your lack of lung is not noted because they know nothing about it; you might even have gotten a better review had you come out about it, but you take a great deal of pride in the raves you've gotten under these circumstances. You sing better than half the dilettantes out there with recording contracts right now, with one less lung. You could sing the shit out of shit with half a lung.

But this performance took almost all the energy you had. You'll just take a break now. You go in for your follow-up appointments, and the doctors find some more spots, not small ones, on your other lung, the lung you do still need. This time, Victor talks you into the chemo and radiation; you still really don't want it, but you're too tired to argue. You could double up on holistic treatments, you think, which you've already been doing: Reiki, acupuncture, crystals, affirmations, aromatherapy. But you agree to do it for him. You see his worry now.

These treatments, however, take the last small reserve of energy in your well. When you're not sitting in the chemo room, you're in your bedroom with the curtains drawn watching *Golden Girls* marathons. You feel somewhat better for brief periods between treatments, enough to plant a few fall flowers out front, catch up on some mending projects, start a new afghan for Betsy, to replace an earlier one you made that doesn't match her sofa very well. Your doctors say you've made significant improvement. You do not feel significantly improved. You're on oxygen most of the time, and that bullshit tank is a pain in your ass to drag around even on better days. Victor and Betsy suggest at least coming down to the living room, looking out at the beautiful backyard to get your spirits up. They don't get it. You don't want to see the life you're not living; you don't want hope for what you're not going to have. But you can't say that to them, even if it somehow wouldn't make them sad, which you know it would. They'd try to cheer you up, rally you; you don't want to be rallied. It's confusing, because you were always such a fighter; maybe you're finally done fighting. You should keep on going, to feel like *this*? Weren't you the one who always told everyone that you were a huge proponent of assisted suicide, that if you had some horrible debilitating illness you wanted one of us to come pull the plug? You never got confirmations from me and Victor about that, and even Audrey, who understands you like no one else and who is a nurse and mother through and through, had said *I don't think so*. You're not going to record; you've known this for years. You've done some good in the world, not enough to make up for the excess of drama you've added, but you've done what you felt you could. Maybe you weren't meant to be an old person. That feels true. You can't picture yourself as a little old lady with a silver perm and unblended rouge. You still look good now; maybe this is meant to be. What is it they say about leaving a good-looking corpse?

Just before Thanksgiving, you're feeling better. You've felt good enough to walk the dog all the way around the block, dragging that dumb old oxygen tank behind you. You're looking forward to having me home. You plan dinner; Victor and Betsy will help, it'll be like always. I fly in from Chicago the Sunday before, but when my cab pulls up in the driveway, you're feeling a little weak. Victor puts you in the car to take you to the hospital to be on the safe side. Your daughter tells you she loves you, you mouth the words back, can't get any air behind them, an apologetic look in your eyes. You know. You totally know. She doesn't know, but you do.

The Year Is 2016

The year is 2016!

—Mom, that's this year.

—Well, this year is the future from where I'm sitting. I'm not looking to go to outer space.

—Thank god.

The year is 2016! So much happened in the year 2015. The people rose up and said *No more!* There were peaceful demonstrations and a new government was instituted. One person, one vote. The stupid electoral college became a relic of the past. I never understood that anyway.

And that was just the beginning! Because of this new, true democracy, all kinds of scientific breakthroughs that had previously been discovered that couldn't have come into practice under the corporatocracy as it was have now been implemented. Cures for AIDS and cancer, cures for Parkinson's. Cures for many kinds of mental illness. Health care is fucking affordable. Alternative healing and therapy are covered! News is news and entertainment is entertainment! Funds for alternative energies are created, funds for public education are distributed fairly! College is free! The employment rate is up! Drugs are legal, and we have new gun laws, which is to say: no more guns at all! which means crime is down, which means prisons are closing. Racism is over. Well, no it isn't. Let's be serious. We have work to do there. But we have new, specific civil rights laws and we actually enforce them. And war is over. More or less.

—That's a miraculous near future you've dreamed up there, Mom.
—Well, why not. You've encouraged me to make shit up.

But you and I still have some unresolved issues. So we plan a trip to Machu Picchu. I've wanted to go there for a spiritual experience ever since I read that Shirley MacLaine book. Shirley herself is going up with us as our guide, along with her personal shaman. We fly into Cusco with nothing we can't fit into our backpacks, as dictated by Shirley, as dictated by the shaman. We are told to get good hiking shoes, to pack layers to take on and off, and to bring two things for the fire: a symbol of something to let go of, and an offering. I ask *What kind of an offering?*; you can tell I look nervous. You say *Mom, you're confusing "offering" with "sacrifice"; she's not asking you to bring a puppy to toss into a pyre*; I laugh. Shirley says *Just a small totem you can carry that has meaning to you that you want to give to the earth in gratitude.* We spend the first night in a tent at the bottom to get used to the elevation—of course, I've performed in cities with high elevations before, but this is eleven thousand feet, and you and I are both already dizzy and we're still at the bottom. Shirley—who told us not to bring anything we can't fit into our backpacks—has a donkey to carry what she needs. She's famous, and the rules don't apply to her, so she has a personal shaman and a donkey. Her shaman doesn't speak English, and though Shirley doesn't speak his language either, she will translate because she understands him psychically. You, I can see, are doing your best not to laugh about this, but I give you a nudge in the side and you let it go.

Shirley lays out a thin mattress stuffed with the hypoallergenic wool of a vicuna, two silk sheets on top of that because she has sensitive skin, and a cashmere blanket on top of that. You and I have one cotton sheet each to lay on the ground, so we put on all our layers and curl up together. The shaman has only the clothes on his back and appears oddly content. Shirley is dead asleep in about two minutes; she snores like a horse, which is hilarious at first, less so when we get no sleep whatsoever. In the morning she wakes us before dawn and we ask why she didn't tell us to pack earplugs, and of course she denies that she snores at all. *Absurd*, she says. *Chop-chop now, it's time for the morning revel.* She leads you out of the tent and adds another log to the fire. *Sit down, sit down.* The shaman hands Shirley what appears to be a bunch of leaves; she proceeds to rub these leaves over our heads and bodies and says a blessing in some unrecognizable language. *Can I ask what that means*, I say, Shirley says *No*. The shaman takes a small bottle from the donkey's pack, hands it to Shirley. She takes a swig, hands it to me, I swig, I hand it to you, you swig. It tastes like dirt mixed with vinegar. We both make faces, hope we haven't just swallowed some kind of hallucinogen. *We are here to heal via becoming one with the earth*, Shirley says, *as all things do. We drink the earth water, we breathe the sacred mountain air, and offer our gifts to the fire as pieces of ourselves.* I am hit with the strong sense that Shirley's version of this ritual is dubious. You, of course, have never had any other sense about it. *We will now contribute to the flames.*

Shirley stands up. *I will offer this watch, given to me by my ex-husband. Om, na na, Om na na.* She drops the watch, encrusted with jewels, into the center of the fire. It's hard not to notice that Shirley's tossed in something that we could probably trade for a house. *Lois.* Shirley gestures from me to the fire. I stand, remove a well-worn birthday card my mother had given me when I turned sixteen, when she suspected I was having some issues with my confidence. She hadn't written much on it, but the poem inside was surprisingly moving, about growing up beautifully; that word was underlined twice, and I knew what she was trying to tell me, though it wasn't her way to gush out loud, and it's signed simply *Mother.* I start to well up as I put it into the flames; you reach for my hand as I sit back down. We go around the circle, watching as various meaningful items are thrown in as offerings. You make an offering of your father's and my wedding bands, tied with a small satin ribbon, meant to express gratitude to us for coming together long enough to make you. When we go around the second time, with our items to let go of, I toss in a small suede pouch that contains two marbles I've had since I was a kid, one of those little ring puzzles that I swear is unsolvable, a photo of myself with the top of my head out of the frame, and a tiny starfish with two broken legs. *Whoa,* Shirley says. *That's a whole lot of metaphor for one little pouch. Is this not supposed to be a safe and loving space?* I ask. *Not necessarily,* Shirley says. You stand up and say *Well, since Shirley already tossed my mom in for me, I'll let go of this instead.* You toss in your puffy-eyed picture first grade school photo and a 2017 calendar. *The past and the future,* Shirley says. *Brilliant. You could take a lesson from your daughter, Lois. Shirley, shut the fuck up,* you say. I bust out in cackles.

We are a united front, victorious against Shirley MacLaine.

—This is pretty ridiculous, Mom. I think I'm going to have to cut it.

—I love this chapter!

—It's all right, Mom, but I don't think it really fits. Something about it feels too obvious. Or too silly.

—Let me have it.

—All right, we'll talk about it later.

Enjoy Your Happy Ending

You become a successful writer. It was meant to be.

—I don't believe in meant to be.
—Well, you should.

You live happily ever after.

—Oh come on now.
—No, look. You do. I can add this, if it makes you feel better:

You write books, you have relative peace of mind, you have a wonderful circle of friends. You have a solid marriage. Maybe you and Ben still disagree about some things, thirty years in—you want to say the perfect wise thing when he's sad, he doesn't want you to do anything; he wants only to be seen, you think he's going to leave every time you disagree; even after decades, this thought, though ever smaller and smaller, never entirely goes away; this makes sense to me now, but you're together, and you're old and it's good even if you still think he's easily distracted when he lets the dogs off-leash at the beach; he thinks you worry too much, all the same *exact* issues as when you got your first dog a few years after you were married; but you're both a little bit right, and this sort of thing is such a small part of your existence—the rest of which is sitting on the porch of your house upstate, reading, having dinners with friends, making very, very occasional appearances after you both retire. Here's the thing: one of you will get cancer, or Alzheimer's, or arthritis, or something, or you won't, neither of you, you'll both grow very old and creaky, and right after one dies, the other will die peacefully while sleeping, of heartbreak like they say, or maybe you'll die in a car crash together because you decided to drive long past the time when you should have stopped. The greater likelihood is that one will be left behind. That's just the deal. Do you want to fully understand that right now? I didn't think so. I lived into my sixties with an unresolved story. You've already had a sort of resolution I never got. You don't have to write a different ending for yourself. The worst could happen to you and you'd be okay. That's the difference between you and me. I know this now. You might have some of me in you, I know you do, but you have way more of your father. I don't know why I didn't know this before. Maybe I did and I didn't want to. Or I did and I didn't want to see that it was a good thing.

Enjoy your happy ending. I mean it.

Acknowledgments

CAPSY THANK-YOUS TO:

Nina Solomon, for reading every draft of every thing, every time. Josh Mohr, Mark Haskell Smith, Gina Frangello, and Jamie Quatro, for your thoughtful notes and for encouraging me with my wacky ideas. Duncan Murrell, for reading that part I left out, and to Lisa Lucas for your late-game read when I was freaking out.

For reading that other book (or wide swaths of it) that I dropped in favor of this book, I give thanks to: Emily Rapp Black, Pia Z. Ehrhardt, Melanie Hoopes, and Bryn Magnus.

To Tod Goldberg and all my UCR colleagues, I give thanks for snickerdoodles and support.

To Donny Ward, I thank you for making that movie or whatever. That was cool.

To Lois, Susan, Rob, Reed, Mark, and all people related to me, or who ever met me, for what should seem like (but are not limited to) obvious reasons. I love you.

To Audrey and Inge, for being so sweet.

To Kirk Walsh, for cheerleading, always.

To Bob, for letting us live at your house.

To my adored Kalamazoo people, who continue to grow in number.

To Ben, for that jacket/coat thing. (And for standing next to me that one day, and always.)

And to Cal Morgan, for being patient with my bangs and making this stuff so much better, always!

About the Author

Elizabeth Crane is the author of the novel *We Only Know So Much* and three collections of short stories: *When the Messenger Is Hot*, *All This Heavenly Glory*, and *You Must Be This Happy to Enter*. Her stories have been featured on NPR's *Selected Shorts*. She is a recipient of the Chicago Public Library 21st Century Award, and her work has been adapted for the stage by Chicago's Steppenwolf Theatre Company. A feature film adaptation of *We Only Know So Much* will be released in 2016.

About the author . . .

About the book

Read on

P.S.

Insights,
Interviews
& More . . .

. . . and Her Stuff

I COME FROM A PEOPLE who like to save things. My father, a professor of musicology, used to save for various reasons, historical preservation chief among them; for my mother, an opera singer who lived through more than a few lean times, it was more a matter of "This might come in handy someday" or "That's still perfectly good." (Even, occasionally, regarding something like a crumpled-up paper towel on the counter. Weirdly, I get that now.) I sometimes think the only people we don't call hoarders are those who can afford extra storage space.

I probably fall somewhere between these two models: *normal human being* and *potential future hoarder*. I myself have carted around any number of boxes of memorabilia dating back to my childhood on the Upper West Side, including, but not limited to: all cards and letters ever written to me; a significant number of rough drafts and/or Xerox copies of letters I've written to others; notebooks and journals that run almost continuously from 1969–present; paper copies and some rough drafts of every piece of fiction I ever wrote, dating from around 1973 to sometime in the last decade, when I decided to trust that I could save things digitally; and non-digital (analog?) photos—I've been an enthusiastic amateur photographer since I was in fifth grade, until I belatedly hopped on that digital train too. I have, currently, three large, heavy archival scrapbooks that my father bought for me when I sold my first book, insisting that now that I was a published author, each and every review—and each and every reprint thereof, in each and every newspaper, journal, or Pennysaver—nay, each and every item on which my name or likeness was ever printed (and especially if it's laminated), I must properly save for my . . . well, having no children, I'm forced to conclude that my father must have envisioned a future in which my archives would matter. I have most of my beloved children's books, though at one point I parted with a few to give to some actual children; I have many, many items that I have knitted, embroidered, or sewed, including an orangey floral corduroy jumper with a matching disco bag; and I have the shredded remains of my very first pair of Calvin Klein jeans, which I got in tenth or eleventh grade when Calvin Klein jeans first came out. (I know there's one reader out there who's pausing over that phrase—*first came out?*—as though Calvins have been around so long as to have no known origin, but they do, and yes, it was a long time ago.) And this doesn't include other sentimental stuff, much of which takes up even more space than all these things made of paper, all of the things that other people made for me—all the sweaters my grandmother knitted me at my request (one "oversized" sweater, so oversized as to require its own archival box), all the afghans my mother knitted for me. (Honestly, I am kind of amazed I was ever able to relinquish the sofa my mother had reupholstered for me, though I suppose I should be grateful that I have some limits.) But it's with regret that I report that lost forever in the basement of my step-grandparents' house in the Bronx (that as far as I know were still there when the house was sold a few decades after they died) was a dollhouse room my father had lovingly built for me, inlaid with real parquet floors. (I live in hope that it's a treasure in a new home somewhere.) I have a vague memory that, in some move, I decided I could finally part with my college notebooks. (I did my best to tear out the notes I passed between friends. I knew what mattered.) In other moves, I let go of my childhood magazine collections: *TV Guide*, *Seventeen*, most of my *Tiger Beat* and *Partridge Family* magazines. (Now that I own my own home, I regret the latter greatly.)

But wait! That sounds like a lot of stuff, right? But what happens when one parent dies, and then the other, is that you get *still more very important stuff*. So add to the list: handmade quilts and more afghans, all manner of needlework, finished and un-, furniture, dishware, glassware, publications, photos, recordings (my mom tape-recorded her performances whenever possible, and taped every voice lesson she ever took, and she may have taped over some of those, but hundreds still remain, and I can't be expected to throw those away, because often the tapes caught her laughing or chatting, and I might want to listen to that someday. If I ever get a tape player again). Add as well all of their memorabilia, plus countless other things they saved that have been moot for years now (like hundreds of movies on VHS cassettes taped off the TV), and *their* lifetime collections of magazines, like *Life* and *National Geographic*. My father was known to say that one of his great regrets was letting go of the *Superman* No. 1 comic book that he bought, you know, new. I'd also like to say that this inventory is really just off the top of my head, and is in no way comprehensive. So, yeah. Stuff.

In a great moment of foresight, before he died, my father catalogued and donated his vast collection of Jew's harps to the Khomus Museum in Yakutia. So that's one fewer set of boxes for me and my sister to put in our attics and look at once or twice over the course of the rest of our lives. I do wish he'd saved me that chest of drawers of eyeglass lenses from my grandfather's shop. I could have really done something with that. ~

The Point, Sort of

ALL THIS TO SAY: in crafting a book like this, you might assume I'd be inclined to comb through these archives. Weirdly enough, I don't especially enjoy looking at much of this material. I did read my journals from beginning to end a few years back, when I was trying to write a memoir, and nothing about the experience was enjoyable. At best it was marginally illuminating, in that I discovered that I remembered some things very differently from the way I'd written about them at the time.

But the point is that I didn't want this book to depict events with any accuracy. I am a fan of whatever you want to call this category of fiction in which authors use their real names for their character names. As someone who has often mined my own history for inspiration, I find that using my real name feels like a fun way to blur the lines further while also not pretending that a story didn't begin where it did. This book began with a simple idea: if I had the opportunity to sit down with my mom, who died in 1998, and dig into what each of us thought we knew about the other person's life, what would be revealed? My hope was to capture something of the essence of these two real people, reflecting who they truly were/are/could have been/could be. The book *Percival Everett by Virgil Russell*, by Percival Everett, blew my mind. There's no way to synopsize it simply, but it explores a father-son relationship, playing with point of view in a way that's unlike anything I've ever read. That no one had ever told me to read Percival Everett before is also mind-blowing, because Percival Everett is so in my wheelhouse that he pretty much built the wheelhouse. Sometimes you don't even hear or think about who builds the wheelhouse you're in, but now I'm working my way through all the bricks Percival Everett laid, believe me.

All this to say that I made the non-decision not to dig too deeply into literal stuff.

Further Ambiguity

Read on

In the following pages, I present to you some literal stuff to peruse that may or may not come from the collected archives of the Crane/Russell/Brandt estate. Any resemblance to individuals, living or dead, is entirely ambiguous. I'll be curious to know if you think that what you see in this assemblage lines up with the story as I tell it, or if you think it matters.

Sunday, Aug. 12, 19

SOCIETY NEWS

Russell-Crane Wedding Solemnized at Church

Marriage vows of Miss Loise Russell, daughter of Mr. and Mrs. Walter Russell, 508 West Fourth street, and Frederick Crane, son of Mr. and Mrs. Baron D. Crane, 601 North White street, Mt. Pleasant, were spoken a ceremony which took place o'clock Sunday afternoon at First Methodist church. The A. D. Steffenson, pastor of church, read the double ring vice.

tar vases and large baskets filled with white gladioli and pom poms. White candelabra completed the setting.

Organ music was played by Mrs. Floyd Scott. Stephen Hobson of Iowa City was vocalist, offering "I Love Thee," Grieg, "O Perfect Love," Barnby, and "How Do I Love Thee," by Lippe.

In Bridal Party

Serving as matrons of honor were Mrs. Robert Evans and the s. Albert Mont- Iowa City. Pat- flower girl. of Mechanics- e bridegroom as rs were Albert loosa and Peter llan McCoid of

given in mar- her. Her gown white organdy, a fitted bodice s. The neckline appliqued em- tiered bouffant to a short train. h veil of pure s attached to a flowers. The g white gloves rescent bouquet and stephanotis. f honor were in

white, was centered with a four tier wedding cake. The bride's chosen colors of blue and white were used in decoration of the guest tables.

Assisting with the serving were Mrs. Elmer Bloom, Jr., and the Misses Barbara Crane, Jane Stanley, Linda Carlson, Nancy Hahm, Caroline Smith, Sue Schmidt, Kay Schauland and Janet Hendrickson. Mrs. Donald Schmelzer had charge of the guest book and Mrs. John Hilton attended the gifts.

The couple left on a short wedding trip and for traveling the bride chose a brown linen dress with beige accessories.

Mr. and Mrs. Crane will reside temporarily at 508 West Fourth street. On Sept. 17, they plan to sail for Cologne, Germany, where Mr. Crane will study on a Fulbright scholarship at Cologne university.

Mrs. Crane, a graduate of Muscatine high school, attended Muscatine junior college and the State University of Iowa. She was a member of Chi Omega social sorority at the university. Mr. Crane, a graduate of Mt. Pleasant high school and Carlton college, received his M. A. degree from the State University of Iowa.

Out of town guests at the wedding were from Mt. Pleasant, Davenport, Oskaloosa and Iowa City, Ia.; Viola, Ill.; Norwalk, Calif., and Pittsburgh, Pa.

basket of light blue daisies.

The best man was Willard Snustad of Mechanicsville. Albert Carlson of Oskaloosa, Peter Salzman and Allan McCoid, both of Mt Pleasant, served as ushers.

Immediately following the ceremony, a reception for the 300 guests was held in the church parlor. The serving table, completely decorated in white, centered a four-tier wedding cake. The guests' ... the bride's chos- ... e and white. Miss ... a sister of the ... Bloom, Jr., Mrs ... Miss Linda Carlson, ... hn, Miss Caroline ... Schmidt, Miss ... and Miss Janet ... rved at the recep- ... ald Schmelzer was ... guest book, and ... in charge of the

... the bride chose a ... with beige ac- ... a short wedding ... will live at 508 ... until September 17 ... sail for Germany ... study at that time ... scholarship at ... sity, Cologne. Ger-

... a graduate of Mus- ... ool, attended Mus- ... and the State Uni- ... She is a member ... ega social sorority ... duated from Mt ... school and Carleton ... ield, Minn. He re- ... A. degree from SUI

... guests were from ... Davenport, Oskaloo- ... Viola, Ill., Norwalk, ... sburgh, Penn.

1941 Lois

MJC

ALL STATE VOCAL CAMP 1953 – *Mixed Chorus*

Further Ambiguity *(continued)*

October 18,1956

Dear Folks,
So glad to hear that the Hudnalls are back. Ican imagine that the kids are happy. I thought about Linda and Pat when I saw that candy, and I do think we will semd them some for Christmas-they would get a kick out of it--don't think it will cost too much. We'll have to find out when we send Christmas packages--we have some ready to send already--and they are absolutely not to be opened before Dec,25-as we had them wrapped and there is no inside wrapping''! Did I tell you that I sent Cathy and Bob a card-well I did but it will probably take an age to get there. Have you heard any more about Carol Sue--that could be serious. We surely got a kick out of your seeing the Cranes. Yesterday ,all our mail caught up with us--five letters and two bills from the conservatory. So we read them in chronolggical order--first one from Baron. Then one from Ruth telling of the outing they had planned for that Sunday. Then yours telling that you saw them. What fun! Then we had another from Ruth telling us about it!! Also a long letter and a clipping from Betty--you'll have to keep me posted on the Muscatine elections--maybe you could send me the clippings from the paper on it. Also, any bit of society news, you could clipp and send. You get so much more weight for the same price -air mail than we do, it wouldn't cost you any extra if you didn't put too much in any one letter. Also, could we right now order an annual Journal to be sent here--we would appreciate it so much. So you have been working alot,

on?? Did I tell you that we are eating Heinz
Say, that front door was a shock! Sorry you
d case of cramps Tuesday, poor Fred felt so
fully, they didn t last too long. And by that
d the Wischets ever get a kick out of it!
nd they preferred to eat butter and sugar on their
uld be sure to write home about his little
does! He is so proud of it. And, could you
mps, and send all different kinds on your letters,
elope, and mark it air mail, or any thing --
chets have a stamp collection and we give them
ave been all the samw kind of 15cent airmail
stany more too have a variety,thank you. They
ves Frau Wischet something to do, being an invaid
before the war, and it was all stolen, and
over, but they did--and the amazing thing is
ny of the stamps, they just have all their
. And they really have a nice and varied collectio
Carolyn,she reallyis excited about the baby.
glad she is so happy. She told me that now I'd
knows, maybe her Daniel Keith will have a cousin!
her, but.....! Oh, Iam enclosing the check
ed in our trunk--it's signed and you may cash
n cash here are cashiers checks or American
t doesn't do me much good. You can save it for
I will need later. One of these days we will
with marks to show where we live etc. We havenT
e.
ne since I lasr wrote,We have each had two voice
s the best either of us has ever had or probably
much vivaciousness(wow that was a word!)
it of into her students' singing, really an
y nice. Last Saturday, after lunch at the
teria where one can get a hat lunch for a mark-
where we usually eat everyday lunch) we took
t of Sülz , the closest suberb,only a f ew
lowshopped. We had several rather nice days
ng again, the usual weather here. Then last
nice restourant in Lindenthal, and walked
he way home. Monday, we visited the cathdral
walked only a fourth of the way of the more
the spire, and both us gave out--Fred feels
places!Saw the gold caskets in which the remais
c.

iining hall, amazongly preserved, since about the year 2oo ad.

ut 10, so I had better stop typing, since it's rather loud—
ght disturb someone. And isn't too hot, anyway!
y night I baked choc. chip cookies—with no brown sugar!
lla, and substituting bk. powd. for soda. The oven was
ifferent & I really had a time, we ate them, but!
, I have finished only 2 sets of towels—Yellow ones
ch and pink for Barbie. I wasn't too satisfied with
t ones—Tried a new design and it didn't turn out as
I expected—Pretty—but could be better. We've
t been lazy lately—we have to register for the
tly soon, & then we'll be able to set up a
ule.

washed again today! What a chore—my poor
are so dry & I practically bathe them in
ream. But that hand scrubbing. Fred carries
upstairs & helps me hang them so I can't
lain. And poor Fraulein Wischet has so much
than I do—3 men in the family. And she
s this house & keeps it immaculate. Scrubs
itchen floor at least—I am not exaggerating—
sometimes 3 times a week! Wow—I like
to be clean, but—!!

ve been wearing my Bermuda's around the
I was afraid at first they wouldn't—
ally Herr Wischet approve—but they seem
a kick out of them. When I have them on—
in—(who I may now call Charlotte, she told me!)
s & say "Bermuda Shorts" which I taught
Herr Wischet has a little harder time—calling
Bermooda's"!

tell all the office gang "hello" for me & not
the men too hard. That Bella! and her raise!
so glad for your raise, I hope by now
have all my awful wedding bills paid and
concentrate on yourself.
ust say, "Goodnite."
—the Cranes have a picture of our house & should
t to you when they're done. We have the front
of the house—the two windows on the third floor
you see.

Just had a hot bath & am sleepy—

Love
Lois

PAR AVION

Soprano with N.Y.C. Opera

Joining company was 'lucky break'

By GILLIAN ROSS

New Yorkers may consider the New York City Opera as simply a fledgeling company, hardly comparable to the well-established Metropolitan, but that's not how a member of the former company sees it.

"I don't think a young opera singer could ask for a better opportunity to further her career than with the New York Opera," declared Lois Crane in an interview yesterday.

And for someone whose career and family are equally important to her, joining the company at the beginning of the season was a lucky break for the young soprano. Admitting that a rivalry did exist between the two companies, Mrs. Fredrick Crane (who likes to be known as Miss Crane professionally), defended hers saying that the New York City Opera was more willing to present experimental works, as well as well known ones, and so often took a chance on audience reaction.

In Montreal for a brief visit, the artist will sing one of the lead roles of Handel's "Judas Maccabaeus," to be presented this evening at 8 p.m. by the Tudor Singers of Montreal. The oratorio will take place in the Church of St. Andrew and St. Paul on Sherbrooke Street.

Equally experienced in oratorio and opera singing, Miss Crane has performed with various companies across the States. "I started off with a company in Binghamton, N.Y., and later joined the Lake George Opera Company for a few seasons," she declared. My oratorio singing experience was gained at university and in various churches."

The mother of a seven year-old daughter "who has been mad about opera since she was four," holds a degree in music from the State University of Ohio and a Rockefeller grant. Both she and her husband, a musicologist, also took a year off and studied music together in Cologne, Germany.

"It is a great boon having a husband who is able to help me with languages — particularly Italian, French and German," she confided, adding that she has the most difficulty with French.

Juggling a career and raising a family pose no problem to the attractive American. Pointing out the importance of a good baby sitter, Miss Crane declared that she found the sitter problem easier since she moved to New York City.

"I have met other women in the same situation and we

Lois Crane

'Madame Butterfly'

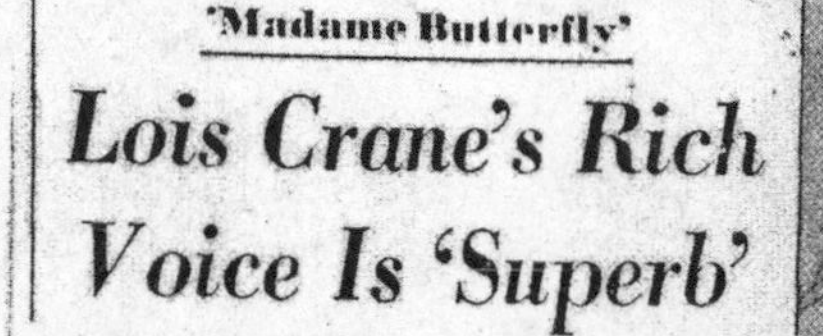

Lois Crane's Rich Voice Is 'Superb'

Lois Crane's marvelously rich soprano voice, used with beautifully controlled power, last night paced the Tri-Cities Opera to a superb performance of "Madame Butterfly" at the Masonic Temple.

Mrs. Crane over the years has developed tremendous strength as a singer.

This permits her to sing expressively, with full tone, but not loudly, when the music calls for quiet singing. Her strength also permits her to sing forte and fortissimo without any strain, any pinching or harshness.

Her voice is a ready tool for any emotional demands of opera librettists, and they are many and varied even in such a tragedy as

acting is int

beauty of fac

bonus for au

Mrs. Crane

a long way

whole story

Guild Night

Puccini class

Carleton Sn

were unusuall

his high stand

the standards

World of

Hollywood an

Milan.

Peyton M. I

tra played a

would have to

afterward in th

Typical of t

Alan Crabb as Goro all sang with lead quality, especially Mrs. Neidorf.

Mr. Snyder also achieved wonders with the lighting, particularly in the dawn at the start of the third act.

Kurt Shell was impressively sinister as Bonzo, Butterfly's properly concerned uncle.

The production will be staged again at 8 p.m. next Friday and Saturday and Oct. 23 and at 3 p.m. Oct. 24.

re to Gram
LOVE YOU
mom

Thurs July 30, 1970

Lufthansa

Boeing Jet 747

Betsy Love!

How do you like this big jumbo jet, another one of the huge new planes? Are you happy now? Is your tummy ok? My flight was tiresome and I have to change planes in Frankfurt to get to M... like you did in Chicago... showed a movie, but I ... sleep. I hope you hav... time with Daddy + all... Cranes. I love you M...

P.S. Don't forget to write

Luftpost
Airmai...

Miss B...

Wed.

Dear LOVE!

Your letter was wonde... This tower is on the top of a huge hill and over looks the city in the valley. We ate dinner here on Mon. night. Now I am working hard. I hope you are well and having fun with Gram. I really miss you alot. Be a good girl, I'll come home as soon as possible. Much, much MUCH LOVE + HUGS + kisses — MOM

STUTTGART, Fernsehturm (211 m)

Miss B...
588...
Ne...

Zürich und die Alpen
Zurich et les alpes
Zurich and the alps

Dear Betsy -
Isn't this a beautiful city? the mts. look like Colorado, but the city is very old fashioned and charming. I miss you so much and I know you are having fun with Grammy. Be a good girl and send me lots of hugs & love.
I love You
Mom

Dec 4, 1970
AIR MA

Hi -
The audition today was very successful & I can hardly wait to tell you about it. Rome is a fascinating city - full of wandering narrow streets & lots of old ruins - I wish there were time to sightsee. Bought you both something from here. Can hardly wait to go home, but must go to London on the way. I hope you are well - I miss my Pumpkin - Love Mom

538 West End Ave
New York
N.Y. 11A
USA

Disneyland
THE MAGIC KINGDOM

Hi
Sweetheart -
Wish you could have been here with me. It was lots of fun and I thought about you all the time! How are you? Write to me
Love & Hugs. Mom

SLEEPING BEAUTY'S CASTLE

Miss Betsy Crane
538 West End Ave
Apt 11-A
New York
New York
10024

Mrs. Frederick Crane holds her five-month-old daughter, Betsy, at their Lathrop Avenue home.

Tri-Cities Opera star enjoys dual role of 'Violetta,' housewife and mother

Cleaning pewter

Egg dressing

SHTOONK
IS ALWAYS
SPELLED
WITH
VERNON
ROYAL
39c
Dont
Read
COMPOSITIONS
DOWN
WITH
PANTS
BONUS PHOTO
exclusive
with
Royaltone
PHOTO SERVICE
FOR YOUR WALLET

Further Ambiguity *(continued)*

is a list of things we have in
1. Shoes 2. Pen-ink splats 3. Date
Same height 5. Jacket-blue 6. Both
7. Both apartments in 500's 8.
9. We both have blue eyes 10. Same
11. Same notebooks 12. Same
cards. 13. Same Spoons 14. Same
Masterpiece 16. "A" apar
Never seen "Andromeda Strain" 18. best
Love Mar

Kidnappings, after kidnappings... So
far, theories in the past year +
the beginning of this year these have
been kidnapped or attempted. This is
from an electric company (I don't know the
name) J. P. Getty Jr., Patricia Hea
Murphy, John Calzadilla, and
Ann was attempted. Thats 6. T
ridiculous

DEAR MOMMY.
I HAVE NEW BOOKS,
I HAVE NEW Pajamas!
I LOVE YOU!
YOU'RE WELCOME.
BETSY

PERSONAL HABITS	[illegible] Weeks	[illegible] Weeks	[illegible] Weeks
Takes off and puts on wraps alone.	S	S	S
Attends to personal needs without help.	S	S	S
Keeps hands and material away from mouth.	S	S	S
Relaxes during rest period.	S	S	S
Listens attentively.	S	S	S
Shows courtesy and consideration	S	S	S
Appears happy and cheerful	S	S	S
Uses soft, well-controlled voice.	S	S	S
Displays self-confidence.	S	S	S
Controls feelings.	S	S	S
Accepts directions and corrections.	O	S	S
SOCIAL HABITS			
Listens when others are talking.	O	O	O
Keeps hands and feet to himself.	O	O	O
Participates in group activity.	O	O	O
Takes turns and shares.	S	O	O
Respects the rights and property of others.	S	O	O
Works and plays well with others.	S	O	O
Responds to signals promptly.	S	S	S

WORK HABITS		
Listens to and follows directions.		
Works independently.		
Stays with a task until completed.		
Puts working tools away when task is finished.		
Does neat work.		
Uses material and equipment with care.	O	O
Assumes responsibility.	O	O
SKILLS & INTERESTS		
Speaks clearly.	O	O
Takes part in group discussion.	O	O
Possesses a variety of interests.	O	O
Shows skill in manipulating crayons, paint, scissors, clay, etc.	O	O
Enjoys singing.	O	O
Participates in rhythm.	O	O
Joins in active play.	S	O
Enjoys stories and poems and listens well.	O	O
Shows an interest in science found in our everyday living.	O	O

EXPLANATION OF GRADE MARKINGS

O - Outstanding Progress
S - Satisfactory Progress
I - Improvement desired

Dear Betsy Love-
In just a little over a week and I'll be able to hug you again! How do you like this beautiful castle? This old city is famous for Mozart and the Salzburg Marionettes - You would love it. I loved your letter. Much, much Love,
Mom

Miss Betsy Crane
601 North White St
Mt. Pleasant
Iowa
USA

BRISTOL
HOTEL KEMPINSKI
BERLIN

Dear Love
I hear from Grammy that you're having fun together. I miss you, but keep busy singing for lots of people. Hope something good comes out of it. Not sure how long I'll stay yet, I'll write more to Gram later. I LOVE YOU.
Mom

MIT LUFTPOST
PAR AVION

Miss Betsy Crane
588 West End Ave
New York 1002
New York
USA

AERIAL VIEW OF DISNEYLAND

Betsy-
Another view of when you're making a snow castle. I was at the beach! Isn't that funny! But, I'm working hard, too & miss you & look at your picture. Hugs & hugs & hugs.
I Love You, Mom

POST CARD
Miss Betsy Crane
588 West End
New York
New York
10024

Further Ambiguity *(continued)*

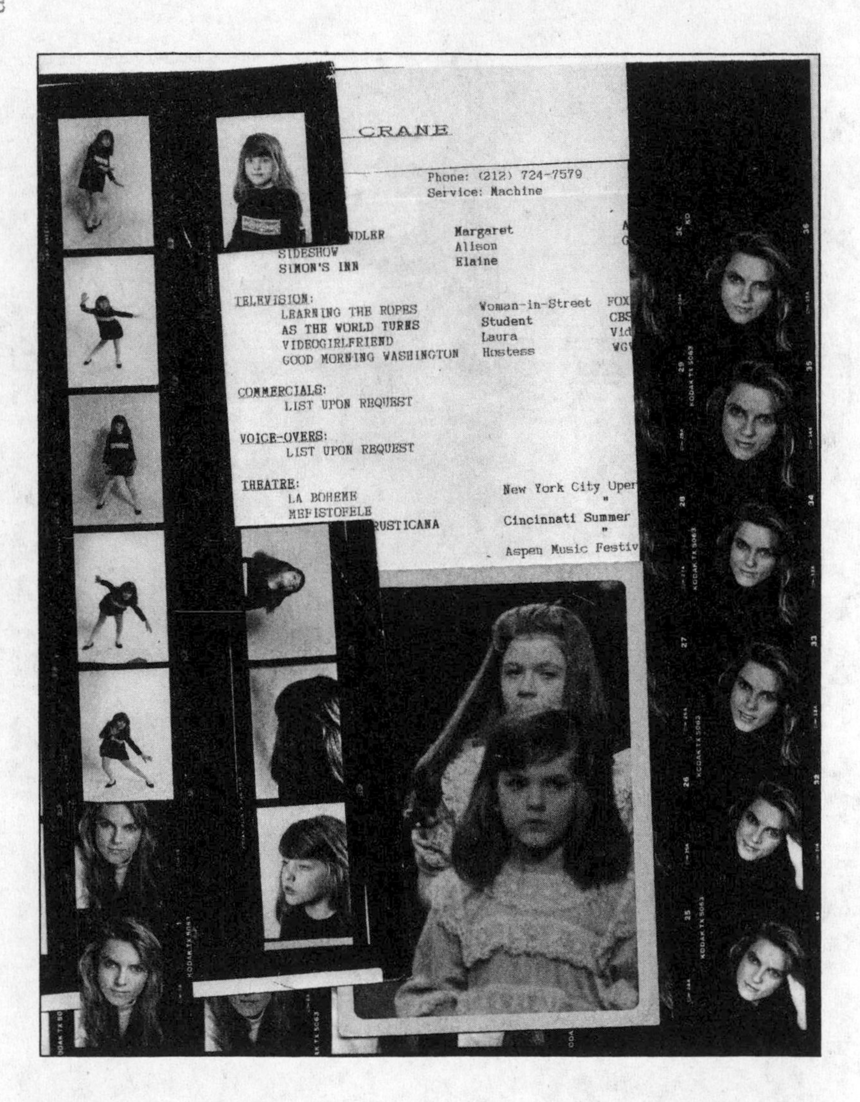

To the Editor:

Never am I so moved to write as when the issue involves food that gets corrupted into some hideous, allegedly improved version of its former self.

Now we have moved past the atrocity of fruit and nuts in bagels into shape distortion, and Mimi Sheraton is right ("Let the Circle Be Unbroken," Op-Ed, May 15).

Perhaps the time is righ[t] for a guidebook. Caffeinated water? No. Coffee or water.

I notice that pizza gets some bit of modification as well. Pick one. Pizza-flavored potato chips? Pizza is good. Chips are good. Can we not decide which we want at any given time?

Just call this toaster pastry something else, and leave the poor, simple, perfect bagel alone.

ELIZABETH CRANE
Chicago, May 15, 2001

though my mother is even more mood-oriented than before the cancer/lung thing. As a show of my faith in her ability to function as usual, I let my mother drive to Taco Bell (when she sends me back into the house to retrieve her *book* — a tattered Week-at-a-Glance calendar/address combo crammed with assorted scraps of paper, napkins, unpaid bills, to-do lists, fabric swatches, and bus tickets, held together by the combined strength of a rubber band and a size 10 ... opportunity for better judgment arises ... ately rejected upon returning to the car ... ng the first glimmer of hope I've seen ... r's eyes in months). This even though ... ore than a little stressed out as a driver ... as attached to an oxygen tank and on ... nd Xanax and antibiotics and whatever ... use she wants a chicken taco *really bad*

Chapter Number Two Original

By now it was Monday, and the ... end was over. The Garfl Family had gotten back last night, but Sammy hadn't seen any of them yet. ... a.m., and Sammy ... Garfl boys shuffle ... shadows. Following, th... Baby Garfl. She ... though, instead of ... Sammy, when she ... She stood on that ... and said, "I am Q... quite a stately ...

"You are?" ask...

"No, Sammy," she...

"Oh," said Samm...

```
Interior.  Day.  MEG's living room.  A lot of information is
revealed right away from the decor.  It is typically New York in
that there is much more "stuff" than there is space.  The only
window looks out on a brick wall and someone else's window.
Bookshelves are crammed with books and knickknacks, and stacks of
books are also piled up on the floor.  There are many picture
frames, dried flowers, needlepoints - lots of feminine touches,
but other things like a rack of baseball hats give more clues
about her life - one bearing a network logo, one from her mother's
soap opera, and a Yankee hat.  Nearby is a bust of Elvis, on which
is a baseball hat that says Iowa.  There are still other things
that indicate her sense of humor - a picture of John Cleese in a
dress posted to the fridge, a watercolor that says "Faith, Hope,
Spam," a Simpsons calendar.  The television is outfitted with VCR
and cable, and there are piles of videos near the t.v. as well.
MEG enters, arms full of groceries, mail, keys.  Before she does
anything, arms full, she finds a finger with which to turn on the
television.   Donahue has on men who can't commit.  Meg
acknowledges this topic briefly with a look of "so what else is
new".  Only after this routine but nonetheless urgent matter is
taken care of, does MEG then kick the door shut, drop the mail,
and walk over to the kitchen to put down her groceries.  She walks
back over to the sofa, where she has dropped the mail, to look
through it.  At least two magazines such as People and Us are
among her mail, and she's opening a few letters as she hears a
familiar male voice.

                         VOICE
                     (defensively)

 ...mpletely honest with every single
 ...rlfriends.

 ...immediately at the screen, to think about
 ...ounds like.  She quickly figures it out,
 ...n, and it's one of her ex-boyfriends, Ryan
 ...name is the caption, "Can't Commit".  MEG
 ...n in horror for a moment, and then quickly
 ....  JOE, a friend, answers. JOE has a guitar
 ...hat we can see, there is a lot of high tech
 ... him, many tapes and CD's, and the otherwise
 ...g bachelor's apartment, such as pictures
 ...d empty beer cans strewn about.  The scene
 ...tween them.

                         JOE
```